Tough Love at Mystic Bay

Elizabeth Sowden

These are works of fiction. Names, characters, places, and incidents either are the product of the author's imagination or are used fictitiously. Any resemblance to actual persons, living or dead, events, or locales, is coincidental.

Tough Love at Mystic Bay text copyright © Elizabeth Sowden
Edited by Rebecca Dimyan

Published in North America and Europe by Running Wild Press. Visit Running Wild Press at www.runningwildpress.com Educators, librarians, book clubs (as well as the eternally curious), go to www.runningwildpress.com for teaching tools.

ISBN (pbk) 978-1-947041-53-0
ISBN (ebook) 978-1-947041-54-7

Printed in the United States of America.

Dedication

This novel is dedicated to the memory of Professor Marvin Frankel (Psychology department, Sarah Lawrence College, 1972 - 2018) whose unforgettable lessons made this book possible.

And to my parents, Cynthia and Ralph Sowden, for their unwavering support.

Book 1

Before School

1

Jess never washes her gi. She claims it's because she's afraid that it will shrink. She says she doesn't need to wash it because she airs it out on the clothesline after every class. But we all know that none of this is true; she refuses to wash her gi because she knows that by smelling like weeks-old sweat, she can get her opponents to tap out sooner. We all try to get to class as early as we can so that we can partner up before Jess gets there.

This morning, I slept a little too late. Then, I hit every single light on Nicollet Avenue. By the time I got to the gym, everyone had a partner to roll with. Everyone except Jess.

Jess is sitting on top of me, pressing the entire weight of her double-D chest on mine. As she smashes my face with her collarbone, the smell nearly makes me choke. It reminds me of my first week in culinary school when one of the chefs opened a tin of fermented herring from Norway and told us if we wanted to be chefs, we had better learn to appreciate strong odors.

Jess shoves one hand into my collar. All I can see is the fire-breathing rooster on the front of her rashguard. My eyes water from Jess's fumes, blurring the flames from the rooster's mouth. As she reaches for the second grip, I buck my hips hard and shift her weight to the side. Finally, I've escaped and she's no longer sitting on me, but before I can think of what to do next, she wraps her legs around my waist and pulls me in guard. From this position, Jess controls my body and restricts my movements by squeezing my ribcage with her knees and keeping my torso pressed tightly against hers. Every time I try to sit up, she pulls me down hard with her thighs. Her hands clamp down onto my arm and she swings her body until it's perpendicular to mine. Even through the thick cotton of my sleeve, I can feel her fingers digging into my flesh. She tries to finish the armbar, but for a split second, her grip loosens and I yank my arm free.

Jess attacks my other hand. She grips my sleeve and shoots her feet over my head, forcing me flat against the floor. My face hits the mat, and suddenly I'm no longer in my jiu-jitsu gym. I'm face down on a concrete floor in a dog cage. I'm fifteen-years-old and a two-hundred-pound man is kneeling on my back. The tropical heat makes sweat drip into my eyes. He bends my arm and twists it hard until the muscles in my shoulder start to tear.

Before Jess can complete her omoplata, I tap hard. She eases up, and I push away from her. As I stand up, I'm shaking and breathing heavily. She stares up at me, bewildered. Sunlight streaming through the grimy windows illuminates the short blond hairs on Jess's scalp and the whitish lashes that surround her ocean-blue eyes. The instructor's disco music, which is playing at a low volume on the gym stereo, re-enters my awareness. All around us, other pairs of grapplers run through various techniques. The mirror at the front of the room is almost completely fogged over.

James, the instructor, makes a joke about Jess's funk, but when he sees my face, he realizes that Jess's nasty gi isn't what's upsetting me.

"Grace," he says to me, "are you alright?"

"Sure," I say, nodding. "I just need a minute."

I go to the bathroom and lock the door. With my back against the wall, I sink down to the floor and sob. It's been more than fifteen years since I was locked in a dog cage at Mystic Bay, but suddenly I feel like it's just happened.

After a few minutes, I feel calm again. I splash my face with cold water and walk back out onto the mat.

"Feeling better?" James asks.

"Yeah," I say, "I'm fine."

James pairs me up with one of the guys. A purple belt named Darrin pulls me in guard and holds me close to his chest so I can't posture up. I inhale deeply, breathing in his Hawaiian Fresh scent.

After class, James and I are the last to leave.

"Listen, Grace," he says as he unlocks his car. The rear end is crumpled and the trunk seems to be held in place by bungee cords and duct tape. The dented driver's side door gives a shudder as James jerks it open. "If Jess did something I need you to tell me. It's really important for me to make sure that all of my students are safe during training."

I shake my head.

"It wasn't anything that Jess did."

The wind picks up. Yellow leaves tumble through the alley. I can feel James looking at me, but I don't say anything more.

"Is there something you want to talk about?"

I shake my head, and suddenly I'm fighting back tears. I never talk about Mystic Bay. Nobody ever believes me when I do.

"Well, if you change your mind, you know where to find me," James says. His car starts with a rumble. I watch his taillights disappear as he drives away.

When I get to work, the stainless steel counters, appliances and exhaust hoods gleam, newly cleaned and ready for tonight's dinner service. Mariachi trumpets blast through a small radio, a sunny contrast to the mellow piano arrangements playing in the dining room. We have a brief staff meeting before we get started on prep.

Soon, the sound of hot oil crackling and my cooks chopping vegetables drowns out my thoughts. Every station is busy. As soon as we send dishes out, new tickets come in. On the other side of the door, the room is dim, with candles in frosted votives burning on each linen-clothed table. Black and white photographs of rain-glossed cobblestones, crowded metro cars and *grevistes* in newsboy caps line the walls. A small alcove hosts a baby grand piano where a musician sits and plays Debussy each night. Most people prefer that side of the door, but for me, the kitchen —with its heat, its noise and its fluorescent lights —is the only side I want to be on.

I place a chicken leg skin down in a pan full of hot, rendered fat. I watch the skin tighten and crisp. When I'm happy with the color, I take the meat out of the pan and pour chardonnay into it until the liquid is a quarter of an inch deep. I set the meat back in it, skin side up this time, and let the meat gently braise in the butter-colored wine.

I nestle the cooked chicken thigh on a bed of *pommes puree* next to a small stack of slim, tender asparagus stalks. A simple dish that's well executed is better than a hundred fancy ones. The pretentious fucks down the street have redone their menu so many times the servers spend their entire shifts running back to the kitchen to ask questions. Greens with grapefruit curd and pine vinaigrette. Deep-fried pork belly with chokecherry yogurt. Salmon carpaccio with smoked raisins and pickled fennel with a rhubarb-and-limoncello reduction. Thirty different kinds of aioli. I wish they'd call it what it is: mayonnaise with a little more flavor.

I think about what David Desmarais, the chef I studied under at Le Cinq in Paris, used to say about restaurateurs like these. *"Imbéciles qui pètent plus haut que leurs culs,"* he'd say. Imbeciles who fart higher than their asses. Chef David was half Moroccan and grew up in Marseille where he got his start, cooking in seaside cafes. His wavy, once-black hair looked as if all the color had simply rinsed out of it. He had enormous, bronze fingers that at first looked too big to be anything but clumsy, but Chef David could dice an onion in seconds. His mantra was *"fais pas le con."* Don't fuck around.

When dinner service is over and I'm helping my staff clean the kitchen and prepare for tomorrow, I overhear one of the new food runners talking to my sous chef, Corey.

"I really want to meet her," I hear her say. She looks like she's about eighteen-years-old. Her hair is freshly dyed black, but I can tell from the roots that it was, until recently, electric blue.

"I've been working with her for years," Corey replies. "She never hangs around. Once the burners go off, she splits."

They're talking about me. After we close up, most of the staff heads out to a bar. They've invited me a hundred times but I've never gone with them. I'm afraid of the questions they'll ask. *What high school did you go to? Oh, really? I went there too. Why don't I remember you? Why don't you ever date anyone? Why don't you ever hang out with us? Why don't you ever do interviews like the other chefs in town? Why do you seem like you're hiding some big dark scary secret?*

"'Night, Grace," Corey says as he changes out of his black chef's coat and into a denim jacket that is too big for his narrow frame. Thick brown stubble sprouts along his jawline. It matches his wild, Romanian eyebrows.

"Have fun," I reply.

"You can come, you know," he says.

"No, thanks," I say, and he gives me a sideways grin before he turns to leave. Corey has been my sous chef for three years. Before he was hired, I became notorious for burning through sous chefs. In my first two years as head chef, I fired three sous chefs and had two more quit. Until Corey came along, I didn't think I'd find anyone I could trust to do things right, but I refused to settle for mediocrity in my brigade. I remembered what Chef David told me: Don't fuck around.

Corey and I walk outside together where he joins the rest of the front-of-house staff. They set off in the direction of the bars on Washington Avenue. They take long, easy steps. Their work is done for now, and they're flush with tonight's tips. They smile and give each other playful shoves. The night swallows echo of their laughter as they disappear around a corner.

I get in my car and put the key in the ignition, but I don't start the engine. My chest feels tight and my eyes are hot. Why can't I be more like they are? Why can't I hang out at bars and laugh and tell stories like a normal person? I shut my eyes and rest my forehead against the steering wheel. A car pulls up next to me. A squad car. I dry my eyes and turn on my car. Last thing I need is some cop thinking I'm drunk. I can't say the alphabet backwards.

At home, I try to sleep, but every time I close my eyes, I hear girls screaming. I hear boys being tossed against the wall. I hear loud, droning self-help recordings. I hear the blast of the alarm, signaling some kid's attempt to escape. I hear the crackle of radio transmitters –a sound that meant someone was watching.

Finally, I reach for my iPhone and open the Netflix app. I watch old episodes of *Frasier* until I fall asleep.

2

Spring, 1998

"Eighth grade fucking sucked," I wrote in LaKeisha's yearbook. "I'm so glad we're finally getting away from this crap-hole. Things are going to be so much better next year when we get to South High. I can't wait. Thanks for being my best friend over these past couple of years. I hope you'll still be my best friend next year and the year after. Love, Grace."

"You can't write that!" LaKeisha said and grabbed a black pen.

"What do you mean, I 'can't write that'?"

"You can't write curse words in my yearbook! And you shouldn't write negative things about our school in it." She tried to cross out what I'd written, but I wrestled the pen away from her.

"You can't censor me!" I cried. "Those are *my* words!"

"Yeah, well, it's my yearbook!"

She tried to snatch the pen back from me, but I hid it in my pocket.

"Fine," she said. "I'll leave your nasty-ass message alone. But when my mom sees it she's going to say you're a bad influence."

"Who shows their yearbook to their mother?"

LaKeisha giggled and crammed her yearbook into her backpack. She took out her compact and touched up her eyeliner. LaKeisha liked to wear heavy black eyeliner, combat boots and a black shawl made of crushed velvet. She wore white lipstick sometimes, too, but the assistant principal always made her rub it off. She had a silver ring through her

9

left eyebrow. I wanted an eyebrow ring too, but my mother said it would make me ugly.

"I still can't believe we're the only Sheridan students to get accepted into the Liberal Arts program at South High," she said.

"Why the fuck not? All the other kids in this school are morons."

"Grace! Watch your language," LaKeisha scolded.

"Come on," I said. "You know I'm right."

LaKeisha's eyes swept the lunchroom. One of the boys dumped a carton of chocolate milk over a half-eaten burrito and shoved it at another boy. A group of girls whispered and giggled and squealed over pictures of Leonardo DiCaprio. A boy in a Smashing Pumpkins t-shirt knelt on the table, playing air guitar and headbanging until one of the lunch aides yelled at him to sit down.

LaKeisha tugged on the ends of her curly black hair.

"Yeah, ok," she said. "I guess you're right. Hopefully when we get to high school, everyone will be more mature."

On the first day of summer vacation, I lazed on the couch, watching *The Montel Williams Show*. The words "Troubled Teens" flashed on the bottom of the screen. An overweight mother with blond, chin-length hair cried as she told Montel about her daughter.

"She talks back. She runs around with boys. She smokes marijuana. She's completely out of control. I just don't know what to do." The camera zoomed in close to the woman's face as she flicked away a tear with her manicured finger.

Montel told the daughter to come out from backstage, and as she walked onto the set, the audience booed. She held two pixelated middle fingers in the air. The audience booed even louder.

"Why do you act this way?" Montel asked the girl.

"Because my mom's a bitch," she said. Another chorus of boos from the audience. Another close angle on the mom, crying.

Montel introduced another guest: the director of Epiphany Lake

Academy. The man wore glasses and a gray suit. He was fat.

"At Epiphany Lake Academy, we rehabilitate troubled teens like your daughter," he said to the crying mom. "We have a staff of licensed therapists who are able to treat anything from ADHD to Oppositional Defiant Disorder, which I believe your daughter has."

The camera cut to the mother's face. She was still crying, but now she smiled, like she was relieved.

"Epiphany Lake Academy is offering a year of free tuition for your daughter," Montel said. "Will you do what's best for her? Will you send her to Epiphany Lake?"

The mother brushed away tears with both hands and nodded vigorously. She reached over and hugged the daughter, who didn't hug back. The camera zoomed in on the daughter's face. She stared blankly at nothing.

I switched off the TV.

I went out to the garage and hauled out my bike. It was dark purple with the word "Giant" painted on the side and plastic tinsel sprouting from the handlebars. I put the kickstand down and left my bike in the driveway while I went back into the garage, hit the button for the automatic garage door, and dashed out as fast as I could while the door closed.

I mounted my bike and zipped through the alley, past garages covered in trumpet vines and backyards with thick, glossy rhubarb patches. I rode up Johnson Street, past the diner that served all-you-can-eat French fries, the bakery with the plaster cakes in the window, Jung's Chow Mein and the abandoned movie theater.

When I reached Lowry Avenue, I made a right turn. I released the brakes and let my bike spin as fast down the steep hill as gravity would let it. Wind stung my eyes and whipped through my hair. For a moment, I thought if I pulled the handlebars up, I could take off like a jet.

At the bottom of the hill, I squeezed the brakes. I looked up. In front of me was a tall Queen Anne-style Victorian house. It was powder blue with white gingerbread and white fishscales under the main gable. All of the windows on the ground floor were boarded up, and some on the top floor were broken. Dark, rotting wood showed through cracks in the paint. The porch sagged ever so slightly.

Every day on my way to school, my bus had passed this house, and I glued my eyes to it. What was in there? Who did it belong to? What did it look like before it went to ruin? And why didn't someone take better care of it? After all, it was clear that the people who built it cared about it.

I dismounted my bike. I crept around to the back of the house, through the weedy yard. A glassless transom window stared down at me like a dark eye. The windows back here were boarded, too, but the door looked like a padlock had been torn off of it. I touched the door. The wood was soft. Even without opening the door, I could smell the house: wet newspaper and mice. I was ready to push open the door, but I heard a car in the alley and I jumped back. The fear of some neighbor catching me made my heart pound. I grabbed my bike and rode away with stories of Victorian ghosts swimming around in my head.

3

I wake up a few hours later. It's still early. I stumble into the living room, where the glow of my laptop screen is the only light. I log onto a web forum called Survivors of the Shadows and search for the thread about jiu-jitsu, the one where someone said BJJ helped him get over his past. I saw this thread a couple of weeks ago and decided to give jiu-jitsu a try, hoping it might help me, too. After that flashback, though, I'm not so sure.

I find the thread and add another message to it:

I've been going to BJJ classes for a few weeks now. But yesterday in class, we were drilling the omoplata, and I had a flashback. Did this happen to you? I'm just not sure I should keep going.

After my message posts, I start scanning other threads. The people on SOS are my only friends, even though I've never met any of them. I keep hoping to find someone I know, but so far I haven't. There are a number of people on here who went to the same schools I did, but at different times. Some of them claim to have heard of me, like I was some sort of legend. That means they were there after me; no one from my time has found SOS yet. Everyone else on here went to other schools. Different names, different places, same shit.

A notification pops up. Someone has responded to my last post. I click on the thread.

Sometimes I get flashbacks just from looking at streetlamps. There is one on my block that flickers and sometimes it reminds me of the floodlights that were on all night outside our dorm. You can't avoid flashbacks. Trying just makes it harder to move forward. BJJ has helped me learn to trust people again. I actually have real friends again. Plus, I'm in great shape. I've lost all the weight I put on after I quit meth cold turkey. It takes time and it won't be easy. But keep at it. - NOLAJack

I'm a little annoyed at NOLAJack for saying he has "real" friends now. Am I not a "real" friend? But I know what he means. I can spend hours on here chatting with people who totally get where I'm coming from, but in the end it amounts to hours spent alone with a computer. At the gym, I noticed the way all the other people hung around after class, talking and laughing and making plans to do things together. I want to be a part of that, but walking out the door is just so much easier.

The light in my living room is turning pink. If I leave now, I can make it to the seven-thirty jiu-jitsu class. I stuff my gi into my backpack and lock the door on my way out.

Once a mechanic's garage, the gym is a squat, rundown building that sits in the shadow of a freeway overpass. The roof leaks, and small animals sometimes find their way inside. When James opened the gym, he pulled down the lifts and spread blue foam mats on the floor, which still smells faintly of antifreeze. One wall is lined with mirrors that fog up on cold days when the gym is full of grapplers working up a sweat.

There are five other people at the gym when I get there. Four of them are sitting in a circle at one end of the mat while Jess sits in her own little corner, stretching. She waves when she sees me. James arrives and asks us to line up by rank. Jess, who has a blue belt, is at one end and I'm at the other. A lowly white belt. James guides us through the warmup and then makes us pair off. He pairs me with Jess.

"Do you remember the side control escape?" she asks me.

I nod. "I think so."

I lie on my back while Jess digs her knees into my side and wraps her arms around me in a suffocating, sweaty hug. With all of the weight of her torso pressing me into the floor, I feel like I can't move at all. A panic rises in my chest.

"Relax," Jess says, without moving an inch, "you got this."

Even though my heart is racing, I shut my eyes and go through the steps James taught us. First, I need to use my arms to create space so that her chest on top of mine. I jam my forearm into her windpipe and she backs off, giving me enough room to turn onto my side and move my hips away from her. Then I wrap my legs around her waist and pull her in guard. I've gone from a submissive position to a dominant one —a position that allows me to decide what happens next.

Jess grins. "See? You got this."

James tells us to switch and give our partners a chance to drill their side control escapes, but Jess offers to let me keep practicing mine.

"You can't stop now," she says. "Your escapes are getting good."

After several minutes of practicing, my thighs are burning and my heart is thundering, but I can escape from Jess's iron embrace without thinking through the steps.

"Thanks," I say to Jess when we're finished.

She winks at me. "Any time."

At the end of class, I peel off my sweat-soaked gi and suddenly feel like I've lost thirty pounds. The other students are folding their damp gis too and making plans to watch tonight's UFC fight together.

Everyone straggles out of the gym and once again, James and I are the last to leave.

"I'm glad you came back," he says. He gives me a knowing look, but he doesn't say anything else.

James locks the door to the gym. I notice a small, pink jewel sparkling in his ear lobe. Just below his ear, there is a white scar that bisects his cheek. I realize I didn't notice it until now because it is partially hidden by his snowy beard. He walks with a slightly bowlegged shuffle, as if his lower back gives him pain.

The sound of a siren careening down Lake Street cuts through the air. After the sound fades, James asks me where I'm headed now. Work, I tell him.

"Where do you work?" he asks.

"Saveur de Vie. I'm a chef."

"Oh, I completely understand. I've worked in restaurants before. It's a hard road. Long hours."

I nod.

"Well, I hope you can keep coming to these morning classes. I need someone who will partner with Jess and not complain about it. You don't seem like much of a complainer."

I shrug.

"Jess has a good heart. It's just that she's somewhat of a…"

"An acquired taste?" I ask, remembering that tin of surströmming and the mushroom cloud of malodorous gas that took over the room as soon as Chef opened it. I remember something she said about how the most offensive-smelling foods are often the most celebrated, how things like surströmming, lutefisk and durian all had their own festivals.

James smiles and gets in his car. "Exactly," he says. "She can be loud and opinionated and is a tough opponent, but people would like her better if they just gave her a chance."

"Sure," I say as I settle into my car. Through my rearview mirror, I watch James drive out of the parking lot.

I drive downtown, but I don't head straight to the restaurant. Instead, I drive to Loring Park and flop down on one of the benches near the pond. I light a cigarette and watch red-winged blackbirds dart in and out of the reeds.

It's a little bit funny that I didn't start smoking until *after* I came home from Mystic Bay.

During my senior year of high school, I had constant nightmares. On more than one occasion, I fell asleep with the light on and woke up screaming, convinced I was back in one of those hellhole boarding schools. My dad took me to a doctor who gave me a sleeping pill, but I was afraid to take it. What if it helped me stay asleep, but I still had the dreams? Instead, I tossed the bottle into the back of the drawer in my nightstand and crept out onto the porch roof for a smoke whenever I couldn't sleep.

After graduation, I got a job working behind the line in a grease pit that was next to railroad tracks opposite a grain elevator. The whole place shook whenever a train went by, and I spent hours on my feet, but I loved every minute of it. We were busy from open to close. The sounds of oil bubbling in the fryer and burgers hissing on the grill were a near constant. I always had a knife, spatula, or spoon in my hand. As long as I was behind the line, feeling the heat from the grill on my face, I felt safe. When I got home, feet throbbing, I feel right to sleep, too exhausted to dream.

While I was studying at the Culinary Institute of America and staging at restaurants in Paris, I was so busy working, slogging through courses on Culinary Math and learning to speak French, I was able to keep all those nasty memories at bay.

Now, I'm an Executive Chef. My job is to develop dishes and teach other people how to cook them. I still work behind the line –I can't stand not to –but somehow it's not the same. Sometimes I think I should go back to slinging hash at a scruffy chophouse, someplace with cheap food and high volume where there's never a slow shift.

In the fine-dining world, no matter what you do, some nights are just way too slow.

In a half hour, I'm supposed to have a meeting with the restaurant staff to go over the week's specials. Except I haven't planned them. Not a single one.

Pull yourself the fuck together, I say to myself as I stub out my cigarette. *They will fire your ass in a split second if you show up without a list of specials. There are a million wannabe chefs in this town who would love to take your job.*

In my mind, I make a list:

Monday: Pan-seared duck breast with raspberry glaze and pommes frites.

Tuesday: Duck cassoulet

Wednesday: Pork Roulettes with Honeycrisp apple stuffing

Thursday: Bacon, potato and reblochon casserole

Friday: Poulet Basquais with gnocchi Parisienne

Saturday: Venison Ragout with mashed potatoes

Sunday: Veal in cream sauce with house-made noodles

I lean back against the bench and exhale. This is a good list. It should please my bosses and my customers. My job should be safe for another week.

Jesus, I think to myself, *I sound like a contestant on Master Chef.* I bury my face in the palms of my hands and rub my eyes.

Sometimes I think about just torpedoing my career by putting weird stuff on the menu – stuff you only see in old cookbooks, like jellied eels, or that mock turtle soup the Victorians used to make out of a calf's head, with a garnish of fried balls of brain.

If I did that, it would probably become the next hipster foodie trend, and I'd end up with my own cooking show on the Food Network. Then my crazy mother could run around bragging to all her frenemies about what a good mom she was to have raised someone so successful. I almost throttled her when I got the job at Saveur die Vie and she said, "Boarding school wasn't so bad after all."

"Fuck you," I growl, imagining my mother's smirk.

"Are you talking to me?" a passing jogger asks. He's wearing skin-tight, head-to-toe black and a skull cap. He looks like he's running from the bank job he just pulled.

"No," I say, my cheeks flaming. I hustle back to my car and drive to the restaurant.

4

LaKeisha lived across the river. One morning, she called me up and said she was bored. She felt like taking a long walk. I told her I'd meet her on my side of the bridge, so I rode my bike down and waited.

By the time LaKeisha arrived, she was in a foul mood.

"I can't go anywhere without guys making disgusting comments to me. Either they're making gross kissy sounds at me, like I'm a dog, or they're telling me I dress wrong. 'That goth shit's for white girls. Dress like a proud black woman.' Some asshole said that to me just a few minutes ago. What does that even mean? And if it's not black guys giving me grief, it's white girls. Like Leanne from school. When I told her I like The Cure, she got, like, offended. Because I'm black, I'm only supposed to like LL Cool J."

She looked at me and waited for me to respond, but I didn't know what to say.

"Come on, Grace. Say *something.*"

We turned and walked down Marshall Street. A one-hundred-year-old brewery with black spires and bricked-over windows cast a long shadow over the sidewalk.

"Leanne's a prissy little bitch," I said, finally.

"Grace, I'm mad about something much bigger than Leanne."

"I know. I know! It's just that…when we talk about race stuff…I don't know what to say. I'm sorry."

LaKeisha sighed. "It's ok. It's fine. It's just…I'm mad."

"You should be mad."

She slung an arm over my shoulder. She wore Dream by Gap; it made her smell like tangerines and violets. "That was it," she said. "That was the right thing to say."

Behind us, the old train shed that once sheltered railcars that brought grain to the brewery stood empty. Across the street, the bar had its door propped open, and the scent of French fries wafted out. Workers on their lunch breaks scarfed down hot ham sandwiches.

"Well," LaKeisha said, "What should we do now?"

I remembered the old blue boarded-up house on Lowry and Polk. I pointed to the foot pegs on the back of my bike.

"Hop on," I said. LaKeisha hesitated. "You won't fall."

My bike shook a little as LaKeisha put her foot on one peg, then the other. Her fingers dug into my shoulders. I flexed my calves. The extra weight made it hard to push the pedals at first, but I curled my toes, gritted my teeth and after a few tough strides, we were speeding up Lowry Avenue.

I felt LaKeisha's fingers relax. A flower bed full of purple irises kicked up a soft scent of licorice. The sun blasted my face. I had only just started to wear deodorant a few months ago; I was glad I had remembered to put it on this morning.

We came up to Central Avenue. The block with the blue house was on the other side. The light was green, and I pedaled hard to get us across. I caught a glimpse of the house, its main gable rising slightly higher than the other houses on the block. A shiver ran down my spine. LaKeisha's fingers twitched.

I stopped in front of the house. The upstairs windows with the broken glass stared down at me. The white fish-scale shingles under the gable looked scarred and worn.

LaKeisha sucked her teeth. "Oh, please. A jacked-up old house? My block is full of those. My mom is buying a house in Richfield so we can get *away* from shit like that."

"Come on! I bet we'll find something really cool in there."

"Like what? Crackheads? When I come to the white side of the river, I want to hang out in all the nice places you got over here."

"*The Wedding Singer* is still playing at Apache 6," I suggested. That theater was almost three miles from where we were. I knew she wouldn't want to walk that far.

"I hate those movies," she said with an eye-roll.

"We could watch TV at my house," I said, "but we don't have air conditioning."

"Fine! We'll go into the musty old crack house. But only for a minute. And we better not get caught!"

"It's *not* a crackhouse," I said.

"You don't know that."

We walked around to the weed-choked yard. Above the door, there was a long, brown scar where a back porch roof used to be. I held my breath as I opened the door. LaKeisha covered her nose with her hand.

I stepped inside and waited for my eyes to adjust. There was a small hallway and a steep, narrow staircase; I figured this was the servants' entrance.

"The family who built the house must have had servants," I said.

I wanted to climb the stairs and explore the servants' quarters. I could just imagine the secrets that the maid and the cook would have known – and kept – about the family that they cared for. There was no way I'd be able to talk LaKeisha into going up there with me. So, instead, we went through a doorway opposite the staircase that led into the kitchen.

The walls were splashed with graffiti. There were white squares on the wall where appliances used to be and a small, wooden signal box mounted to the wall. It was so old that the labels had almost completely worn away. I recognized it because *Upstairs, Downstairs* was one of the only shows my mom and I could agree on when we were trying to find something to watch.

"I wonder if this still works," I said as I ran my fingers over it.

"What is that?"

"It's a servants' call box. See here where it says 'bedroom'? Someone in one of the upstairs bedrooms would push a button and this square would light up. That would let the servants know that the person in that bedroom needed something."

LaKeisha nodded silently and glanced absently around the room. I could tell that the servants' call box didn't interest her, but my mind was swimming in daydreams: girls in rustling taffeta, elaborate dinners, Christmas trees covered in candles—just like in the books that came with my Samantha doll.

LaKeisha and I sat on the floor of the parlor, underneath a mistletoe of old, tangled wires that once connected to a chandelier. The room was dark except for threads of sunlight that seeped through the gaps where the boards on the windows had been hung unevenly. Because the windows were boarded, the house stayed cool.

"What do you think high school will be like?" LaKeisha asked. "I think it's going to be great. I can't wait to start," she said, without waiting for me to answer.

"Well, it will *have* to be better than middle school."

"Homecoming dances, pep rallies, prom," she said wistfully. "I can't wait."

"I'll just be happy to be away from mean, nasty people," I said, as I remembered Leanne giggling and whispering into Candace's ear, while her eyes remained fixed on me. Whenever Leanne stared at you while laughing into someone else's ear, you could be sure she was starting a rumor about you. She told everyone that LaKeisha worshipped the devil and that I gave blow jobs to the skater boys.

A few months ago, she started a rumor that LaKeisha and I were lesbians. Other kids shouted "dykes!" at us for weeks. One day at recess, LaKeisha and I sat by the fence, watching the cars go by on University Avenue. The asphalt was warm, and the shadow of the chain link fence made a diamond pattern on LaKeisha's tights. Suddenly, one of the boys ran up to us, screamed "dykes!" and beaned us with a kickball. As he turned to run, LaKeisha whipped the ball back at him and it bounced off of his shoulder. He ran and told the teacher.

LaKeisha almost got suspended. We told them over and over again that he threw the ball at us first but it wasn't until the teacher confronted him and he confessed that they decided to let LaKeisha off the hook.

When I got home and told my mother, I thought she'd be angry – with the principal, with Leanne, with the kid who threw the ball – but instead, she said, "Maybe you and LaKeisha should spend less time together."

"I can't wait to try out for plays. And marching band. Maybe I'll even try out for cheerleading."

"You?" I said, stifling a laugh.

"What? Who says you can't cheerlead in combat boots? Anyway, what about you? Have you signed up for anything?"

"Swim team," I said.

"But you have to smile the entire time and put Jello in your hair!"

"Not synchronized swimming! The swim team! Competitive swimming. Relays. Races. The 100-meter butterfly."

LaKeisha laughed. "Girl, I'm hungry. Let's get out of here."

We peeked outside to make sure that no one would see us leave the abandoned house, and left through the door that we had used to come in. LaKeisha took a little bottle of Dream by Gap out of her purse and we both doused ourselves in it so no one would smell the moldy house on us.

We walked back down to the Subway on the corner of Lowry and Central where we split a foot-long tuna sandwich and a bag of potato chips. Half an hour later, LaKeisha said she had to head home. I walked with her as far as the bridge, then hopped on my bike and rode away.

5

The gym is locked when I arrive for the seven-thirty class. I lean against my car and sip a macchiato while I wait for James to arrive and open the gym. I didn't sleep well, and I'm anxious for the caffeine to kick in.

Across the street, a Somali man parks his minivan and unloads his family. His wife wears a long black hijab; their little girl's hijab is bright pink. She takes her mother's hand. The family disappears into the building across the street. Before the door closes, the little girl turns and waves at me.

As I wave back, Jess pulls into the parking lot. She drives a 1969 Pontiac GTO with pipes loud enough to wake everyone in the neighborhood.

"James isn't here yet?" she asks as she gets out of her car. She glances at her phone and finds a text from James. "Oh, he canceled class today," she says. "That happens sometimes," Jess explains. "He has this insomnia thing…"

I'm annoyed. I have that problem too, and I still managed to show up. Plus, I didn't get any text. So I was just supposed to sit here and wait for an hour like an idiot? People fucking suck.

"Do you want to get breakfast or something?" Jess asks.

For a second, I'm tempted to accept her invitation, but instead, I lie and say I had better run some errands before work.

Two hours later, I drive to the restaurant. My cell phone starts to ring as soon as I arrive at work. The call is from my mother. I let it go to voicemail. Last time we spoke, she started in again on her diatribe that sending me to the program "couldn't have been all bad" because I "turned out OK."

"Right mom," I spat at her, "I have a good job and I'm not a crack whore, so of course that means *you* didn't make any mistakes."

She said something like "Oh, come on," and I hung up on her. I've been avoiding her calls since. I light a cigarette and listen to my mother's voicemail. For an entire minute, she yaps brightly about how her friends ate at Saveur de Vie and were so impressed with my food. "I'm so proud of you, sweetie!" she says. I chuck the phone into the back seat. Back when I was working at my first job at Marek's Tavern, she called my dad nearly every week and pitched a bitch fit, insisting that he convince me to quit working there. The idea of me serving onion rings to mechanics and pipefitters embarrassed her for some reason. Now she's "proud."

How does she think I got here?

I crush my cigarette and toss it away.

"You really need to quit smoking," says Corey. He has a Minnesota Twins logo tattooed on the side of his neck. During baseball season, he always insists that the kitchen radio is tuned to the game broadcast. Some of the cooks complain, but I don't care what's on the radio.

"Thanks, *Dad*," I say to him.

"Smoking dulls your taste buds. How can you be sure that your dishes taste right if your taste buds aren't firing on all cylinders?" Corey recently quit smoking. I can smell the nicotine gum on his breath.

"Are people complaining about my food?" I ask as I button up my chef's jacket.

"Not that I know of," he admits.

"So why are you lecturing me about my smoking?"

"Because it's bad for you! It's 2015. The only people who still smoke are people with serious problems."

"Says the guy who used to smoke two packs a day."

Corey crosses his arms over his chest. He's so skinny, his chef jackets are always too big for him. "I never smoked that much."

"You did, too," Nate, the barback, says as he rushes between Corey and me, carrying a case of Stella Artois. I give Corey my best 'told you so' look.

"I'm just concerned about your health," Corey says.

"Well, Corey, I'm touched that you care so much but what you should be concerned about right now is the *pâté en croûte*. That phyllo dough isn't going to roll itself."

Corey flashes a lopsided grin and takes a mound of chilled dough from the walk-in. He rolls the dough while I carefully butter and stack each paper-thin sheet. Phyllo dough is always a two-person job; at least it is in my kitchen.

"I can't get over it," Corey says.

"Get over what?"

"I've never, ever worked with an Executive Chef who is as hands-on as you. Most of them just stroll in, put on a jacket, look at what everyone's doing, take their jacket off and go sit at the bar."

"That's because all the chefs you worked for had given up," I reply, painting sunshine-colored butter across a delicate sheet of dough. Before Corey joined my brigade, he worked at a kitschy tiki bar down by the river. The owner is an anorexic blond who perches on a barstool while she spies on her employees. Chefs never last more than a few months there. She tried to get me to work for her once, but I told her no way. I visited that kitchen once and saw the staff putting pasta that had already been cooked into plastic bags. I could never work for someone who would serve subpar-textured pasta and charge $12 a plate for it. I don't care how high-volume her restaurant is.

Most people would lose their appetite if they could see what their food looks like before it comes to the table: half-cooked bacon congealing on racks, icebergs of mashed potato waiting to be thawed, plastic-wrapped manufactured biscuits destined to be reheated. I always promised myself that when I had my own kitchen, I wouldn't run it that way. People can warm up frozen potatoes at home. It doesn't feel right to charge them for it. That's why almost everything we make is made to order and all of our meat and produce is delivered fresh every morning. It costs more and it's more work, but my customers get what they pay for, and if someone ever decides to tour my kitchen, they won't be surprised by what they see.

"Ok, that's sorta true. But still," Corey goes on, "you're way different from other chefs. It's pretty cool."

I don't do it for you, I think. I keep it to myself. It's better if I let him think I do it to be a good boss and not because I'm a crazy person who loses her shit when she's not keeping busy with work.

Corey starts in on industry gossip: a sous chef at Patty Mayhem's got fired for snorting cocaine in the bathroom; a General Manager at Hunger is having a torrid affair with a barely-legal server; Northern Spike's quasi-celebrity chef flipped out on a customer for requesting mustard.

I nod, but I'm not really listening to what Corey is saying. I don't find this nearly as fascinating as he does. Besides, if I want to catch up on scene gossip, I can always go read those stupid foodie columns. They love a good scandal. They're constantly calling me to set up an interview. I've been ducking them for months, but I'm running out of excuses and my boss is getting short on patience.

A tray of chicken and duck breasts has been marinating in the fridge since just before closing last night. Corey dices them finely for the pâté while I cut tiny leaves and roses out of dough.

Once the pâté is ready to bake, I slip out for a quick smoke break. I glance at my phone. There it is; I don't know how I missed it earlier: the text from James.

6

In July, the "back-to-school" commercials started to air on TV. Swim team practices were scheduled to start in August. I needed a swim cap and goggles, which meant that my mom and I had to go shopping at the mall. We drove up to Apache Plaza so I could get swim gear at Sportmart and a new backpack from Herberger's.

"This place is depressing," I said to my mom as we passed a Fanny Farmer with aluminum gates guarding its empty shelves. The letters on the marquee used to glow bright green, but now they were dark and gathering dust. A dry fountain sat in the center of the court. A girl wearing combat boots and a streak of pink dye in her blond hair sat on the edge of it, sketching something in a notebook.

My mom sucked her teeth. "Would you look at that girl's hair?" she said. "Grace, if you come home with hair like that, I'll cut it off myself."

My stomach tightened. I glanced at the girl, hoping she hadn't heard, but when I looked closer, I noticed she was listening to a Walkman. I let out a small sigh of relief and followed my mother into Herberger's.

She went off to look at shoes for herself. I wandered through the Junior Miss department alone. I wanted to dye my hair like the girl by the fountain. I wanted electric blue or neon green. I couldn't understand what my mom had against hair dye. It was just hair. It wasn't like dying your hair automatically made you a pot smoker or got you pregnant.

I found a Smashing Pumpkins t-shirt and a black hooded sweatshirt with a multi-colored star in the middle of it. A pair of JNCO jeans caught my eye. I checked the tag: the bottoms were thirty-four inches wide. I took it off the rack to get a better look at the bright red logo on the back pocket.

"Grace!"

My mom appeared out of nowhere and ripped the jeans out of my hands.

"If you think I'm going to let you walk around looking like some sort of freak, forget it," she hissed.

"Jesus, Mom. I was just looking."

She thrust the JNCOs back onto the rack and shoved an armload of l.e.i. jeans at me.

"Oh, Mom, these have flowers on them," I protested.

"Yeah well it wouldn't kill you to look a little more *feminine* for a change," she said, ushering me into a fitting room.

I closed the door and sat on the little bench. What was so wrong with JNCOs anyway? I wondered. Just because they were super baggy and popular with skater boys didn't mean I was going to use them to smuggle drugs to school. I mean, it wasn't like I was looking at miniskirts or crop tops or belly chains like the slutty, prissy girls in school wore. They were just pants.

I took off my clothes and stood in front of the mirror. My thighs were a little chubby, but I wasn't fat, in spite of what some of the boys at school teased. One of them even said, "Do you eat a lot? Is that why your ass is so big?"

"Who's fat?" I asked myself as I looked at myself sideways.

I pulled on the l.e.i jeans. The big roses appliqued on the legs were ugly. I put on the Smashing Pumpkins shirt and when I saw the way it looked on top of the rose jeans, I wanted JNCOs more than ever.

"Grace? Do those jeans fit?"

"They fit fine, Mom," I said.

"Then let's get going. I have a lot of other errands I have to run."

I handed the pile of clothes to my mom, and she took them to the checkout counter. She said nothing about the Smashing Pumpkins shirt. I smiled as the clerk folded it.

As we left the mall, I looked for the girl with the pink streak in her hair, but she was gone. I flipped a penny into the empty fountain. I wasn't sure what to wish for, but since the fountain was dry, it probably didn't matter.

7

After two months of daily jiu-jitsu classes, I have learned most of the basic submissions and am beginning to see how all of the positions, escapes, passes, chokes and sweeps all fit together. I can do a lot more without getting tired, and I can move faster than I could before. I haven't worked on my body this much since that first semester of 9th grade when I was on the swim team.

I've worked with everyone in the class, but I'm starting to prefer working with Jess. She's tough, and with her, I can work the technique without worrying that I'm being too aggressive. She also gives as good as she gets, and I often leave the gym with constellations of tiny bruises on the undersides of my arms, where my skin got caught between her knee and the mat.

I still haven't accepted her invitations to hang out after class. I think she's given up. I just couldn't bring myself to say yes.

I write all this in a message on SOS to NOLAJack.

NOLAJack's family sent him to a roach-infested camp in Samoa when he came out to them as gay. He became dangerously thin thanks to intestinal parasites and was covered in scabies most of the time. The staff there routinely locked him in a coffin-sized box as punishment from some infraction or other. He participated in a plot to kill one of the younger kids after a rumor went around that the camp would shut down if someone died there. That camp went by the name Arcadian School for Boys, owned and operated by the same fucks who ran Epiphany Lake Academy and Mystic Bay.

These places always have such pretty names. Blue Horizon Academy. Revelation Ranch Academy. Andromeda Wilderness Programs. Aspirations Academy for Girls. New Direction Ranch. Emerald Valley Therapeutic Boarding School. Healing Sun Residential Treatment Center. Academy at Echo Canyon. They are all over the US and in foreign countries too, but no one ever talks about it. No one except us.

NOLAJack offers a simple reply: *Keep at it.*

If he can get on with his life, I can, too. Right?

I navigate away from SOS and open my email. There's a note from my dad. The message says, "Came across this old photo while rearranging my bookshelf. Thought you'd get a kick out of it."

It's a picture of my dad and me from when I was studying in France. Dad had come to Paris to visit me and we'd taken a weekend trip to Auxerre in Bourgogne. In the photo, Dad has his arm around me and we're standing in front of a three-tiered fountain and half-timbered medieval houses. The cobblestones under our feet are slick with rain.

I remember that evening. We found a small cafe where we drank Chablis and tasted the proprietor's ancient family recipe: *tourte de groins de porc.* The host explained that it was pig snouts, diced and slow-simmered, tossed with tarragon and stuffed into a rich pastry crust. After sightseeing in the rain all afternoon, the *tourte* made us warm.

I mull over the thought of putting it on the menu at work. It could be our special on Saturday night. People would probably be too scared to try it. I would probably get sacked. My stupid mother wouldn't be able to brag about her "star chef" daughter to her idiot friends anymore.

I write my dad back to thank him for the photo, then I pick up my phone and call our pork supplier.

The next day, Corey shrieks when he opens the crate that's just been dropped off by the pork supplier.

"Jesus!" he cries. "What *is* this?"

"Oh, relax," I say. "They're just pig snouts."

He looks at me like I've just peeled my face off, revealing a jiggly, multi-eyed alien head.

I don't get a chance to respond because that's the moment when the GM comes into the kitchen, hands-on-hips, staring at me. His spiky orange hair stands straight up and the tops of his ears are turning red.

"What the *hell* did you put on the menu?" he demands. "*Tourte de Groins de Porc?!* You put *groins* on the menu?!"

"It's French for 'snout,'" I say coolly.

"Right," he says, "like that makes it ok. Who's going to want to eat pig snout pie?"

I shrug. "I don't really care if people eat it or not."

Corey stifles a giggle while the GM rolls his eyes. "You are so completely full of shit," he says.

"Hey," I shoot back, "Who is the chef here? My job is to make the food. Your job is to sell it. I don't give two fucks about what you have to do to sell the food I make."

"You won't be the chef here very long if you keep doing shit like this," he says and storms back to the front of the house.

Without another word to anyone, I drop the snouts into a vat of boiling water.

A few hours later, after the snouts have been cooked, cooled, chopped and sautéed with butter, garlic, shallots and tarragon, I layer the meat over sliced potatoes and pastry sheets packed into a vacherin mold. My boss walks into the kitchen just as I fold the final layer of pastry dough over the top of the round *tourte*. I take leftover bits of dough and cut them into the shape of tiny pigs.

"Is this the 'pork groin' that's got Max into such a tizzy?" the owner asks, peering at me over the tops of her white-framed glasses.

"It's a delicacy in Bourgogne."

She nods. "How are you going to serve that?"

"In individual slices with a side of steamed green beans."

"How much did those cost?" she asks.

"Next to nothing."

"Alright," she says, and leaves the kitchen.

I add the little pastry pigs to the crust of the *tourte* and slide it into the oven.

The orders flood in. So many people order the 'pork groin' special that after the first hour of service we have to take it off the menu. During a brief lull between the first and second seating, Max walks into the kitchen. He hovers over my shoulder while I plate an order of lamb shoulder in a ruby port sauce.

"Can I help you?" I ask without turning to face him.

"I owe you an apology. I thought no one would order that pig snout thing. But they all thought it was so weird they just had to try it. And they loved it. You have really good instincts. We should all trust you more."

He's got his hand on the back of his neck and he stares at a spot on the wall before finally making eye contact with me.

I turn around and hand him the lamb shoulder. "Yes, well, remember this."

The last seating of the night begins to wind down, and Corey and I get the kitchen ready for the next day. The owner comes in and perches on a stool.

"Grace, the profit margin on that pork snout tort is huge. I think we should put it on the regular menu."

"Sure," I say. I glance over at Corey who gives me a sidelong look. "If that's what you want to do."

On my way home, I stop at the dive bar down the street from my apartment. Inside it's dark except for the fake Tiffany lamps that hang over the pool tables and the glow of the pinball machine. I order a Jack and ginger. "With a Little Help from My Friends" comes on the jukebox

– the Joe Cocker version. I glance around for a place to sit when I hear someone shout my name.

It's Jess. She motions for me to join her.

"This is my wife, Michelle," Jess says. The woman standing next to Jess extends her hand for me to shake.

"I never thought I'd see you in here," Jess says to me.

"I leave nearby," I explain. "And I needed a drink."

"Rough night?"

"Kind of. I tried to get fired. But I failed."

Jess screws up her face, then laughs. "What do you mean you tried to get fired? What did you do?"

"I put something weird on the menu. I thought it would get me in trouble. But people liked it."

"Grace works at Saveur de Vie," Jess explains to her wife. "She's the head chef."

"That sounds like a great job! Why would you want to give that up?" She studies me from behind her Prada glasses.

I don't know what to say. I don't *really* want to get fired.

"I don't…" I say, "I guess the stress just gets to me sometimes."

Michelle smiles. "Believe me, I understand. I'm a lawyer."

Jess orders me another drink. She starts talking about the gym, quoting jokes that James has told and telling stories about gruesome injuries. I nod along, but there's a fog seeping into my brain. My neck feels stiff. I start to drift. I can't hear anything Jess is saying.

The clacking of the flippers on the pinball machine finally brings me around. I can't stay here. If I don't leave now, I might not make it home in one piece. The last time this happened, I nearly walked in front of a light rail train.

"Hey, you know what? I better get going."

"Why?" Jess asks. She almost looks hurt.

I reach for an excuse. "I…have to get up early tomorrow. And you do, too. Remember?"

"Right," she says. "Bright and early, on the mat. Still…" she glances at her watch. "It's kind of early. You have time for one more round, don't you?"

"Sorry," I mumble.

"Ok. See you tomorrow, I guess."

The moment I step out onto the street, I regret leaving. But I don't turn around to go back in. One part of me wants to sit with Jess until the bar closes. Another part wants to go home and draw blackout curtains on the world.

I sit in my car and rest my head on the steering wheel. I say to myself: *why can't you just be normal?*

8

Swim practice started early. It was dark when I woke up, and the morning glory blossoms were just starting to open. Because my high school didn't have a pool, our team had to use one at a school across town.

The water was cold and biting, but after several laps, I felt hot all over.

"You're pretty fast," the coach said to me just before practice ended for the day. "If you can keep up that pace, I'll put you on the Varsity squad."

By 8:30 I was home. I ate two bowls of Oreo O's and fell asleep on the couch, watching Montel Williams give makeovers to frumpy wives.

"That's amazing!" LaKeisha said later when I talked to her on the phone and told her what my swim coach had said. "You can be captain of the swim team, and I'll be the lead in the school play! We'll take over that school before we're sophomores! We're going to look so great in our orange and black letter jackets! I can't wait to see how many pages we get in the yearbook!"

"School hasn't even started yet, and you're already thinking about the yearbook?"

"It will be a million times better than the pathetic ones we had in middle school."

"Well, let's hope so." I stood over the stove, pouring a box of Kraft macaroni into a pan of boiling water. The phone cord wasn't quite long enough to reach the stove.

"I hope we get lots of the same classes. Are you going to take French?"

"Spanish." I stirred the macaroni.

"No, take French with me! Or Japanese."

"It's not like we won't have plenty of other classes together. You're taking Algebra, right?"

"Geometry. But we'll probably have 9th Grade Composition together. I hear everyone has to take that."

"Right."

"Oh, Grace, we're going to have so much fun in high school! Dances, boyfriends, band trips! It's going to be wonderful!"

An inexplicable wave of sadness hit me. I decided I was just hungry and poured the water out of my pan of macaroni. I tore open the packet of bright orange cheese and added milk.

"I have to go," I said to LaKeisha. "I'll call you tomorrow."

I threw a trivet onto the kitchen table and set the pan of macaroni on it. I ate straight from the pan and didn't stop until it was all gone.

By the end of the week, the coach had divided the swim team into Varsity and JV squads. I made Varsity. I was the only freshman to make the Varsity Squad. There were four senior girls, two juniors, a sophomore and me. The captain of the team was a small, wiry Hmong girl named Mai Lee. At last year's State meet, she took first in the 100 butterfly.

"Swimming is in my blood," she told me. "My parents swam across the Mekong River to get away from the Viet Cong. My father taught me to swim as soon as I could hold my head up."

I smiled nervously. For someone so small, Mai Lee was kind of intimidating.

The coach had us swim five 400-meter sets. I thought about what Mai Lee said, about her parents swimming across a river to safety. I imagined bullets skimming across the top of the water. I imagined bad guys chasing me in speedboats. I pictured the shore in front of me: just a few short meters to freedom. As I completed my last set and touched the wall, I looked up and realized that I'd finished before the other girls.

When I got out of the pool, I felt like I was floating. Before I went to the locker room, the coach said to me, "City Time Trials are next week. I want you to swim the 500 freestyle. I think that's going to be your event."

At the city time trials, I swam the 50 meters freestyle, the 500 freestyle, and swam 50 meters freestyle in the 200 individual medley relay. My team won the relay, but I came in third in both of my other two events. My time for the 500 was just over five minutes.

"Sorry I didn't do better," I said to my coach.

"Don't be sorry!" he said, squeezing my shoulder. "You've got all season to work on your speed. You'll win plenty of heats this year."

After time trials were over, I sat in the car with my mother. "It really looked like you were going to win that second race, but then that other girl started to pull ahead of you, and you fell further and further behind," she said.

"I'm sorry I wasn't good enough for you," I grumbled. I reached over and turned the radio to the alternative station.

"Oh, Grace, lighten up," she said as she turned the music down.

"Do we really have to go to this stupid bridal shower thing?" I asked. I was exhausted and hungry. I just wanted to plop down in front of the TV with a big bowl of pasta.

"Yes. Your dress is in the back seat."

An ugly, burgundy velvet empire waist dress stared back and me from the rear of the car. The plastic it was wrapped in crinkled as I grabbed a hold of it.

"I hate this dress," I complained.

"Tough. We're stopping to pick up Grandma. You can change at her house."

The dress was uncomfortable. It pinched under the arms and flattened my chest. I remembered that my mother bought it for me before I *had* a chest.

"Hurry up, Grace," my mother called as I struggled with the zipper.

"This doesn't fit me anymore," I said as I came out of the bathroom. "Can't I wear something else?"

Mom rolled her eyes. "Grace, we're going to be late."

"But it's really uncomfortable!"

"Oh, you'll be fine. Come on, let's go."

"That dress *does* look awfully tight," Grandma said, but Mom was already out the door.

I sat in the back seat, staring out the window as we drove to the suburbs. Every time I inhaled, the dress squeezed a little bit more.

We arrived at my cousin's house twenty-five minutes later. I carried in the gifts. An elderly aunt came up to me and asked, "Gracie, is that you? You're so grown up!"

Mom put her hands on my shoulders and said in a cheery voice, "She's our *Varsity* swimmer!" I fought the urge to ram an elbow into her ribs. Earlier, when she picked me up from the pool, all she'd wanted to talk about was how I'd let that other girl pull ahead of me. Now she wanted to brag about how I had made the varsity squad?

"Oh really?" Aunt Pearl asked. She turned to me with an expectant look.

"Tell her about your time swimming the 500, Grace," Mom said. I looked up at her in disbelief. For an instant, her eyes darkened and I felt her pinching the skin under my arm.

Moments later, I followed my mother out to the car.

"You embarrassed the shit out of me," she hissed. She slammed the car door as she got into the driver's seat.

"You *pinched* me!" I shot back. My cheeks flamed.

"I just wanted you to talk! I wanted you to tell Aunt Pearl about your swimming so I could be proud for a change."

I barely had time to shut my door or put my seatbelt on before she put the car in reverse and stomped on the accelerator.

"Proud?" I wanted to ask her why she suddenly wanted to be proud when she didn't seem proud at all after City Time Trials. I wanted to ask her why making the varsity squad only mattered when someone else was standing there. I wanted to ask her how Grandma was supposed to get home since we'd given her a ride and now we had just left without even telling her. But I couldn't make the words come out.

"Yes, proud. I do everything for you. Can't you do something to make me feel good for five minutes?"

When we got home, I went straight to my room and tore off the tight dress. I found a notebook and wrote in it, "I fucking hate my mom. She's a phony two-faced bitch. She should have gotten a cat instead of having a kid."

I put my *In Utero* CD into my Discman and turned the volume all the way up.

9

At the restaurant, I find my staff gathered in the kitchen, standing with their backs to the door. I'm about to read them today's specials – chestnut soup, goat cheese and cauliflower soufflé, duck with honey and figs – when Corey whirls around and shoves his iPhone into my face.

"Look!"

On the screen is a picture of the *tourte* I made the day before. "'Scrumptious Snouts at Saveur de Vie'?" I read aloud. "What is this?"

"It's Eater!" Corey says. "The blog. They write about restaurants all over the country and have like 300,000 followers on Twitter."

"So?" I say, tossing his phone back to him. His expression flattens.

"What do you mean, 'so'? How can you not be excited? Eater is, like, the Roger Ebert of food, and they just gave you a rave review. You should be jumping for joy right now."

I shrug as I button up my chef's jacket.

"I don't get you," Corey says, clearly disappointed. "It's like you don't even care."

"Has it ever occurred to you that some people care too much? Go get the figs out of the walk-in."

I suddenly feel like my lungs are hardening. My boss is definitely going to want me to do an interview now and it will be even harder to put her off and my name and face will end up on some blog or newspaper and my mother will see it and gloat and tell everyone what a great mother she is and 'Mystic Bay' wasn't bad because I turned out ok even though she never had to live in a fucking dog cage or watch girls be forced to eat their own vomit or listen to creepy self-help tapes on blast every goddamn day or…

"Grace!" Corey is by my side, furiously patting my sleeve with a damp towel. "Jesus, Grace, your sleeve caught fire. Are you hurt?"

I pull back my sleeve to look at my skin. It's fine. The flame didn't burn me.

"What the hell happened?" he asks.

"Brain fog. It's nothing. I'm fine."

"Do you need to go home?" He asks.

"I just need a minute," I reply, and step out onto the loading dock to get some fresh air. The loading dock once faced a weedy parking lot. I used to be able to watch the traffic on Washington Avenue and glimpse the river beyond it, but now the lot is a construction site. Right now, all that's there is a grayish skeleton that will eventually hold up a condo tower. A jackhammer echoes in the narrow alley. That sound would drive most people crazy, but I like it; it clears away the fog.

10

On my first day of 9th grade, I stood in line in the windowless cafeteria, waiting to pick up my class schedule. As I waited, I watched two older girls shriek and hug each other.

"I can't believe we're finally seniors," one of them said. The back of her shirt listed all the stops Green Day made on their most recent tour. Traces of green dye stained the ends of her hair.

"Guess what?" The other girl asked. "I got a car! We can have lunch off campus." Her sweatshirt told me that she was on the soccer team. The two girls disappeared into the crowd. The line inched forward.

I gave my name to the woman behind the table, and she handed me a small square of paper with my classes on it. I asked her how to find room 215. She raised her voice so that I could hear her over the loud hum of kids reuniting after the long summer.

My first class was empty except for a black-haired girl wearing all black, sitting in the first row.

"LaKeisha?"

She beamed when she saw me. "Sit here!" she said, slamming her hand down on the empty desk next to her.

"I'm so happy you're in this class! I got lost looking for this room."

"I have a feeling that's going to happen a lot."

LaKeisha leaned close and lowered her voice. "Well, here's one thing I do know: some of the older kids like to prank freshmen by saying there's a pool on the third floor, but the school doesn't have one."

"Yeah, I know. I'm on the swim team, remember? We do all our practices at Southwest because they have a pool and we don't."

The room quickly filled. A low rumble of conversation began but died down as the teacher entered the room. He walked silently to the blackboard and wrote his name in chalk. When he turned around, heat flooded my cheeks. The teacher – Mr. Kyeong – had thick black hair that fell into his eyes and dimples that punctuated his movie-star smile. I could see his biceps through his button-down shirt.

"Good morning class," he said brightly, "I'm Brian Kyeong, and this is 9th Grade English. While I pass out your reading lists for the semester, let me tell you a little about me: I'm from Los Angeles – the heart of Koreatown, to be exact. I came to the University of Minnesota on a baseball scholarship and decided to stay here and be a teacher. In the spring, I coach the baseball team. We're going to work hard this year, but we're going to learn a lot. Any questions so far?"

Do you have a girlfriend? I blinked hard as if that could erase the question from my mind.

"What about you?" he asked. When I realized he was looking at me, I felt like I'd just plunged into a tub of ice water. He handed me a reading list.

"Me?"

He nodded, still smiling.

"Um…" I scanned the reading list as fast as I could. "*A Tree Grows in Brooklyn* is one of my favorite books…but that's not really a question."

I sank a little in my seat, my cheeks flaming.

He laughed. "No, but it's a good answer."

I felt a rush of relief when someone behind me raised a hand.

An hour later, LaKeisha confronted me in the hallway.

"You're in love with our English teacher!" she squealed.

"No, I'm not," I said, and made a big show of trying to get my bearings.

"Yes, you are. All during class, you looked at him with the same look you had last year when you were crushing on that skater kid."

"Well, I'd love to stay and talk about this more, but my next class is Spanish and that's on the third floor."

As I made my way to the stairwell, she called after me: "Whether you like it or not, we're gonna talk about this!"

That afternoon, I found a note in my locker. I unfolded it and found a drawing of two stick-figures kissing. One had long hair that stuck straight back. The other one was holding a shopping bag. "Grace + Mr. Kyeong 4Eva" was scribbled underneath.

The next morning, I got to Mr. Kyeong's class early. LaKeisha punched me in the arm as she took her seat next to me.

"Why is he holding a grocery bag?" I asked her, holding up her artwork.

"It's a briefcase."

"You seriously cannot draw for shit," I whispered to her. She responded by making a kissy face and pretending to fondle herself.

"Too much coffee this morning, LaKeisha?" Mr. Kyeong asked, winking. A tiny gold chain glittered around his neck; the charm on the end was tucked under his collar. He told us that our first unit of the semester would be memoir.

"How can a writer take something that they remember and make it real for someone else?" He asked as he twirled an un-capped dry erase marker between his thumb and forefinger. Slowly, I raised my hand.

"Details?"

Mr. Kyeong flashed his megawatt smile. "Is that a question?"

My cheeks flushed a little. "By focusing on details – very specific ones."

"That's right, Grace," he said, still smiling. I smiled back, feeling warm all over until LaKeisha jammed her mechanical pencil into my ribs.

"The first book we're going to read is a memoir by Irina Ratushinskaya," Mr. Kyeong said as he wrote the author's name on the whiteboard. "Irina Ratushinskaya is a Russian poet. During the Soviet period, she was a dissident. Can anyone tell me what a dissident is?"

LaKeisha's hand shot up. "A dissident is someone who disagrees with the government."

"That's right, LaKeisha. Now, here in America, we're all free to be dissidents. The constitution guarantees our *right* to be dissidents. But in other parts of the world, people who speak out against their governments end up in political prisons. And that's what happened to Irina Ratushinskaya."

Mr. Kyeong passed out copies to the book to everyone. On the very first page of the book, there was an author's note, which he read aloud to the class:

"'Readers may wonder, quite justifiably, how much of this book is truth and how much is fiction? The answer is that there is no fiction at all; I do not have enough imagination for it.' Why do you think she wrote this?"

"Maybe because she really didn't tell the truth," LaKeisha said.

"What makes you say that?" Mr. Kyeong asked.

"Well, my mama always says, if a first thing out of a man's mouth is 'I hate drama,' it really means he secretly likes it. So, like, if you have to say you're telling the truth, maybe you're really not."

I raised my hand. "She's afraid people won't believe her. That doesn't mean that what she has to say isn't true."

LaKeisha turned to face me: "If she's telling the truth, why should she worry that people won't believe her?"

I had no answer for that one. We both looked at Mr. Kyeong, who was beaming at us. "This is a great debate, ladies. Unfortunately, we're running out of time. For your homework tonight, I want you all to read the first chapter of *Grey is the Color of Hope* and write a memory of your own. It doesn't have to be too long – no more than a page – but be sure to focus on the details."

The bell rang and the classroom quickly emptied. I stayed behind. I held my breath and slowly walked up to Mr. Kyeong's desk.

"Hey there," he said. "What can I do for you?"

"Oh, it's nothing…I was just wondering what kind of necklace that is."

He pulled it out of his collar and revealed a flat disc with lines like a basketball and the words Los Angeles Lakers written across it.

"I'm hoping for a good season," he said, winking.

During the two hours between the end of the school day and the start of swim practice, I wrote my memory for Mr. Kyeong's class.

When I was nine-years-old, a new family moved into the house next door to ours. They had a dog. He was a Rottweiler. My dad said he was small for his breed. His name was Dino.

They kept Dino outside – even when it was raining or cold. They didn't feed him very much either. I used to take lunch meat from our refrigerator and offer it to him by sticking my hands through the chain link fence. The first time I fed him, he stood very far away from the fence and just sniffed the air. I think he was afraid to come to me, but he walked over very slowly. He sniffed the pimento loaf that I held in my clenched fist. Then, he snatched it and ran to the other side of the yard, where he ate it.

After that, I fed him every day. He became less and less afraid of me. One day, he licked my fingers. His warm tongue tickled.

A few months after they first brought Dino home, I saw the man come home from work. He slammed his car door. He opened the gate and kicked Dino in his ribs. Dino yelped. I yelled for my dad. He said if the neighbor did that again, we would have to call the police.

Sure enough, the next day, the man kicked Dino again. Harder this time. Dino cried and laid down on the ground. My dad made a phone call. Someone came and took Dino away – to a better family. I never saw him again. I'll always remember the lesson my dad taught me: when someone does something to hurt someone else, you've got to speak up.

I started to write, "That was before my dad moved out of the house and my mother started acting crazy," but I scratched it out.

11

The snouts ended up on another food blog. It was an amateur blog by some writer desperate to make a name for herself, so I didn't stress out about it too much. But now someone at the *Star Tribune* has noticed, and they want me to do an interview. I've been ducking this journalist's calls all morning. I can't believe he hasn't given up.

"You are popular today," Jess says as my phone rings for the third time since class started.

"Some reporter keeps calling. Wants me to talk about some dish I made."

"Why don't you just answer? I'd be psyched if someone from the newspaper wanted to talk to me."

I don't answer. Jess is on her back with the soles of her feet pressed against my hips. I'm standing opposite her, gripping fistfuls of her pant legs in each hand. My objective is to get her legs out of the way so I can mount and submit her, but her legs will not move.

"Miss Grace," James says to me as he walks over to our corner of the mat. "Lock your arms out straight and use your body weight to move her legs. Have you seen the giant kettlebells she likes to throw around? If you try to out-muscle her, you're going to lose."

I follow his advice, shooting my legs back so that I'm leaning most of my weight on Jess's shins. Her legs collapse, and I move them to the side.

"Good," James says, "now take mount." She grunts a little as I put my knee across her solar plexus and then slide it to the floor. I sit on her, my knees digging into either side of her ribcage.

"Scoot up a bit," James says. "Sit higher on her chest so she can't buck you off." I do as he says. I watch Jess's face redden. She glowers up at me through her white lashes. She digs her elbows into my thighs and I can feel the bruises forming already.

"Jess isn't going to let you stay there very long. From here you can do a choke, armbar, americana — just about any submission you want. But do it before she escapes."

I decide to try a collar choke; by grabbing a handful of fabric on either side of her throat, I can choke Jess with her own gi. I slide my right hand into the right side of Jess's collar and grab a handful of the stiff blue cotton. Before I can slide my left hand in for my second grip, she tosses me onto my back, takes mount and chokes *me*.

I tap out as a cloud of silvery fireflies forms in my head. My tongue feels numb. As the fireflies fade away, Jess's face comes into sharp focus. She winks at me and squeezes my shoulder.

"Let's do it again," she says, flopping onto her back.

After class, I look at my phone and its long list of missed calls. Jess asks me a question and I say "sure" without having any idea what I've agreed to. My ears are ringing and I have a sharp pain right above my eyes. Why won't this writer just leave me alone?

I arrive at work an hour later. My head still hurts even though I've taken ibuprofen. Before I can button up my chef's jacket, my boss calls me into her office.

"The *Star Tribune* wants to talk to you."

"I know," I mutter, staring at a photo that sits on her desk. It's a snapshot of a man standing on a narrow street in Paris, with a tiny cafe in the background. I recognize the cafe. It was run by an Algerian family who made the most incredible lamb stew. They served a hearty portion and fluffy couscous to go with it for just five euros. I ate there a lot while I was staging at Le Cinq.

"I don't know what this phobia you have about interviews is about, but you need to get over it," she says. She sips her coffee. The glasses with the white frames hide the fine wrinkles around her eyes. Her dark hair is pulled back into a tight ponytail.

"Wouldn't you rather speak to them? You're the owner."

"But you're the expert on French food," she retorts. "Call them back."

Defeated, I skulk out of her office and head for the loading dock. I light a cigarette. My stomach aches like I've just swallowed an apple from a poisoned tree and my shoulders feel heavy. I hold my phone up to my ear. The reporter's cheerful voice makes me relax a little.

"Your torte of pig snouts has really taken off," the reporter says. "How do you account for that?"

"People are lemmings."

The reporter just laughs. "Can you tell me about the dish? Where does it come from? Where did you first taste it?"

I explain that it's a traditional recipe from Burgundy and that an elderly neighbor I had in Paris made it for me once. I tell him it's an ancient recipe that was first documented in the fourteenth century.

"They should really serve it at the Renaissance Festival," I tell him. "It would be way more authentic than those turkey legs."

I hear him chuckle and stifle a cough. He says something about Europeans using ingredients that Americans won't. Then he tells a joke about England and kidney pie.

"Europeans are better at using the whole animal," I say. "It's more ethical." Some chef in Chicago said this once. I remember reading about it while I was in culinary school.

He says he has enough and thanks me for the interview. I end the call and put my phone in my pocket. My hand is shaking.

That afternoon, the *Star Tribune* article goes live online. Everyone in the restaurant is excited except for me. I just feel this vine of dread sprouting in the pit of my stomach, reaching up to strangle me. If he used that thing I said about lemmings, my boss is going to lock me in the freezer. I scan the article quickly. I sound sophisticated and polished. Professional. And yet I don't feel any better.

Thanks to the article, the dinner service is packed.

By closing time, I've forgotten my anxiety, but it rushes back in the moment I glance at my phone. Three missed calls, all from my mother. I delete all three of her voicemails without listening to a single word.

At home, my phone rings again, but this time it's my dad.

"Gracious," he says to me, "did your mom call you?"

"Three times," I say.

"Did you talk to her?"

"Nope." I light a cigarette. It's my last one. I debate going out to buy another pack. I don't want to go out, but I know I'll regret it in the morning.

"I did," he says. "She was foaming at the mouth. Wanted to know why you wouldn't answer the phone. I said, 'probably for the same reason I wish I hadn't.'"

I laugh. "I bet that went over well."

"Like a lead balloon," he says.

"Oh, God, Dad, I knew this would happen. I really didn't want to do that interview. I tried to get out of it."

"Grace...it's okay to be successful."

"I just want to cook." Suddenly I feel like I'm going to cry. *Damn it, don't!*

"I know, Gracious."

For a few minutes, he doesn't say anything and neither do I. My eyes feel hot. Somewhere outside, a group of men is playing basketball in the dark. I can hear the ball hitting the pavement.

"I have to get to sleep," I say, finally.

"Good night, Grace," he says.

As soon as I hang up, I realize I have a text from Jess. *Meet me in the lobby at the Uptown.* That's right. Jess invited me to see a midnight movie with her at the Uptown Theater. For a minute, I consider not going, and start working on an excuse. On the other hand, at the movies, I won't have to talk, and I *am* out of cigarettes. I change into more comfortable clothes, grab my car keys and head out to meet Jess.

12

During the second week of school, we had our first swim meet. After Sixth Hour, we got on the bus and rode out to the suburbs while The Barenaked Ladies blasted from the radio. I rested my head against the window and watched rundown houses blur.

I was nervous. I volunteered to swim in three events: 50 freestyle, 500 freestyle and the Medley Relay. The coach had already given me his pep talk: "Don't worry about your time or how you place. Just work hard like you've been doing in practice."

I tried to take the coach's words to heart, but I knew that if I didn't do well, I could lose my spot on the Varsity squad. The older girls had told me about girls from previous years who were fast during practice but choked during swim meets and had to be moved over to the JV squad. They made it seem like getting bumped down to JV was the worst thing ever.

"You can't letter if you're JV," Mai Lee had said, as she slid her thin, muscular arms into the big leather sleeves of her letter jacket. I desperately wanted a jacket like that.

The pool at Edina High School was clean and bright with no missing tiles on the deck. We changed into our swimsuits in the Boys' locker room. Our suits were plain black racing suits, but the girls from the Edina team had theirs custom made: emerald green with "Edina" printed in neat white script down the side.

"Stuck up bitches," Mai Lee said as we huddled around her. "Let's kick their snobby suburban asses."

In my first heat – the 50 freestyle – I took second place, losing to the Edina swimmer by four and a half seconds. During the 500, Mai Lee knelt at the shallow end of the pool and held numbered cards in the water to help me keep track of what lap I was on. Through the first eighteen laps, I held a steady pace. I blocked out both of the other swimmers in the lanes next to me and imagined I was crossing the English Channel or the San Francisco Bay. Then, on the 19th lap, the card at the end of the pool turned bright orange and shook back and forth.

I took one large breath and plunged my face into the water. I kicked and stroked hard without stopping to exhale even once. When I reached the wall, I somersaulted and pushed off the wall with my feet. My heart thundered in my chest, and I could feel my cheeks flaming, even under water. I touched the wall and lifted my face out of the water. I let the air out of my lungs and panted hard. I grabbed the handles on the starting block and pulled myself out of the water. That's when I noticed my teammates jumping up and down and cheering.

"You won, Grace!" the coach said, clapping me on the shoulder. Mai Lee dropped the cards on the deck and trotted down to the other end of the pool. She wrapped her arms around me and lifted me off my feet. As she set me back down, I heard someone shout my name. Quickly, I scanned the crowd for familiar faces.

It was my dad.

I hadn't seen him in almost a year. Because he moved out without talking to a lawyer first, the judge said he'd given up his visitation rights or something like that, and because he didn't even call for a long time after that, it seemed like he didn't really care. But now, according to my mom, he was trying to get weekends.

A few days ago, I'd overheard my mom talking on the phone, saying, "If he thinks he can just waltz back in and take my kid, he can just forget it. I'll make sure he *never* sees her."

What if I *want to see him?* I wondered.

I walked over to the bleachers where my dad was sitting. "Hey there, Gracious!" He said and wrapped me in a bear hug.

"You're doing *great* out there!"

"How did you know I had a meet today?" I asked him.

He released the hug and reached into his pocket. He showed me a small stack of folded pages. "Your grandma faxed me a copy of your schedule," he said. He meant my mom's mom. I didn't know she talked to my dad.

"I'm so proud of you," he said. "I'm going to come to all your meets and cheer you on." He paused and got this look on his face, like a dog who'd just peed on the carpet. "If that's ok with you, I mean."

"Sure," I said. He smiled and I stood there without saying anything for a few minutes before I told him I had to get back to my team.

Mai Lee won the 100-meter butterfly and we crushed the Edina team in the medley relay. The judges scored the meet in our favor; my hands burned from slapping high-fives with my teammates.

"This is a great start to the season," the coach said. "Let's keep it going!"

On the car ride home, I closed my eyes and tried not to listen to my mom talking. "The only reason your father showed up at that meet is because his lawyers told him it would make him look good."

She had missed the meet because she'd had a meeting with *her* lawyers.

"He doesn't care about this family. He wants to get back at me. That's all this is. I can't believe he has the nerve."

I reached over and turned the radio to 93.7. Gwen Stefani sang about living in captivity.

"Would you turn that down? I'm trying to talk to you." She had her hands on her hips. She had gotten so much skinnier since my dad left. The yellow plaid mini skirt with the matching blazer showed how spindly her thighs were. Her hair was salon-shiny and freshly dyed blond.

She's so lame. She thinks she can become Kate Moss, I thought.

I turned the volume down and waited. Streetlights flicked on as we cruised past the part. Lights glowed in the windows of old houses.

"I won tonight," I said. "I swam the 500 and won. I helped my team win the medley relay. We won our first meet of the season. We're 1 and 0. Are you going to say anything about that?"

She sighed. "Grace, can't you ever think of anything but yourself? You're the most selfish kid I've ever known."

13

Jess waits for me in the lobby at the Uptown Theater. She's leaning against the wall with her back turned toward the glass door. She's wearing work boots and a leather jacket. From behind, it's easy to mistake her for a man, thanks to her broad shoulders and short hair. This neighborhood was once full of people who looked just like her: punk rockers and tattoo artists who didn't care how weird you were as long as you weren't a narc. Most of those folks are gone now; they've been displaced by prissy corporate types. I wonder if that's what I like about Jess — that she reminds me of a different time.

"Hey," I say to her as I tap her on the shoulder.

"Hey! I wasn't sure you'd make it," Jess says. I don't tell her how close I came to bailing out on her.

"Where's Michelle?" I change the subject.

"She's at home. Knocked out. She had a long day of lawyering. Besides, midnight movies have always been my thing. Well, that and jiu-jitsu."

Jess hands me a bag of popcorn and a ticket. I reach for my wallet so I can give her cash but she waves me off.

"Thanks," I mutter, sheepishly. I follow Jess up to the balcony. As the lights dim and the opening theme to *Life of Brian* begins to play, I find myself trying to remember the last time I was in a movie theater sitting with people who weren't total strangers.

It was in high school. It was after I got out of Mystic Bay and was back at South High. LaKeisha invited me to go to a movie with her and some of her friends. They would've been my friends, too, if I hadn't been sent away, but by the time I got back, I was just someone they "kinda remembered" from freshman year. I didn't really remember them at all.

We went to the movie theater at the Mall of America and saw some stupid comedy. Every time LaKeisha laughed, she nudged me with her elbow. She had always done that. Even when we were in elementary school watching movies like *Aladdin,* she would nudge me every time she laughed. It never bothered me. But that afternoon in high school, her nudges made me flinch. Each gentle poke made me tense waiting for the next one.

Finally, I snapped and shoved her hard, then got up and walked out of the theater. I paced around near the concession stand, where popcorn leaped over the sides of a steel kettle and blue raspberry slushies churned slowly in a translucent vat.

"Grace, what is the matter with you?" LaKeisha asked as she stomped toward me. My heart raced as I backed away from her. "Ever since you came back to school you have been acting crazy."

"I told you," I panted, suddenly noticing that I was struggling to catch air, "what they did to me."

She rolled her eyes.

"Quit making up stories," she said.

I showed her my middle finger and walked away. That was the last time we spoke.

Popcorn erupts from Jess's mouth as she laughs, snapping me out of my memory. I look over at her, half expecting her to nudge me, but her elbow stays on her side of the arm rest. She catches me looking at her and winks.

As the movie draws to a close, and the man hanging from one of the wooden crosses begins to sing "Always Look on the Bright Side of Life," the whole theater swells with song. Jess's voice carries over all of them. Her voice is brash and gravelly, but never off key.

Moments later, we file back out into the dark city streets. We say goodbye and drive home. I walk up the stairs to my apartment with that song still bouncing through my brain. It isn't until the next morning that I realize I forgot to buy cigarettes.

14

My dad showing up at my swim meet really set my mom off. She threw a fit one weekend when LaKeisha invited me to sleep over.

"You never want to spend any time with me," mom accused. It seemed to come out of nowhere, especially since she hadn't asked me to do anything with her before I told her that LaKeisha had invited me over.

We were in the kitchen. The dishwasher hummed and the radio was on.

"Geez, Mom. I just want to hang out with my friend. I did all my homework, I did all my chores and I don't have any swim meets this weekend. I don't see what the problem is."

Mom crossed her arms. "You think you can rely on your *friends*? Your friends will turn their backs on you one day. I'm all you've got."

I looked away from her. A ray of sunlight lanced through the window. A commercial for diamond rings droned over the radio waves.

"I asked you *last week* if I could stay at LaKeisha's today and you said yes. I don't get why it's a problem all of a sudden."

The dishwasher clicked over to the rinse cycle.

"You used to love spending time with me. Remember? You loved it when I let you play with my old Jill doll."

I rolled my eyes. "I'm not five any more, Mom. I'm almost fifteen. There's a big difference."

The radio played a song from the '60s.

"Grace Meredith, I work my fingers to the bone to put a roof over your head. A little affection now and then would pay for that."

The whole room blinked red. I pressed the sharp edge of my thumbnail against the bone in my wrist.

"I don't owe you shit," I spat back.

"Watch your language," she said, wagging her finger. "Do you know what my father would have said if I'd talked that way to him?"

I leaned against the dishwasher. It was warm.

"Mom, do you remember that ad you put in the newspaper? 'I'm fair, honest and always on time!' Well, you're not being honest or fair to me right now."

The song on the radio faded out. A DJ introduced the next one and in that moment, I thought of all the other kitchens around town that were tuned to his voice. I suddenly felt a yearning for those imaginary kitchens; like being somewhere on vacation and desperately wanting to go home.

"Fine," she relented. "Go to your friend's house. I could use a night off from you anyway."

An hour later, we pulled up outside of LaKeisha's house. It was a small, 1940s-style bungalow with white siding and mint-green shutters.

"Ugh, this neighborhood," Mom muttered. "I don't even like driving through here, much less dropping you off here."

Except for a vacant lot across the street, the rest of the houses on the block looked just like LaKeisha's: modest, post-war, tidy.

"Don't worry, Mom. It's not like your clients can smell North Minneapolis on you when you're showing houses in Wayzata."

Mom actually laughed. "I love you, Grace," she said, and opened her arms for a hug. The words she'd spoken earlier were still fresh on my mind. As I let her arms encircle me, I resisted the urge to shove her away. She smelled like the perfume counter at J.C. Penney.

LaKeisha's dad greeted me at the door. He wore his hair in dreadlocks tied back with a black bandana. LaKeisha's parents owned a little diner that was down the street. "We're so happy to have you here, Grace," he said as he led me to LaKeisha's room.

Marilyn Manson's eyebrowless, porcelain-white face hung directly above LaKeisha's bed. His lips were deep red like he'd just eaten a live duck.

"I cannot *believe* your parents let you have that," I said, as I admired the poster.

"Oh, they hate it," she said, "but they don't think posters are worth fighting about. My dad says that back in the day, people thought Ray Charles was scandalous. Can you imagine?" She laughed.

"Does that mean your grandparents got mad when your dad listened to Ray Charles?"

LaKeisha shrugged. "My grandparents worked a lot. I don't think they had time to get mad about music."

"My mom works all the time. She still finds time to get mad about…everything."

LaKeisha cocked her head to the side. "Really? Your mom seems so nice."

"She's a bitch," I said, looking past LaKeisha at the vacant lot across the street. A small cement staircase stood alone in the grass, leading nowhere.

"Come on," LaKeisha said, "she can't be that bad."

I didn't argue. LaKeisha changed the subject. "Oh, I can't believe I forgot to tell you! Remember how I got a callback for 'A Winter's Tale?'"

I nodded.

"I got a part! I'm going to be Dorcas, a Shepherdess in love with the Young Shepherd."

"Your character's name is Dork-ass?"

LaKeisha let out a squeal and grabbed hold of the hood on my sweatshirt, pulling it over my eyes.

"That's awesome," I said, pushing the hood away from my face, "Just think: by senior year, you'll have the lead roles in all the plays, and I'll be captain of the swim team."

"And we'll take the cutest guys to the prom."

I watched a pair of young boys chase each other through the vacant lot. A boy with cornrows and a red shirt whirled and launched a Nerf football at the kid who ran behind him. The second boy dropped the ball.

"What guys? I can't think of anyone cute," I said.

LaKeisha rolled her eyes. "Oh, please. That's because you're so busy drooling over Mr. Kyeong that you never notice anyone else."

The mention of Mr. Kyeong's name made my face tingle.

LaKeisha's dad drove us to Roller Garden, but before we left, LaKeisha pulled out a can of spray-on hair dye.

"I can't," I said. "My mom will have a fit."

"Chill out. It's washable. It will shampoo right out."

LaKeisha gathered a large tress of my hair and sprayed neon blue dye onto it. After it dried, I ran my fingers through it. I thought I looked cute.

After breakfast the next morning, LaKeisha and her dad drove me home. My house was empty, but the radio was still on. I needed to wash the blue dye out of my hair, but when I went into the bathroom and looked at my reflection, I decided I could keep the blue dye in a little longer. After all, Mom wasn't supposed to be home until about supper time. She had appointments all day.

I sat on the couch with an Anne Rice novel. I got pulled so far into the story about witches in a dilapidated New Orleans mansion that I completely forgot about the time.

I hadn't heard my mom come in, but now she was standing in front of me. I looked up.

"What the *hell* is that in your hair?" she demanded.

"Relax, Mom," I said. "It will wash right out."

"My clients are some of the most wealthy and influential people in this city. Do you think they'll work with me if I have a daughter who looks like a rock and roll druggie?"

I closed my book. "Mom, are you deaf? I *said* it's temporary. It's washable."

She put her hands on her hips. There was a smudge on her elbow and her nylons bunched around her ankles. "Why did you do that? To make me look stupid? You had no right to do that without my permission."

I threw my book onto the floor and stood up from the couch. "I don't need your permission. It's *my* hair!"

She stomped out of the room and returned with a pair of scissors in her hand. "I told you that if you dyed your hair I would cut it off!" She grabbed a fistful of my hair. I heard a loud metallic scrape as she separated the scissor blades.

"Mom, stop," I said, but she didn't let go. I grabbed the hand that held the scissors. All of the hours of swimming must have made me strong, because I out-muscled her in a mid-air arm wrestle. The scissors clattered to the floor.

"It washes out!" I shouted.

"THEN GO WASH IT OUT!" Her face became a beet, her eyes glassy black beads. All the creases around her eyes suddenly seemed deeper.

I had never heard her bellow like that. As I walked to the bathroom, I shook. The water turned quickly from cold to hot – too hot, but I didn't turn it down. My mother was a bitch. A cunt. A worthless, ugly old cow. I wanted to scream, to break the shower tiles, to smash my mother's face like a rotten Jack O' Lantern.

Instead, I held my wrist up to my lips and sank my teeth into my skin. I stopped just before the skin broke. I'd left behind a series of tiny, half-moon indentations, arranged in a football shape.

The blue dye swirled around my feet, disappeared down the drain.

The next day at swim practice, Mai Lee noticed the strange bruise on my wrist.

"What the hell is that? It looks like someone bit you," she said. The little half-moons had all turned black and blue and bled together.

"I was…just practicing giving hickeys," I lied.

Her eyebrows jumped. "Looks like you need a lot more practice."

15

I start going to the movies with Jess on a semi-regular basis. We see a lot of old movies, like *Barbarella, Easy Rider* and *Harold and Maude.*

One Sunday morning, after seeing *The Way We Were,* I'm on the phone with my dad explaining why the movie made no sense to me.

"What's with you and all these movies from the seventies?" he laughs.

I explain about Jess.

"Good, Grace," he says, his tone suddenly serious. "I am glad you're making friends."

I don't say anything. Dad changes the subject.

"We turned another one," he says, referring to his network of parents whose kids are survivors, like me. They have meetings once a month to talk about the industry and sometimes when one of them finds out that another parent is planning to ship their kid off, they stage an intervention to talk them out of it.

"That's good," I say. I know he wants me to get more involved, but I can't do it. The thought of listening to some woman rattle off all the reasons why her kid deserves to be shipped off makes my hands tighten into fists. If I went to this intervention thing, there is a ninety-percent chance I would end up in jail.

In addition to his parents-of-survivors group, Dad also writes a blog and keeps track of schools all over the country. He knows more about this shit than I do.

"Mystic Bay has been reincarnated. It's Misty Harbor RTC now."

"Misty Harbor? That name is even stupider than Mystic Bay."

"Yeah, it is. They claim that Misty Harbor is in no way affiliated with Mystic Bay, but they employ all the same staff."

"Barf." For a second, I flash back to the rainy mornings at Mystic Bay, when the sky was oyster-colored and droplets of water hung suspended in the air until noon. I shudder. I fish around for my cigarettes, jamming my hand in between the cushions on my couch.

"Don't barf yet: there's more. Epiphany Lake is reopening. The website lists some guy named Arthur Crenshaw as the owner."

"Crandell using a fake name?" I ask as my fingers bump into a half-empty pack of cigarettes. I drop it onto my lap and pull one out.

"Yeah," Dad says, "but he's such a moron. The website is registered under his actual fucking name. I posted a screenshot on my blog and got a five thousand word email from this Crenshaw character. He starts out by insisting that this new school has nothing to do with Crandell, then spends eight paragraphs *defending* Crandell. Dumbass doesn't know whether he's coming or going."

Ash tumbles from the end of my cigarette onto the floor. "Makes sense to me. It's the same old shit."

I hear a dog barking in the background on my dad's end of the line. He still lives in the duplex he and I moved into after he got me out of Mystic Bay.

"How's work?" Dad asks.

"Okay, I guess."

"Just Ok?" he sounds surprised.

"Now *Bon Appetit* wants to talk to me."

"That's great!"

"No, it isn't."

Dad sighs, "Gracious…."

My phone beeps. "I'm getting another call," I say. Dad and I trade goodbyes, and I hang up, but I let the other call go to voicemail.

Misty Harbor RTC. I type the words into the search bar. I click on the link, and when the site pops up, I see images of the same, ugly bunkhouses tucked in a dark grove of scruffy pine trees. The name is new but the rest is the same. My spine rattles.

I log onto SOS and write a post that links to Misty Harbor RTC.

It was on SOS that I first learned about the fate of the schools I attended. The horror stories of what went on at Mystic Bay finally caught up with it. Bad press dogged the place until the Dominican government ordered it to close. Rumors about it reopening started circulating a year later.

Enrollment at Epiphany Lake started to slow down. Then, the recession hit. Suddenly, no one could afford to drop thousands of dollars to ship their kids away. Epiphany Lake closed permanently.

Until now.

That's what these assholes do. They get away with their bullshit as long as they can, then when they have to shut down, they wait a while and pop up again after the dust settles. The owners of these places sometimes get arrested, but rarely do they ever wind up facing any real prison time.

In Utah, where "wilderness therapy" programs take kids on forced marches through the desert, a sixteen-year-old girl died of heat stroke while on a trek with the Challenger Foundation. Two former employees of Challenger went on to establish North Star Expeditions. North Star was supposed to teach survival skills and self-reliance, polishing surly brats into perfect young adults.

There's a famous story about a kid named Aaron Bacon who went on an expedition with North Star. While they were on trail, the kids were only allowed to light campfires using a bow drill which isn't easy unless you're a scoutmaster or hard-core survivalist. Anyone who couldn't master it wasn't allowed to eat their share of the group's rations. Because he never got the hang of the bow drill, Aaron had to eat what he could catch, surviving on scorpions and raw lizards.

Aaron began to experience abdominal pain, but when he told the counselors about it, all they did was mock him and accuse him of faking. They took away his sleeping bag, forcing him to get through the below-freezing nights on unforgiving ground, under cold desert stars. His nose bled. He lost control of his bowels. His vision went dark and he became delirious. Through it all, they called him a liar and refused to get him to a doctor. Someone did try to save him, fed him oatmeal and brown sugar and let him lie in the shade of a juniper tree. But it was too late. Aaron Bacon died of a perforated ulcer. The motherfuckers who wouldn't get him help were tried for negligent homicide, but they didn't serve any time. They got off with community service and probation.

That was in 1995. More than 20 years later, the same shit is still going on.

My phone rings again. This time I answer it. It's Jess.

"Grace! Thank God! I really need your help! Can you come over right away?"

"What's the problem?"

"Michelle is having some of her law school friends over and she put me in charge of the food."

"So?"

"I burned everything!"

Jess's house is royal blue with black gingerbread and a porch that curves halfway around the front of it. A slate walkway leads me to the front door, which is wide open. A smoke alarm is going off inside. There's creeping phlox on both sides of the walkway, but it's dormant now. I try to imagine what it looks like in summer; little white blossoms everywhere like a blanket of stars.

I can smell canola oil and scorched cheese even before I step into the house. Jess is in the kitchen, standing on a step ladder and flapping a damp towel at the smoke alarm above her head. There are empty Lean Cuisine boxes all over the kitchen table and little black plastic trays jammed into the sink. A pot on the stove has smoke rising from it and oil pouring down its sides.

Finally, the alarm stops shrieking and Jess climbs down off her ladder, her face red and beading with sweat.

"What the hell are you trying to do here?" I ask, picking up one of the Lean Cuisine boxes. It has a picture of macaroni and cheese on the front.

"Trying to make deep fried macaroni and cheese bites," Jess replies, drying her forehead with the back of her sleeve. "I saw a video online. You're supposed to take the frozen stuff out of the tray and slice it up into squares and then fry it."

"And they are supposed to be Cajun or what?" I ask as I peer into the still-smoking pot and fish out a blackened mac-and-cheese square.

"The first batch didn't cook! They were still frozen in the middle. So I cranked up the heat."

"How many did you put in at once?"

"As many as I could fit! Why?"

"When you add too many things to hot oil, it lowers the temperature. That's why the first ones you put in didn't cook through. The trick is to cook a few at a time," I explain.

"Oh…" she says, "Well…now what?"

"I'll go pick up some stuff. You just get this stuff out of the way, and I'll take care of the rest."

Forty-five minutes later, I return to Jess's house with a sack of groceries. All the evidence of Jess's mac-and-cheese mishap is gone. Jess helps me carry the groceries in.

"What can I do?" she asks.

"Nothing, I can take care of it," I say. Jess looks disappointed. "But if you really want to, you can help chop the ingredients for the stuffed eggplants," I add.

I hand Jess the roma tomatoes and kalamata olives. "I need these diced petite," I instruct.

I take twelve baby eggplants out of the grocery sack and wash them gently before slicing each one in half and scooping out the young, tender-but-firm flesh. I cube the flesh and saute it in olive oil along with the tomatoes, olives and a bit of fresh garlic. Just before I take the mixture off of the heat, I add a pinch of salt and a squeeze of lemon juice. I carefully stuff each of the twenty-four eggplant halves, topping each one with a crumble of Bulgarian feta and sprinkle of seasoned breadcrumbs, then I slide them into a hot oven.

Next, I show Jess how to remove pith from blood oranges, and put her in charge of the blood orange and red onion salad. While keeping a close eye on the eggplants in the oven, I begin assembling the mortadella-and-provolone paninis, going through the steps in my head until I settle into a familiar rhythm.

By the time Michelle and her friends arrive, Jess and I are laying the food out on the table. The house suddenly fills with chatter as I heat sugar on the stove to make a ginger syrup for the granita. I mix in prosecco and lemon juice before pouring the mixture into trays and sliding them into the freezer.

Now that both the stove and oven are turned off, the kitchen feels cold. The energy that's been humming in my brain, the high I've been riding, is starting to drop. I feel like I might cry. A shrill peal of laughter from the dining room makes me flinch. No one will care if I leave, I reason, and I can text Jess the instructions for the last step for the granita. I grab my car keys and coat, intending to just slip out without anyone noticing, but Jess catches me.

"Grace, you can't leave!" she says. "I need you to keep me company. I hate conversating with Michelle's lawyer friends."

She yokes her arm around my neck. "Come on. We can watch old UFC fights in the den. Plus, I squirreled away some of the food. After all that work, I wasn't about to let them have it all!"

I hear that high-pitched laugh again. It makes my heart beat faster.

"It's quieter in the den," Jess reassures me, and I follow her down the hall.

"I can't thank you enough for helping me out like this," Jess says. She turns on the TV. Conor McGregor stares down his opponent. The referee gives them the signal to start the fight. "I'm sure this is the last thing you wanted to do on your day off."

"I like working," I reply.

"Well, I still appreciate it. I can't believe I was going to serve squares of fried Lean Cuisine! You have opened my eyes. I will never use food hacks I find online ever again."

I laugh. "In that case, it was worth it."

16

The day after my mom came at me with the scissors, I sat in Mr. Kyeong's class. We were discussing Anna Akhmatova's poem *Requiem*. Mr. Kyeong wanted us to talk about the similarities between Irina Ratushinskaya carving poems in soap while in a political prison, and Anna Akhmatova waiting for hours outside the prison, standing in line in front of a woman with blue lips.

Irina is inside the wall and Anna is outside, but they're both in prison, I wrote in my notebook. But I didn't raise my hand to say it. I let my classmates' voices blend around me while I went back to my living room. I watched my mother lift the scissors over my head. *Instead of letting them clatter to the floor, I snatch them away from her. I grab a fistful of her hair and yank it hard. The scissors barely close around her hair, but when I'm done, she has a huge, jagged bald patch right on the side of her head. She touches it with her hand and wails.*

Mr. Kyeong walked by my desk. He glanced at my notebook and saw what I had written. "Grace?" He prodded. "You don't have anything to add to this discussion?"

I shook my head.

LaKeisha raised her hand to ask why we had to read about Russians instead of slaves in the south.

"Look at the syllabus," Mr. Kyeong said. "We have an entire unit devoted to African-American literature coming up. For now, let's stay on task, ok?"

He seemed annoyed. I'd never seen him annoyed before. I wondered why it bothered LaKeisha to read about Russia, but I didn't care. I wanted to go somewhere and sleep. I wanted to pull the covers over my head and hide in the dark. But I didn't want to go home.

The bell rang. The class quickly emptied, but before I could leave the room, Mr. Kyeong called my name.

"Grace, is everything ok? Usually, you're very good about participating in class, but today you were so quiet. I'm concerned."

I didn't want to say anything, but I felt something crumble inside me. My lip trembled and tears dripped from my eyes.

"It's my mom," I confessed. "She's always yelling at me. She has to control everything that I do. And yesterday she tried to attack me with scissors."

Mr. Kyeong's face darkened. "Grace, that's very serious."

I nodded.

I felt his hand on my shoulder, gently squeezing. If he had moved just an inch closer to me, I would have collapsed into his arms. But he stayed exactly he was, with a soft hand on my shoulder.

"It sounds like your mom needs help," he said.

I nodded again.

"We can make sure she gets it. Will you let me talk to the school counselor about this?"

"Yes," I said, quietly.

"Good," he said, giving my shoulder a final squeeze before his hand dropped away. I missed the warmth immediately. "You're one of my brightest students, Grace. I hate to see you with this black cloud hanging over you."

As I left Mr. Kyeong's room, I found LaKeisha hiding behind the door.

"Ooh! Grace and Mr. Kyeong, sitting in a tree! K-I-S-S-I-N-G!" she teased.

"Oh, shut up!" I growled at her and left her standing alone in the hallway.

The next day, I was in my first class for barely five minutes before I was called into the counselor's office.

"Mr. Kyeong says you're having some trouble with your mother," she said. She was an older lady with a pile of white curls on her head. Her shirt had little teacups printed all over it.

"Yes," I said.

"We feel it's best to reach out to her to see if we can help her get the kind of help she needs. We'll be calling her today."

"Ok," I nodded. I felt nervous, but I didn't know why.

"I would also like you to meet with me once a week," she said.

"What about my classes?"

"We'll make sure you don't get behind," she said.

There was a picture on her wall that looked like a five-year-old drew it: a big yellow sun and a red stick figure with its arms pointing up.

"Ok," I said.

"How do you feel now?" she asked.

"Nervous," I admitted.

She nodded. "That's normal. But we are going to do what we can to help things get better."

I nodded. We sat in silence for a while and she let me go back to class.

17

For the holidays, my boss insisted that I had to put something special on the menu — something "even crazier than the pig snouts." I decided on roast venison. I used a Victorian technique of threading strips of jiggly white pork fat through the venison to tenderize and caramelize it. Then, I instructed the servers to carve it tableside. That way, when the meat was cooked and wheeled out into the dining room, it created a kind of subdued floor show.

Two days after the first of the year, Corey came running into the kitchen, screaming, "We're in the *New York Times!*"

Marvelous Venison in Minneapolis has been on the *New York Times'* "most emailed" list for more than a week.

I can't stop sweating.

My dad tries to convince me that I'm worried over nothing.

"Do you think there's some sort of secret police that goes around arresting chefs for attracting the attention of the *New York Times?* You are totally unhinged, my dear," he says.

I don't tell my fears to anyone else, but I can tell they all think I'm nuts for not being happy about the articles. I bury my fears, but it's like cramming too many boxes into a closet. Open the closet door even a crack and it will all come tumbling out.

18

That day in June when LaKeisha and I broke into the abandoned house on Lowry wasn't the last time I visited it. No one ever seemed to notice me slip into the house, so I went there whenever I needed a quiet place to be alone. I went there so often, I knew every corner, every doorway, every shadow of that old empty house.

The house had two staircases: a wide one with meticulously-turned spindles and a rounded bottom step, and a very narrow, very dark staircase with plain, unvarnished steps. They both led to the bedrooms upstairs, but the large one was for the family to use, and the narrow one was for the servants.

Most of the spindles on the grand staircase were still intact, and the banister was smooth underneath a thick coating of dust. The floorboards were a little warped, but still sturdy. They always groaned a little as I ascended.

There was more light upstairs than downstairs. All of the windows downstairs were boarded up, but the windows upstairs were not. Daylight and cold autumn air filtered through their broken panes.

Most of the rooms were empty, except for the room that faced Lowry Avenue. One of the windows was missing altogether, leaving a wide gap that let in wind and ice and rain. A small bed caught the dry leaves that blew in through the window as if someone had placed it there to do just that. One gray afternoon in September, I stood near the window and looked down at the street below. Across the street, a man raked his yard.

Cars cruised up and down the street. A pair of kids my age carried sandwiches from the Subway shop on the corner. Their hooded sweatshirts hid their faces.

One of them looked up at the glassless window, saw me, and pointed. The other looked up at me, his eyes wide with shock. I stood as still as I could. One grabbed the other's sleeve and they ran, disappearing around the corner. It was kind of fun, being a ghost.

The school called my mother to express their concern. But instead of agreeing to make an appointment with the counselor they recommended, she demanded that I be pulled from Mr. Kyeong's class. The principal caved immediately. The next day, I would have to go to Ms. Jensen's class instead, a teacher I'd never even met.

I slammed my bedroom door. My mother stood on the other side, yelling something about how I needed to wake up and realize what a terrible person Mr. Kyeong was and that he was probably trying to sleep with me and how she was going to make sure he got fired. I found my Discman under my pillow, opened it, snapped *In Utero* in place, and turned it up so loud that it drowned out my mother's voice.

In the morning, I didn't go to school. When I reached the bus stop, I just kept walking, and before I knew it, I was running.

I didn't stop until I reached the abandoned Queen Anne. I crept in through the back door and bounded up the narrow, tilted servant's staircase. The sun hadn't risen yet so it was still dark, but I didn't need light to find my way around.

When I reached the front bedroom, I threw myself down onto the bed. I buried my face into the mildewed bedspread and cried. No one was around; no one would hear. I gathered handfuls of cloth in my fists and let out a scream. Then I sighed and stayed silent while tears continued to drip from my eyes.

After a while, I felt calmer. I lay on my back and stared at the ceiling, watching the shadows of the bare tree branches outside stretch every time a car went by. Just as the tight feeling in my chest began to ease, I heard sirens. At first, I thought they sounded like they were going in another direction, but suddenly, the walls of the abandoned bedroom were splashed with red and blue light.

My body tensed all over. I held my breath. I heard footsteps; someone was downstairs, in the kitchen.

"Come down from there," a voice called. "It's ok. We're not going to arrest you. Just come out of there. It's not safe for you to be in here."

Slowly, I got up from the bed. I rubbed my damp face. I walked down the hall, toward the back staircase. A flashlight beam blinded me.

"Come on down, it's ok," the officer said again.

I carefully descended the staircase and took hold of the officer's outstretched hand. She led me to her car and gently helped me into the back seat.

"One of the neighbors heard someone screaming," the officer said, her eyes meeting mine in the rearview mirror. "When they realized it was coming from inside that creepy old house, they thought it was a ghost." She chuckled.

I pretended to laugh, but as the squad car got closer and closer to my house, my chest tightened. The sky began to pale, with hints of strawberry and peach beginning to show through the lattice of empty tree branches on my block.

The officer gripped my arm lightly as she walked with me up the stairs to my mother's house.

"Do you want to talk to me about what's going on?" the officer asked. "If there's a problem, I might be able to help."

I shook my head.

"Are you sure, honey? Last chance." She said this just as she pulled up outside my house. I shook my head again.

My mother answered the door.

"Good morning, ma'am," the officer said. "We caught your daughter trespassing in an abandoned house on Lowry Avenue."

"What?"

"I wouldn't be too hard on her, ma'am. Kids will be kids, and it's hard for them to resist an abandoned house. But those places are dangerous and there's a reason we want kids to stay out of them."

"Is she going to be charged?" My mother asked.

The officer shook her head. "No. We'll let her go with a warning this time. She'll be fine – so long as she doesn't do it again."

My mother smiled. "Of course. Thank you, officer."

The officer nodded and left. My heart sank as I watched the taillights of her squad car disappear. Once the officer was gone and I was inside the house, my mother's smile vanished. She grabbed my hair and pulled so hard that I fell to my knees.

"What is wrong with you?" she demanded. "I give you everything and this is how you thank me? You run away and break into places where you don't belong? You skip school? You embarrass me by coming home in a police car, in broad daylight for all the neighbors to see?"

She let go of my hair and slapped me hard in the face.

"I never wanted to have you. You know that, right? I never wanted any kids. But I had you anyway and have worked my fingers to the bone for you and you're not grateful for anything. Well, that's it. I've given you everything and it's never been enough. I'm done with you."

She bared her teeth and I noticed the lines around her lips that she tried to cover with concealer. She got in her car and drove off, leaving me alone in the house for the rest of the day. When she came home that evening, she knocked on my bedroom door.

"Grace? Are you in there? How about we order a pizza? I stopped at Blockbuster and rented some movies. I got you those sour gummy things that you like too."

I remained silent and waited for her to walk away.

I didn't go to school the next day either and my mom didn't say anything. When the school called, no one picked up.

19

After another sleepless night, I meet Jess at the gym for open mat time. While I wait for her, I sit on the mat and watch two purple belts roll. The blue foam mat is cold enough to numb my toes. The windows are edged with a delicate frost. Opposite the sweat-fogged mirrors, punching bags hang from the ceiling in a row and they tremble every time one of the purple belts slams the other on the mat. A man-sized grappling dummy sits slumped against the wall, a cast-off gi tied around his black cordura torso. The stereo blasts Donna Summer's voice over a spongy Disco beat. A bell rings, signaling the end of a three-minute round. The two purple belts stop grappling and rest, breathing heavily as they wait to start again.

"You look like shit," Jess says when she arrives at the gym.

"I couldn't sleep."

Jess and I kneel on the mat facing each other. We perform the secret jiu-jitsu handshake — a hand slap followed by a fist bump — and wait for the bell to ring. As soon as it does, Jess flattens me. Before I can do anything about it, she's sitting on me and hunting for a submission. As she slides her hand into my collar to get a grip for a choke, I try to buck my hips and roll her over, but Jess releases my collar and slams her hand onto the mat, bracing herself so I can't move her. Every move I make, she counters immediately, forcing me to stay in the same position. Her body on top of mine feels like a sack of wet grain. My muscles burn even though I've barely moved at all. Finally, I jam my elbows into her thighs, twist my body to the side as hard as I can, and pull my legs out from under her, trapping her in guard.

I grab her sleeve with one hand and the back of her head with the other, pulling her down against my chest. Jess postures up so she can pass my guard, and as she does she lets out a grunt. Something about the sound makes my brain crackle. A memory flashes: Crandell, that fat sweaty hog, grunting in my ear as he attacked me in an isolation shed at Epiphany Lake.

Rage electrifies every muscle in my body. As she sits up, I shoot my legs up as hard as I can, wrap them around her neck and pull her back down. Every muscle in my thighs is twitching. I grab the back of her head and shove her face into my crotch. I use my legs to form a pretzel-knot around Jess's head and neck; from here, I can choke her with my thighs. I squeeze with all of my strength and watch as her face takes on the color of an eggplant. She slaps the mat and for a split second, I forget to let go.

Jess coughs as I release her.

"I'm sorry," I tell her. My heart is hammering at my ribcage.

"For what?" she asks as her face returns to its normal color. "That was awesome. You're a fucking warrior."

"I thought maybe I went too hard. I kind of went to a bad place. I wasn't thinking straight."

Jess pats my knee. "I get it," she says. "I think that happens to everyone at least once. It's a fight-or-flight type thing."

The bell rings.

"Hey," one of the purple belts says to me as he crosses the mat, "I saw that triangle choke. Good for you."

"When you postured up, I had this memory pop up and I just reacted…"

"I totally get it. The mat is a great place to work through shit. Jiu-jitsu saved my life," she says. "Did I ever tell you that?"

I shake my head.

"It was four years ago…or five. I think it was five. Anyway, I was crazy in love with this girl named Kizzy. She had this gorgeous ballerina neck, was really sweet and un-fucking-believable in bed. But she was totally fucked up. Sometimes her eyes would go blank and she'd just stare off into space. Then she'd freak out and throw things or hit me. One time she came at me, swinging her arms like fan blades. She backed me against the wall. Finally, I threw her to the ground and pinned her down until she calmed down. I remember thinking, 'if I was I guy, I'd get arrested, and I'm only defending myself.'"

I wait for her to continue. My body is cooling down, and my sweat is starting to make me feel cold. I hope the heater kicks on again soon.

"The scariest part was that sometimes she'd get that way, all glassy and vacant and ready to ignite, and then – like say we were out in public somewhere – then when she saw someone she knew, she'd snap right out of it. It scared me so much to know that she could control it. Once I asked her if she could control her Piss Jar Monster – that's what she called it – around other people, why couldn't she do that for me? So what did she do? She back-handed me in my eye. She was wearing a ring I'd given her, and the prongs ripped open my eyelid." She shuts her right eye and points to a small, crescent-shaped scar with her pinky.

"Oh, and I was driving when this happened. Because I was bleeding and could only see out of one eye I almost missed a stoplight. The front end of my car was halfway into the intersection when I slammed on the brakes. There just happened to be a squad car on the scene at the time. This grizzly, old cop came over, took one look at me and my bloody eye, and Kizzy sitting there as if nothing had happened, and told me I needed to press charges against her for assault."

The heater fires up, blasting warm air over both of us.

"Did you?"

She shakes her head. "I couldn't. I loved her. I always felt like I had to protect her. Didn't matter though. Three weeks later, she got arrested. She had been missing for three days. It turned out that she had gone on a bender and was blackout drunk when a cop caught her with her Daisy Duke's around her ankles, pissing in somebody's yard. I used all the money I had to bail her out. I was so mad at her. I demanded to know why she had taken off like that. You know what she did? She took a swing at me. She missed, but I hit her back. Hard. I punched her right in the space above her collarbone. She collapsed onto the floor. I'll never forget the look on her face. She was...shocked."

Jess stares at the frost-edged window while she tells her story. I follow her gaze and notice a trio of Somali girls in bright hijabs and Disney snow boots on their way to school.

"What did you do?" I ask.

"I cried. She cried. We fucked...that's the thing. It was all so addictive. All of it. The raw sweet passion and the dark sticky tar-pit of misery shit. That's why it took me so long to leave her – because I craved it all."

She pauses. The Somali kids have reached the end of the block and are waiting at the stoplight.

"I finally left her after that fight. The next morning she had this huge bruise in the middle of her chest. Like a big, purple rose. I wanted to throw up when I saw it because I'd done that to her. I knew if I stayed with her, I'd have a Piss Jar Monster inside me too."

She finally turns her gaze away from the window and looks at me. Her expression is too intense, and I have to look away.

"You know, people think that if someone cheats on you or lies to you or hits you that your feelings for them should automatically disappear. But that's not how it works. Because that would be sane and sanity has fuck-all to do with love."

"So how does jiu-jitsu fit into all this?" I ask.

"Oh, right. I forgot that's why I was telling this story." Her expression softens a little. "I felt like shit after that relationship. I felt bad because I'd been in it, and I felt bad because I was out of it. I missed her, and I hated myself for missing her. I walked around with a pain in my chest and an upset stomach 24-7. I started going out drinking every night after work. I would hang out at the bar for hours, drinking six or seven beers a night. I was on my way to becoming a raving alcoholic. But one night, there was this older guy in the bar. He noticed I was on my fourth beer and said, 'you can't drown memories you know.' Then he said I should try his jiu-jitsu class. The next day, I came here."

"And the rest is history?"

She smiles. "Pretty much. I just fell in love with it, you know? For that hour, I was able to block her out of my mind. And the more I trained, the more I thought about jiu-jitsu instead of all the things that made me feel bad inside. One night, I was about to go to sleep when I realized I hadn't thought about Kizzy in weeks. That was a fucking great feeling. But if James hadn't been in the bar that night, who knows where I would have ended up?"

"You know," I say, slowly, "She sounds a lot like my mom."

"Oh yeah?" Jess re-ties her lavender belt into a perfect fortune cookie-shaped knot.

"Yeah, you know, doing everything possible to make you want to get away from her while acting like a big victim. That sort of thing."

"Do you still talk to her?"

I shake my head. "I never pick up when she calls. All she ever wants is to rant at me for not appreciating what a great mother she was. Of course, when she can't reach me, she harangues my dad, but at least he doesn't mind taking one for the team."

Jess lets out a soft chuckle. "Divorced?"

I nod.

"My folks are these pseudo-liberal Catholics who are, like, the only straight couple on the planet who has experienced Lesbian Bed Death. If it weren't for the church, they'd have split up ages ago. Meanwhile, they both have side pieces that they pretend the other doesn't know about. Yet, when I was going through that whole mess with Kizzy, they were like, 'We love you but you need to reconsider this homosexual lifestyle.'

I got sick of their benevolent homophobia and haven't talked to them since."

"So, we're both orphans?" I joke.

Jess squeezes my shoulder. "This gym is kind of like a family. A family of misfits." Then, she throws her arm around my neck, gripping me in a headlock where the fumes from her sweaty pits are enough to make me black out.

"Welcome to the family, sis!" she grunts.

Remembering James' instructions, I grab her wrist, shrug my shoulders and step behind her, twisting her arm behind her back the way cops do before they slap on the cuffs. With my other arm, I reach around her neck and squeeze. She taps out.

"Nice rear-naked choke, Miss Grace!" James shouts at me from the other end of the gym.

"It really was," Jess says with a cough.

A bell rings, signaling the end of open mat time. We have to leave so that James can close up the gym.

I fold up my gi top and tie my belt around it. As I reach for my coat, I ask, "Whatever happened to her? To Kizzy?"

"She was in jail for a while and in and out of hospitals after that. Then, a couple of years ago, Kizzy married a straight guy and had a baby. She's been arrested a bunch of times for strangling her husband and gone to court-mandated therapy, but from what I hear, she hasn't changed. And he's still with her."

"Shit," I say as we step out into the cold. Next to the building, a crab apple tree with tiny frozen fruits still clinging to its branches trembles in the wind. "That poor bastard."

"Better him than me!" Jess exclaims.

I remember the string of short-lived relationships my mom plowed through after I came home from boarding school. "I'm pretty sure my dad said the same thing."

James pulls the door shut behind him, causing icicles hanging from the gutter to snap off and land in the snow. "What are you two ladies chatting about?" He asks as he locks the door.

"Dysfunctional family dynamics," I reply.

"Ah," he chortles. He points to the lettering screen-printed onto his hoodie. "Jiu-jitsu is therapy. Remember that."

Jess and I trade glances. We both smile.

20

I went back to school, but I didn't go to my new English class. I hung out in the library instead. The librarian got suspicious, called the assistant principal, and I got in-school suspension. My swim coach told me that the administrators wanted him to cut me from the team. He was sure he could get them to reconsider as long as I promised to stop skipping class.

At home, the answering machine was full of calls from the school. They used phrases like "deeply concerned," "family counseling," and "avoiding out-of-school suspension." I tried to erase them before my mom heard, but it didn't seem to matter. Ever since the morning I got caught in the abandoned house, she'd seemed serene. Happy, almost.

The day I got in-school suspension, I expected her to yell at me and pull my hair again, but instead, she just absorbed the news and signed the slip of paper they made me bring home.

"You're not mad?" I asked.

She turned and smiled. She wore pink lipstick. "Everything's going to be just fine. I've taken care of everything."

She walked out of the room, leaving me alone to wonder what the fuck she was talking about.

In the hallways at school, I hid when I saw LaKeisha coming. I felt bad about telling her to shut up and I was afraid she thought I'd become a loser for skipping school and getting suspended.

I almost wished I could go to a different school.

One week after I got picked up in the squad car, I came home from swim practice to an empty house. My mother had left a note on the refrigerator telling me to reheat leftover chow mein from Jung's. I dumped it onto a pile of dry noodles and stuck it in the microwave. I didn't usually like Jung's chow mein very much; it was mostly celery and little chunks of ham floating in a cornstarch-y sauce. But I was hungry after swim practice, and I devoured every last salty bite. I rinsed my plate and set it in the drying rack. I took a Citra from the fridge and settled onto the couch. I watched *Frasier* and *Will & Grace*.

At 10:00, I turned off the TV and went to bed.

I had a dream that I was swimming. The pool got longer every time I reached the end. I was exhausted. I wanted to get out, but the pool kept growing as if someone were dropping pools from the sky, end-to-end. *Just keep swimming*, I told myself. *Just power through.*

I heard footsteps on the deck. Maybe it was my dad, come to take me home?

The footsteps got louder. I woke up. Two large men stood next to my bed, staring at me in the dark.

I lunged for the window.

One of the men grabbed me and threw me face down on the bed, wrenching my arm behind my back. I screamed for my mom, screamed for her to call the police.

The light flipped on and my eyes ached. I watched as the second man opened my dresser and took some clothes out. He threw them at me.

"Get dressed and let's go," he said.

"Where?" I asked.

They wouldn't say.

"We can do this the easy way or the hard way," the man holding my arm said, "But either way you're coming with us."

I screamed for my mom. Finally, she appeared in the doorway. She crossed her arms and leaned against the doorframe. "You're going with them," she said.

"What? Where?"

"Somewhere you'll be better off," she said. "Just do what they say."

I stared at her. Her gaze was icy and hard, but there was a little bit of a smile, too. It was the same look she had when she got off the phone with her divorce lawyers. I glanced at the second man, who had a face like a pile of old stones. The first one was still restraining me, his large hand cutting off the circulation to my wrist.

The sooner I do what they say, then the sooner this — whatever it is — will be over with and I can get back to normal.

"Can I at least have some privacy?" I asked.

"Why? So you can escape? Just hurry up and put your clothes on."

My face burned. I turned my back to them to make sure they saw as little as possible. When I was dressed, they handcuffed my wrists behind my back and led me out to their SUV. As I climbed into the back seat, I turned and looked at the house. I thought I'd see her watching from the porch window, but the house was completely dark. She had already gone back to sleep.

The engine roared to life. As the car backed out of our driveway and turned onto the street, I noticed that the clock on the dashboard read 4:04 am.

The men wouldn't tell me where we were going. I was hungry, but something told me not to ask for food. The sky's edge turned pink, revealing a long stretch of highway: we were on 169, heading north.

The man driving the car switched the radio on and tuned into KQRS. The morning show was on and the host was saying something racist about Hmong people.

It's probably going to be fine, I said to myself. Maybe just a few days in the woods or something. Or maybe a week helping out on a farm. Or joining some sort of church mission.

As the sky brightened, the scenery changed; strip malls and gas stations gave way to rows of tall pines lining the road like toy soldiers. Two hours passed, then three. The KQRS radio signal bled out into static. The man turned the dial until he found the only station that came through, a country music station. We took an exit for a town I'd never heard of and cruised through a McDonald's drive thru. One of the men tossed an Egg McMuffin onto my lap.

We must be close, I thought, but we drove back onto the highway. I paid close attention to the signs as we passed Grand Rapids and merged onto Highway 2. The roads seemed to get narrower and narrower, and the rows of pines thicker and darker. The radio signal fizzled out again. I closed my eyes and listened to the crackle of the static.

"Hey," one of the men said, turning around from the front seat to glare at me, "you'd better not be sleeping back there."

"You woke me up at 4 am," I countered, "I'm tired."

"You're really lucky," he said, "you're about to get a much-needed attitude adjustment. This place is going to be really good for you."

"Then why won't you tell me where it is?"

He glowered but said nothing.

Highway 2 became 46. Then 71. I'd never been this far north before. Were they just going to dump me off in Canada and leave me to find my own way home?

Finally, we turned off the highway. We passed through a sleepy town's main street, lined with old wooden buildings like something out of a western. Small farmhouses dotted the road. Then, the car slowed. The turn signal clicked and made my heart race. We turned onto a gravel road, and right near the start of it there was a large sign that said 'Keep Out.'

As we drove down the road, passing more 'keep out' and 'no trespassing' signs, I noticed several log cabins tucked behind the trees.

We came to a clearing and a large gate with a sign on top of it: Epiphany Lake Academy.

21

My phone rings while I'm at work. I take it out to the loading dock. It's my dad. He doesn't usually call when he knows I'm working.

"Grace," he says. "I have to tell you something. I wanted to make sure you heard it from me."

Across the alley, a welder is working on a steel joist, sending a shower of sparks into the air. Against the backdrop of fresh snow, the orange sparks light up like New Year's Eve.

"What?"

"It's about Epiphany Lake," he says. I can hear clacking sounds on the other end of the line, his coworkers hammering away on keyboards.

"What about it?"

"It's being marketed as a school for girls now. It says that this is a new phase for the same school. It uses the 'same educational model that Epiphany Lake Academy created in the '90s. This time, the school will focus exclusively on one of the most vulnerable populations: teenage girls.' That's from the site. And there's a list of 'success stories,' kids who went to Epiphany Lake and have made good since."

More sparks hit the air. My knees shake. I leaned my back against the wall so I wouldn't stumble.

"How...how many kids are on it?" I ask.

"Just one so far," dad says. "You."

"Me?"

"It links to your *New York Times* articles."

My chest feels like it's been stepped on by a horse. I slip, but I manage to catch myself before I fall. I'm shaking all over.

"I've already spoken to my lawyer," dad says. "She's writing up a desist letter as we speak."

"This is why I didn't….I told you….I didn't want…"

"It'll be ok, Grace."

"Crandell. That piece of shit."

"I know, Grace."

"That asshole, rapist piece of shit."

I hang up the phone.

The snow is an electric blanket of blue velvet. My head buzzes. I'm chilled and shivering. I need to get warm. I slip my phone into my pocket and head back into the kitchen. I light one of the burners, cranking up the gas as high as it will go.

I hold my hand over it, letting the flames toast my skin.

"Grace, what the hell are you doing?" Corey shouts.

"Getting warm," I say.

My whole sleeve is ablaze.

A white stripe appears on my forearm. Corey grabs me by the shoulders and steers me to the sink to blast my burn with cold water. My spine rattles like I'm on a rollercoaster with no safety bar.

"Grace, why did you do this?" Corey asks me. I can't answer. The room is turning black like someone has pulled the curtains shut on my world.

I fade away.

Book 2

Away at School

1

As the SUV idled outside of the main gate, the driver pulled out a walkie-talkie. I didn't know it then, but the crackling sound it made would soon become very familiar to me.

"Transport here," he said. "Fourteen-year-old female."

Female? I don't even get a name? I wondered.

A flat voice responded, but I couldn't understand what she said. I heard a buzzing sound, and the gates slowly parted. Gravel crunched under the tires. We pulled up to a large log cabin; it looked like it had once been the main lodge of an old resort. It had a large, triangular window under the gable and a deck that wrapped around. It was probably pretty when it was first built but the deck railing had spindles missing and the big window looked like it hadn't been washed in years.

The driver turned off the car, and the other guy yanked my door open. "Get out," he ordered. I picked up my backpack and followed them into the lodge.

It was dim on the inside. I noticed a strange smell: a heavy scent of mildew, and a fainter scent of scorched cheese. A woman met us at the door, a walkie-talkie holstered on her hip. The driver handed her some papers.

"How was she?" the woman asked. She barely even looked at me.

"A little lippy but compliant for the most part."

The woman nodded. The men turned and left. I listened as their car started, drove down the gravel path and disappeared on the road we'd just come in on. My heart raced. I felt dizzy. I didn't know what this place was all about. But I knew I was stuck here.

"This way," the woman said, still without looking at me. I followed her to a small, windowless room. She closed the door.

"Strip," she ordered.

"What?"

"Take off your clothes. Now."

I folded my arms across my chest. "You can't make me do that. I have rights."

She smirked. She took her walkie-talkie out of its holster and spoke into it. It sounded like she was talking in code.

I heard footsteps in the hall. Two girls entered the room. One of them showed her teeth, exposing braces with several brackets out of place. The other had an oily face, pulsing with zits. They looked like they were only a little bit older than I was — sixteen or seventeen. They stood behind the woman and waited.

"Take off your clothes," she said, "or these two will do it for you."

Rage gripped me. *If I run at them hard enough, I can knock them over. I'll just run until I get back to the highway.* I bolted. They tackled me, shoving my face into the cheap carpet. The plastic threads scratched my cheek. The woman held me down while the other two yanked at my clothes. I thought maybe they would stop at the shirt, but I felt somebody tugging at the strap on my bra.

I raised my face from the floor and shouted, "Get the fuck off of me!" A hand on the back of my head jammed my face into the rug again. Another grabbed both of my breasts and then drifted down to undo the button on my pants. I kicked but that only made my pants come off faster. Every time I lifted my face from the floor, a hand in my hair shoved it back down.

I heard a car on the gravel outside and screamed as loud as I could. Maybe someone would hear me and come in and help. I heard two car doors slam, and two sets of footsteps in the hall. They both passed me and my screaming without breaking stride.

The girls' hands groped every part of my body. Somebody jammed two cold fingers into my vagina. I screamed into the mildewed carpet. The woman sat on my back and held my legs so I couldn't kick.

"That's it," the zitty girl said. "No contraband. She can get dressed."

They let me up. The first woman threw a plain red sweatshirt and a pair of stained khakis at me. She told me it was my uniform, the clothes I'd wear from now on.

"You fucking assaulted me," I shouted, "I'm going to sue you."

The three of them laughed.

"Should we put her in The Shed?" asked the girl with the tumbledown braces.

The woman shook her head. "No. It's her first day. Give her a break." She left the room and the girl with braces followed her. The Zit Queen stayed behind. She had this weird grin on her face as she held two of her fingers under my nose.

"Smell yourself," she said. "You stink."

I shoved her hand away. She laughed and left me alone in the room. The door locked behind her.

For an hour, I pounded on the door and yelled for someone to come and let me out. When no one did, I sank into a corner and pulled my knees up to my chest. I felt light-headed and sort of syrupy, like the way I felt whenever I took cold medicine.

I thought of my mother. Did she know this place did strip searches? What would she think if she saw this place? *She would probably be more upset by the way the place looks than how they treat me*, I thought, bitterly.

And what about my dad? Did *he* know about this place? Did he agree to it too? Was my mom right – was his showing up at my swim meet just a show? What if he didn't know? He'd find out eventually. What would he do then?

Finally, the door opened. A girl stepped in. She looked like she was only a year or so older than me. She didn't have braces or zits but her hair was greasy.

"I'm Julie," she said. She didn't smile or offer me her hand to shake. She was tall and slender with the muscular build of someone who ran cross-country, but her eyes looked vacant and her complexion had no color. "I'm an upper level. For the next few weeks, I'll be your buddy. My job is to help you understand how the program works. The only people you may speak to are the staff and me. You do not speak until spoken to, and you do not go anywhere without me."

She handed me a laminated card on a lanyard and told me I had to wear it around my neck at all times. It was a list of all of the program rules, I had to memorize them all by tomorrow. They were printed in very small type.

Julie led me out of the main building and across the campus to the cabin I would share with her and thirty other girls. As we walked across the dormant grass, she explained that all of the students were divided into 'families' of fifteen girls or boys each. (The boys had their own cabins; we did not speak to or look at the boys – Julie pointed to rule number 58 on the card.)

"Our family is 'Liberty.'"

"Yeah, right," I said, rolling my eyes.

Julie's eyes narrowed. "Watch yourself," she said, her voice low. "Our family is Liberty," she repeated, "and we share this cabin with the Karma family."

The cabin smelled like the inside of a clothes-hamper. Our side of the cabin was a plain room with fifteen bunk beds. Julie assured me that the Karma side of the cabin was identical. There was one bathroom for all thirty girls. She showed me which bunk was mine, and I set my backpack on it.

"It's lunchtime," she said. "We'll join the rest of our family in the dining hall."

As we walked out of the cabin, I glanced up and noticed that there was a white plastic device mounted on the frame of the main door. Was that an alarm? An alarm that would go off if you opened the door from the inside?

We walked back to the main lodge but entered through a different door. I suddenly realized why I'd smelled scorched cheese when I first arrived. We picked up our lunches in the chow line: grilled cheese sandwiches burnt black on both sides. Julie found our family. They shifted over to let us sit. Julie introduced me to them. A couple of them said 'hello' in monotone voices, but the rest of them said nothing. I realized they must have been on the same 'level' as I was.

A recording played over a PA system. It was a man's voice, and it was loud – almost too loud to let me hear myself think.

"The key to success," the voice said, "is to realize deeply that everything that happens to us in life starts in our own minds."

If that's true, I wondered, *then when did I imagine this place?*

During my first night at Epiphany Lake, I hardly slept at all. Right before Shutdown, staff came around and gathered up all of our shoes and put them in a locked box at the end of the hall. The doorway to our cramped room with its fifteen bunks stayed open all night, so while the room was dark, lights from the hallway blazed in.

Down the hall, someone in the Karma family was crying.

A spot on the ceiling was discolored from water damage; it was shaped like Australia. I stared at it while girls around me slept.

There were six levels at Epiphany Lake and five categories of rules. To move up a level, you had to earn three hundred points. You could earn up to ten points per day. If you broke one of the rules, you would lose your points. Breaking a Category 1 rule meant losing a day's points. Category 2 would cost you thirty points. Category 3 meant losing a week's worth of points and Category 4 meant losing a month's worth.

If you committed a Category 5 offense, you lost all of your points and had to start the program over. Julie told me that when she first arrived here, she saw a girl try to hang herself because she'd been a level

6 and had lost all of her points. She had been in the program for almost two years.

I looked at the card with the rules I was supposed to memorize and noticed that under Category 5 offenses, 'self-harming or threatening suicide' was listed.

"So, what happened to her if she got a Category 5 after they had taken all her points away?"

Julie lowered her voice. "Staff came into the room in the middle of the night and took her away. We never saw her again."

"Where did they take her?"

Julie shrugged. "Mystic Bay, probably. Whenever anyone really acts up, the staff threatens to send them to Mystic Bay."

"Where is that?" I asked. But by then, the staff were coming around to collect our shoes, and Julie couldn't answer me.

Did that mean there was a place that was even worse than this one?

Three-hundred divided by ten, times six. I would be at Epiphany Lake Academy for at least six months. Less than twenty-four hours ago, I was in the back of a stranger's SUV, thinking I'd only be going away for a week or two.

I bit my lip to keep quiet as tears streamed down my face.

Finally, the Karma girl stopped crying, and I drifted off into a thin sleep.

In the morning, I woke up to a staff member shouting that it was time to get up. The other girls got up quickly. I followed their lead. Once we were dressed, we formed a line and waited at the door. We couldn't "cross out" or "cross in" to rooms without permission.

As we waited for the staff to come around and give us permission to leave the cabin, I noticed that one girl was still in bed. Like me, the girl was a Level 1. I glanced at Julie and watched her eyes scan the girl in the bunk.

When the staff came into the room, Julie raised her hand and said,

"Andrea is still in bed." Andrea was a heavy-set girl with short blonde curls. She had gotten in trouble twice the day before. Once for forgetting her notebook, and once for asking for salt at dinner. Later, I learned that Andrea was sent to Epiphany Lake because she had run away from a fat camp and this was her punishment. I watched as the woman walked over to Andrea's bunk and poked her in the back.

"What are you doing still in bed?"

"I'm sick," the girl moaned. I *had* heard Andrea coughing throughout the night. I thought about speaking up, but Julie was the upper level, and she had told the staffer that Andrea hadn't gotten out of bed. *Don't try to help people if you want to get out of here,* I thought.

The woman rolled her eyes and reached for her walkie-talkie. "Liberty has a faker," she said. "You and you," the woman said, pointing at Julie and the girl behind her, "get this manipulative little shit out of bed."

Immediately, the two girls abandoned their places in line and rushed over to Andrea's bunk. They grabbed her arms and legs and yanked hard, causing her to flip in midair and land face down on the floor. Watching this, I flashed back to yesterday's strip search.

Julie held Andrea down while a second staff member entered the room. She knelt down and looked straight into Andrea's eyes.

"You think you can manipulate us? You think you can make us feel sorry for you by pretending to be sick?"

"I'm not pretending!" Andrea cried.

"You're all liars," the woman said. "You're all here because you're lying, manipulative brats. Now quit wasting everyone's time and get up."

Andrea refused.

The two women grabbed her and pulled her to her feet. She cried.

"Please! I'm sick!"

"You can get in line with the other girls or you can go to The Shed," one of the women said. Andrea whimpered a little, but she took her place in line.

We finally crossed out of the bedroom and out of the cabin, to a field where the three other families of girls were already gathered. They all stood in neat rows. A man stood in front of them. I would soon learn that his name was Crandell, and he was the owner of Epiphany Lake.

Once we took our place in the rows, Crandell said, "Since we had to wait for Liberty, you're all doing a double set!"

I had no clue what he was talking about.

"One hundred jumping jacks!" he shouted.

I was lucky. All those months of swim practice meant one hundred jumping jacks, burpees and bear crawls weren't that difficult for me. But many of the other girls struggled to keep up, including Andrea, who collapsed in front of me.

As she lay inert on the dead grass, Crandell stood over her, shouting. I wanted to tell him to leave her alone, but I knew if I did, I'd lose my points for the day, and that would mean staying here one day longer than I already had to. The only way out was to learn the rules and learn them fast.

I worked through my second set of jumping jacks while Crandell bellowed like a drill Sergeant from some corny low-budget war movie. Considering the gut that slumped over Crandell's belt, I guessed that he *had* learned his technique from movies and not actual military service.

Strings of spit flew from his mouth as he called Andrea every name he could come up with: Liar, Manipulator, Fat Cow, Loser, Trash Heap. Finally, he radioed to someone else on staff, and within minutes, Andrea was hoisted off the ground again and hauled away to some part of the campus that I couldn't see.

After exercise time was over, we filed into the cafeteria for breakfast where bowls of cool, congealed Cream of Wheat waited for us. The hard exercise made me feel strong and clear. *That's the flaw in their plan*, I thought. *By helping me stay in shape, they're helping me keep the strength I'll need to run away from this place. They think we're all lazy. But we're not.*

From breakfast, we went straight to group therapy. We shared our sessions with the Promise family. We all sat in a circle in a windowless room, on hard plastic chairs. On the other side of the circle, a girl cried.

"The only reason you were raped," said a female counselor – the same one who had pulled off my shirt the day before – "is that you put yourself in that position. You have to take responsibility for yourself."

"You're a *slut!*" shouted another girl. "You wouldn't even be here if you weren't so busy trying to make guys like you."

One by one, the group went around the circle, telling the sobbing girl that she was a whore, a skank, a loser, and that her rape was her own fault.

What the fuck kind of therapy is this? I asked myself.

By the time the group was done with her, she was crying quietly, unable to take her eyes off the floor.

"Well, group," the counselor said, "We have someone new here." Her eyes landed on me. She was smiling. "This is Grace."

Slowly, thirty pairs of glassy eyes turned in my direction.

"Grace, tell the group why you're here."

I looked to my left and to my right. The other girls were just staring at me, waiting. I closed my eyes. I wished I could disappear.

"We're waiting, Grace," the woman said, her voice already taking on an edge of impatience.

I didn't know what to say. Was I at Epiphany Lake because I'd gotten caught in the abandoned house? Or had my mom planned to send me here before that happened? Julie told me I wouldn't be able to call my mom until I reached level 3. I couldn't even ask her why she'd sent me away.

"Well, I guess since my parents' divorce, my mom and I just haven't been getting along." I looked down at my feet. I was wearing the flip-flops they gave me after taking away my Airwalks. Underneath, my socks were already filthy. Everyone in the circle wore the same flip-flops, the same dirty socks.

The woman's face iced over. "Is that all?"

I glanced around again and saw that the other girls were waiting for answers, too. "….and I got caught trespassing in an abandoned house."

The woman pressed her lips together until their outer edges turned white. "Grace, we all know you're lying. We all know you did more than trespass in an abandoned house. You did drugs in there. You had sex."

What the fuck is she talking about? Did my mom tell her this bullshit? The skin between my brows pinched. "No," I said, "I just went inside. Just to explore. Just to get away from my mom."

"You're in denial," the woman spat.

"I am not," I insisted.

"You *are* in denial," said another girl. It was Julie. "You can't move forward in this program until you take responsibility for what you've done."

"That doesn't make sense. How can I take responsibility for something I didn't do? For something that somebody is making up?"

"You're the one who is making things up," the counselor said. She was almost smiling.

"When I first came here, I lied, too," Julie said, "I said that I had been caught with just one cigarette. I stuck to that story for weeks. It wasn't until I finally admitted I had lied and smoked methamphetamine that I was finally able to be accountable for my behavior and move forward in the program."

My pulse began to race. I wanted to scream that I wasn't making anything up, that I'd told the truth, and that I didn't understand why they expected me to confess to things I didn't do.

But the therapy hour was up.

Therapy was followed by lunch and another self-help tape: *Negative thoughts attract negative outcomes. You must defeat all negative thoughts. By thinking negative thoughts, you say to the Universe, I want to fail.*

In the afternoon, we sat in a classroom, reading silently out of textbooks. My book looked like someone had left it out in the rain. I tried to smooth out the rippled pages, but the deep valleys just wouldn't flatten out.

After I finished reading the chapter and taking the very easy quiz that came with it, I glanced out the window and, for the first time, noticed the lake. It was still and silvery under the gray sky and edged with scruffy pine trees. From where I sat, it was hard to tell just how big it was.

"Hey," a voice said. It was a junior staff member – a recent graduate of the program – who monitored us from the front of the room. "Are you making run plans?"

"What?" I asked.

"Stop looking out the window. If I catch you doing that again, that's a Category 3."

I sat back against my chair and stared down at my warped text book.

Dinner that night: 'lasagna' made from condensed tomato soup and cottage cheese.

As we left the dining hall and walked single file back to our cabin, I saw tiny lights out of the corner of my eye. I realized: somewhere on the other side of that lake, there's a house, and all its lights are on.

Before Shutdown, I understood what Julie meant when she said I would never get through the program if I didn't "confess" to doing drugs and having sex: I'd only earned three of my ten points that day.

I remembered what she had said: *When I first got here, I lied, too.* It *was* just one cigarette that she had been caught with.

2

Expand your consciousness to receive positive energy from the Universe.

For an entire week, I refused to "confess" in therapy. The counselor called me a worthless liar, an ungrateful brat, a manipulator. Each time, the other girls repeated what she said, screaming at me like I was ruining their lives by refusing to admit I was a druggie whore.

On the fourth day of this, their screaming reminded me of something Mr. Kyeong had taught us about choruses in Greek plays. Then I remembered Mr. Kyeong's glossy black hair and marquee smile and realized he might as well be floating among the stars along with the Hubble Space Telescope. I dropped my head and cried.

When I looked up, the other girls all stared at me expectantly, as if they all knew this was the moment I'd finally admit that I'd snorted cocaine and sucked dicks.

I dried my eyes, crossed my arms and planted my feet on the floor. I said nothing else for the rest of the session.

But something made me change my mind. Andrea, who'd disappeared after the staff accused her of faking being sick, was back in our cabin. Because Andrea was on Level 1 like me, she couldn't tell me where she'd been. But Julie caught me up to speed.

"They put her in The Shed," Julie told me.

The Shed was a tiny cinderblock cabin tucked away behind the boys' bunkhouses. It had four rooms, each with a dirt floor and wooden shelf to sleep on. Kids went to The Shed when they committed major infractions, like refusing to exercise or swearing at a staff member. Stays in The Shed could range from a few hours to several weeks.

"When I first got here," Julie whispered, "A girl from Karma family got put in The Shed. She stayed in there for three months."

A cold shudder passed through me.

If I didn't give them the confession they wanted, it would take 100 days to get to level 2. At that rate, I'd be in this log cabin crap-hole for almost two years. *It's just not worth it*, I told myself. *I'll just give them what they want so I can get the hell out of here.*

I sat in the circle with everyone waiting for me to talk. I stared at my feet; my socks were filthy. My mother would never have let me leave the house wearing such dirty socks. She wouldn't have much cared for the rest of the Epiphany Lake uniform either. The faded khaki pants and baggy maroon sweatshirt were what she would have called 'frumpy.'

"You're wasting time, Grace," the counselor said, impatiently.

I shut my eyes. There was a rattling sound coming from one of the heating ducts, but the room felt cold. I pictured the abandoned house, the front bedroom with the broken window and the bed covered in leaves. *Maybe if I wish hard enough, when I open my eyes, I'll actually be there.*

When I looked up, all I saw was two dozen pairs of eyes staring at me, all with the same dull-black sheen. Would my eyes look like that soon, too?

"The abandoned house had a bed in it. It was upstairs, in a room with a broken window. It was one of the only windows of the house that wasn't boarded." I paused. The noise from the heating duct seemed to get louder.

"There was a streetlight right outside that window and the light would stream in. It made it kind of romantic. Anyway, there was this guy from school. He came into the house with me one night. He was afraid to go up the stairs, but I went first and showed him that it was safe, and he followed me. Once we got into the bedroom, we laid down on the bed and started making out. He put his hand down my pants and I didn't stop him."

I quickly swept the circle to get a sense of whether or not they believed me, but their expressions hadn't changed. Just that same, empty look.

"You're not telling the whole truth," the therapist said.

"I had sex with him in the abandoned house and we smoked weed together after," I said, hoping she would be satisfied and start grilling somebody else.

"The whole truth is that you *lured* him into that house."

"I lured him into the house," I repeated after her as I'd seen some of the other girls do.

"You took off your clothes and seduced him."

"I took off my clothes and seduced him."

"And the man you had sex with was your teacher. Mr. Kyeong."

For a split second, I imagined it: running my fingers through his satiny black hair as he sucked on my nipple through the fabric of a flimsy lace bra. The thought made me feel sore *down there,* and I wished I *had* had sex with Mr. Kyeong.

This bitch wants a confession, I thought, *I'll give her the wildest fucking confession she's ever heard.*

"I took off my clothes and seduced my teacher, Mr. Kyeong. He didn't want to at first. He said I was too young. But once I was naked he didn't stop me from unbuttoning his shirt and feeling his biceps. I kissed his abs, and I unzipped his pants and kissed his hard dick. His huge, hard dick."

The rattling stopped. Most of the faces around the circle remained unchanged, but a few of the girls smirked with amusement.

"He fucked me three times that night. From then on, he met me in that abandoned house every day and did everything I wanted. He brought me a little cocaine once because I'd told him I wanted to try it.

I snorted it off of an antique mirror while he fingered me. It was the best thing I've ever felt."

The room fell silent. Somewhere outside, there was the crunch of tires on gravel and the faint sound of a dog barking in the distance. There were no dogs at Epiphany Lake, which meant that dog belonged to someone who had nothing to do with us. Normal life was only as far away as a dog's voice could carry.

I waited for the therapist to ask me one of those dumb leading questions, like "how did that make you feel" or "don't you think you were acting out because your dad left?"

Instead, she glowered at me for a moment and then looked away.

"Girls," she said to the rest of the group, "let's let Grace know how we feel about what she did."

One by one, the other girls took turns shouting at me:

"You're a complete slut!"

"You're a filthy whore. No one will ever want you."

"You'll never stop being trash until you admit that you *are* trash."

"Your poor teacher must have felt so dirty after having sex with you."

"Why don't you apologize to your mother for ruining her life?"

The last person to shout at me was Julie: "You're disgusting."

By the time they were done, I shook all over. I wanted to grab each of them by the hair and shove their faces into the ground. But that would mean a trip to The Shed, or maybe something even worse. I thought about Mr. Kyeong. I thought about LaKeisha. I tried to count how many days it had been since I saw them last and already I couldn't remember. I dropped my head and cried.

The rattling started up again.

When therapy was over, we stood in a heel-toe line and waited for permission to walk across campus to the study hall. Suddenly, we heard shouting. A boy sprinted across campus, clearly heading for the gravel road. Two other boys chased after him. They caught up with him and tackled him. He landed face down on the gravel. When they picked him up, his face was bleeding. They hauled him off to The Shed.

By the time I had been at Epiphany Lake for six weeks, I learned to shout mean things at the other girls just as they shouted at me. In fact, I got really good at it:

"You're a complete waste of space," I said to a girl who'd confessed to stealing money from her parents to buy marijuana. "You're a burnout and a loser. You should call your mother and apologize to her for stretching out her uterus. In fact, you should tell her that you are sorry she didn't abort you."

It felt good to say those things to her. After all, she was the one who had told me that Mr. Kyeong must have felt dirty after having sex with me.

However, any good feelings I had about therapy disappeared when I got a letter from my mother:

Grace,

I am extremely shocked and saddened to learn the extent of your deplorable behavior. The school told me that you confessed to having sex with your teacher and doing drugs. Unbelievable! I suspected there was something going on between you and that gook teacher. He definitely cared about you too much. Now that I have confirmation I know that I will never, ever let you go back to that school. I will send you to Argentina if I have to. And Mr. Ching-Chong should be arrested.

I tried so hard to raise you right and this is how you repay me. You better pray that this school straightens you out – if it doesn't, I'm washing my hands of you forever.

Sincerely,
Your mother

I suddenly felt like I was buried up to my neck in snow. What had I done? Would my mother get Mr. Kyeong sent to jail? Would he have to quit teaching? Would he hate me forever?

Then again, if he went to jail I wouldn't have to see him, and at least *he* would get a lawyer. And besides, he'd deny everything. His lawyers would want me to testify, and I'd be able to say I was forced to lie. Maybe this could turn out to be a good thing. Maybe my story of sex with Mr. Kyeong could turn out to be my ticket out of here. Maybe there would even be a big investigation. Police would raid Epiphany Lake and take photos of the grungy cabins and kids in the Shed. Crandell would get tossed in jail and every kid here would be set free…

I read the letter again. *I suspected there was something going on…* She must have told the school about her suspicions. That's why the therapist mentioned Mr. Kyeong. My mother probably told them all of this before I even got here.

I pictured her sitting in her office, talking on the phone, glossy brochure in hand. *My daughter's so ungrateful…and that teacher has the nerve to say I'm a bad parent.* I pictured her looking serene as the person on the other end agreed with her every word.

I wondered how she had described Mr. Kyeong during that call. Did she refer to him as *that gook teacher, Mr. Ching-Chong*? Why was *I* the one who had to be locked up? My mother was the one writing racist shit and making fun of Mr. Kyeong's name like a third grader. It was just like that joke the kids used to tell on the playground. *How do Chinese people name their kids? They throw a fork down the stairs and listen to it go 'ching, chang, chung.'*

I crumpled the letter.

I decided not to think about my mother anymore. Instead, I dreamed that Mr. Kyeong would realize that my story was a signal that I needed help and come racing to my rescue. I imagined him tasting my nipple through the lace of a flimsy bra.

The counsellors noticed that I could run faster than most of the other girls, so when a girl tried to run, it became my job to chase after her. A week before Christmas, a new girl joined the Liberty family. Snow fell as we stood in a heel-toe line, waiting to go to dinner. The new girl was standing at the back of the line when she simply turned and started to run.

Chasing after her wasn't easy. After the first snow, we all received program-issued boots with the laces taken out. The boots flopped off the backs of my heads as I ran, allowing snow to fall inside, stinging the soles of my feet. It made me mad, and it wouldn't have happened if the new girl hadn't tried to run. It was all her fault. When I caught up with her, I threw my arms around her waist and fell on top of her. I held her face down in the snow and waited.

A counselor sprinted over to us. I heard the crackling of her walkie-talkie.

"Pick her up," the counselor ordered. I stood up and pulled the new girl up with me. I gripped her arm tightly. Melted snow dripped from her red, wet face. There was more crackling over the walkie-talkie.

"Copy that," the counselor said when she spoke into it. Then she turned to me. "Take her to The Shed."

That was the first time I saw the inside of The Shed. It had a dirt floor and chicken wire stapled over a narrow window. A plank on the wall served as a bed. Someone had scratched graffiti into the wall: "ELA is prison. Give me freedom." Bleach fumes burned the back of my throat. Still gripping the new girl's arm, I shoved her hard and watched her fall backward onto the dirt floor. She started to cry. The counselor closed the door and locked it behind us. As we walked away from The Shed, I could still hear the girl crying.

That night, I couldn't sleep. *She brought it on herself,* I told myself as I stared at the Australia stain on the ceiling. *She should never have tried to run.* I tried to forget that the girl had only been on campus for a few hours, had never even seen The Shed, and had no way of knowing that she would end up there. Well, soon she would learn: the only way out of the program was to work through it.

3

In January, I finally reached Level Two. It was Martin Luther King Day. All the kids back at my old school had the day off, but for us it was just another day.

Reaching Level Two meant I could speak without permission. Three other girls were promoted to Level Two at the same time. After being the same 'family' for weeks without saying a word to each other, we could finally talk. But we still had to be very careful about what we said. We still couldn't speak while standing in lines or during meal times. We also weren't supposed to talk about the riot that happened at another program school in Costa Rica, but rumors still managed to flow through campus.

Even though Level Six was the highest, Level Two was actually the hardest to reach. Some people never made it out of Level One. Andrea, the girl who was tackled for refusing to get out of bed, was one of them. She stayed on the lowest level for two years until she turned eighteen and left Epiphany Lake with nothing more than a fifty dollar bill and a bus ticket to Minneapolis.

Two days after my promotion, staff woke us up earlier than usual. They told us to get dressed and assembled both the Karma and Liberty families in the hall.

"Liberty family, you're going on a field trip. The Karma family is going to stay here and disassemble some of these bunk beds."

We all wanted to know why, but no one dared ask.

Finally, a girl said, "Why do they get to go on a field trip?"

"Talking out of turn – that's a category 1 violation," the woman said. Then, she laughed: "You lost all your points before 7 am. Good job!"

The girl dropped her head and wept silently.

We lined up in single file and marched deep into the woods, until we could no longer see the bunkhouses. There we waited in silence for what seemed like hours. Because it was winter, there was hardly any sound at all, but I did hear the occasional car on a distant road.

I looked at the other girls and thought, *there are fifteen of us, and one member of staff. We could all run from her and she wouldn't be able to catch us.* She still had her walkie-talkie, though. She could radio back to the main camp and make sure Crandell's truck was there to meet us if we made it to the road. Still, there were more of us. If three girls held her down, we could get that radio away from her. We could leave her alone in the woods without it, with no way to contact anyone. We could turn it on and pretend to be her, tell the people at the main camp that we are on our way back when we're really halfway to town. If we all made it to town, there's no way the police would bring all of us back.

But nobody grabbed the woman around her throat. Nobody wrenched her arms behind her back. Nobody reached into that holster and snatched her radio away. We all just stood there saying nothing, listening for cars and dreaming about life somewhere else.

The sun hit its noon-day mark when we finally started back for the main camp. My heels were numb from the snow that had fallen into my boots. My stomach growled. I imagined all the foods I wished I could have: blueberry pancakes, sausages, orange slices.

When we got back to our cabin, the Karma girls were putting bunk beds back together. As I waited for one of them to finish so that I could put my sheets back on, she told me in a whisper what had happened: a state inspector came to evaluate living conditions at Epiphany Lake. If the inspector had seen how crowded the bedrooms were, the school would have been in big trouble. So they sent three families out into the woods and hid some of the bunk beds so it would look like the school had fewer students than it really did.

I wondered: did the inspector see The Shed?

For a week after the inspector came, the food was way better: salads with crisp lettuce, slices of roast pork with noodles and gravy, fresh fruit. But after that, we were back to soggy iceburg lettuce, bland boiled chicken and syrupy canned pears.

4

When you complain, you make yourself into a victim. - Eckhart Tolle

In February, the snow piled up so high that we had to push hard on the cabin door just to get outside. It was thirty-five below zero nearly every day. One morning, we stood outside the cafeteria waiting to be let inside for breakfast. Each breath I took stung my nostrils. I lost feeling in my toes. A girl in line ahead of me, who was from down south and wasn't used to the cold, shivered violently.

Every morning we seem to stand out here a little bit longer, I thought.

I had just been promoted to level 3, which meant I got the privileges that came with it: I could use condiments at meal times (butter, sugar, salt, mustard, ketchup), have a Hershey bar once a week and wear my hair down.

Julie had been promoted to level 5 so she got to move out of our cabin and into a cabin for upper levels that was closer to the edge of campus. In upper level cabins, kids could cook their own food, listen to music and watch TV. As a level 5, Julie could walk across campus by herself, without having to march single-file while staring at the back of somebody's neck. She also got to leave campus and go into town, even see a movie at the single-screen theater now and then. In a few months, if she did everything right, she'd reach level 6 and graduate the program.

There was one other privilege that came with being a level 3: I was allowed one twenty-minute phone call every other week. During the call, a staff member sat in the room with me, watching, listening, ready to disconnect the call if I said anything negative about the program.

The first time I spoke to my mother, she sounded bright and cheerful; I wondered who was sitting in the room with *her*.

"Gracie!" She sang, "It's so wonderful to hear from you! I can't believe it's been almost four months since I talked to you last!"

The last time I'd spoken to my mother was the night the two men came and took me away in the middle of the night.

"I'm sure it's cold up there," she said. "Are you staying warm? Working hard?"

"Yes," I told her. "They keep us very busy."

Every minute of our day was scheduled, and every day was the same.

"Well I've been getting good reports," she said. "It sounds like you're really starting to learn. I think you're on your way to becoming the woman I know you can be."

"What kind of woman is that?" I asked.

"You know, when I tell people that you're at boarding school, they all think it's some elite college prep school. I wish that were true," she said with a sigh.

So do I, I thought. *Do you know that our cabin smells like dirty laundry? Do you know that I'm using a history textbook that was printed in 1976? Do you know that last night, they served us noodles topped with gobs of mayonnaise and called it 'alfredo sauce'?*

"This is better than an elite college prep school," I told her. "We learn the kind of lessons you can't find in a book. I know now that if I complain, I'm just making myself into a victim. I bet kids in those fancy schools complain all the time."

Mom laughed. I couldn't remember the last time I'd heard her laugh.

"Plus, we work out all the time. I can do fifty pushups in a minute. That's enough to get into the army."

"That's wonderful," she said, "But I hope they don't make you do *too* many – you don't want your arms to get all bulky. You'll look like a Russian peasant!"

She laughed again. I glanced at the timer that sat on the table. I had eighteen minutes left.

"Have you talked to Dad?" I asked.

There was silence on the line. When she spoke, the sunny laugh was gone from her voice, and I could picture the change in her facial expression that went with it. "Your father abandoned us. I don't know why you'd ask about him."

"Because he's my dad," I said.

"Grace, I want you to focus on your emotional growth," she said. "Can you do that?"

"Sure, Mom," I said, and handed the phone back to the staff.

"You still have seventeen minutes left," she said in a low voice. She was new and a lot nicer than most of the people on staff. She was one of those people who genuinely wanted to help kids. She wouldn't last long.

I shrugged. She took the phone and put it back on its hook.

They finally let us into the cafeteria. Blood rushed to my toes, making me feel like my boots were on fire. I was hungry. While standing in line, I fantasized about what I wanted to eat: crisp home fries topped with steamed broccoli, bell peppers, onions, scrambled eggs and cheese. Instead, someone handed me a bowl of watery oat meal that wasn't fully cooked. White oats floated on top of gray water.

I poured sugar into it slowly so I could watch the sparkling crystals fall into the water and dissolve.

Later that day, they gathered the girls and boys together. Most of the time, therapy was sitting around in circle calling each other ungrateful sluts, but every few months, they brought everyone together for a 'seminar.' The seminars lasted for hours, starting at ten in the morning and stretching late into the night, until we marched back to our cabins, feeling exhausted and hollow.

We folded up all of the tables and chairs in the cafeteria and moved them aside. With all of us kids crammed into the cafeteria, the room shrank very quickly. We sat on the cold floor and pretended that it wasn't making our ass cheeks fall asleep.

That was the day we played the "Titanic" game.

Patrice, one of the therapists on staff, told us all to lie down on the floor and shut our eyes. She told us to imagine we were on the deck of a ship, feeling the sun on our faces.

"The water below is a clear blue," she said, her voice low and soothing. "It matches the sky above. Feel the cool wind on your face. Grip the deck rail with your hands and feel the power of the ship's engines speeding forward. You're an immigrant dreaming of a new life in America. You're full of excitement and hope. Your heart is full of dreams."

I breathed in deeply and, with my eyes shut tight, imagined I was Kate Winslet, making out with Leonardo DiCaprio on the bow while the ship sailed into the sunset. I sank into my reverie, rewriting history as my mind drifted: *The telegraph operator on the Californian stays on duty just fifteen minutes longer and receives the Titanic's distress calls. The Californian steams at full speed and brings all of the Titanic passengers on board. From the deck of the Californian, Jack and Rose watch the Titanic slip under the water. A few days later, the ship arrives in New York Harbor. Jack and Rose get off together. They go to Coney Island, holding hands on the Ferris wheel as they smile into the sun.*

Suddenly, there was a loud crashing sound. My eyes snapped open and Patrice, Crandell and other staff were banging their hands on tables in unison. I felt sleepy. Confused.

"The ship is sinking!" Crandell shouted angrily. The sound of his voice made a shudder cascade down my spine. "There aren't enough lifeboats! If you want to live, you'll have to fight for your life!"

We were each given one minute to stand on a chair and give a speech, defending our right to live. I stood in a long line, waiting my turn. I didn't listen to the other kids' speeches; I was too nervous. My heart was beating fast like it did when they made us do hundreds of jumping jacks.

I suddenly wished we *were* doing jumping jacks instead of playing this game, though I wasn't sure why.

When it was my turn to stand on the chair, my throat tightened and my knees shook. I felt the hard, smooth surface of the chair through my dirty socks.

"The clock is ticking," Patrice barked. "Does your life mean so little to you that you won't speak up for it?"

Not a single word formed in my mind.

"45 seconds!" Patrice barked again. "Open your mouth or you'll die!"

Out of some corner of my memory, I remembered a poem by Irina Ratushinskaya that I'd memorized to recite for Mr. Kyeong's class. I took a deep breath and as loudly as I could, recited the poem aloud:

"I will live and survive…and I will tell of the best people in all the earth. The most tender but also the most invincible. How they said farewell…how they waited for letters from their loved ones. And I'll be asked, what helped us to live, when there were neither letters nor any news…and I will tell of the first beauty I saw…a frost-covered window…a blue radiance on a tiny pane of glass."

When I finished, my throat was dry, almost sore. I glanced at Patrice. She looked up at me and twisted her face. I couldn't tell what she thought of the poem, but at least she didn't yell. She simply nodded which meant I could step down and it was the next person's turn.

After everyone had given their speech, it was time to vote.

Crandell chose one girl out of the crowd and made the rest of us get into a single-file line that snaked around the perimeter of the room. We were supposed to walk up to her, one by one, and wait for her to say "live" or "die." She could only vote to save three people.

"Live," she said to the first person in front of her. Her voice seemed small and far away; I was all the way at the back of the room. "Live," she said again. "Live."

Everyone who walked up to her got to live, until Crandell said, "That's it – that's three." He stared the girl down, his eyes narrow.

"Do you know what your mistake was?" he asked.

She shook her head. Her eyes began to shine.

"You filled the boat but didn't save yourself."

"I –"

"Doesn't your life mean anything to you? Are you really that ungrateful?"

The girl looked confused as she furiously rubbed her eyes.

"No," she said, weakly.

Crandell bent low and drew his face very close to hers. "You're pathetic," he spat. "If you think your life is worthless, *you're* worthless. Get to the back of the line."

I watched her take her place in the back of the line. She wrapped her arms around herself and cried, her head hanging.

"Every day, you all make choices." Crandell bellowed, "When you choose drugs, you choose death. When you choose sex, you choose death. When you choose to disobey your parents or skip school, you choose death. What choices will you make today?"

The game went on so long I had no idea what time it was. I was hungry. My feet hurt from standing on them. *Titanic* continued to play in my head: Rose lept from the lifeboat and ran through the corridors of the sinking ship, just so she could be with Jack as long as possible. Jack kissed her and told her she was stupid for throwing away her seat on the lifeboat.

At the front of the line, a tall boy with broad, football player's shoulders burst into tears when a girl screamed, "Die!" in his face.

Crandell would have agreed with Jack. He would have said that Rose was an ungrateful brat for jumping off the lifeboat. Was he right?

I had watched *Titanic* in my mind twice by the time I got close to the front of the line. A boy told me to live. I felt a rush of joy. This boy I'd never seen before thought I deserved to live. I wanted to throw my arms around him and kiss him, but I knew we'd both end up in The Shed if I'd done that.

Finally, it was my turn to fill the lifeboat. My body was buzzing because we'd been playing this game for an entire day, and I hadn't eaten since the watery oatmeal. I knew I had to save myself. I knew I had to choose survivors carefully.

The first person who walked up to me was a thin blonde girl who looked at me with zombie eyes. I knew she was tired and hungry like everyone else, but because there was no spark in her eyes, I shouted, "Die!" She walked to the back of the line, the look in her eyes unchanged.

The next was a boy. He had blue eyes like Leonardo DiCaprio, so I let him live.

Before I could decide the next person's fate – a small boy, no older than twelve years old – Patrice stood behind me.

"Imagine that this person is your mother," she said to me. "Every time you disrespected your mother, you told her to die. How many times did you tell your family to die? Will you tell your mother to die again?"

My mind flashed on the night my mother came after me with scissors and threatened to cut the blue dye out of my hair. Rage flared up in my chest. "DIE!" I shouted. The boy's face crumpled and his narrow body shook as he cried.

I only had two more 'live' votes. I needed one to save myself, and I was saving the other for Julie. She stood in line, her arms crossed, her face stained with tears. There were thirty people between us.

"DIE!" I shouted. I watched their expressions change every time I shouted. I made a game of it, counting the faces that changed and the ones that didn't.

Finally, Julie stood in front of me. I looked straight into her wet eyes. I didn't see sadness or hope. Only a question: *Will I live or die, Grace?*

"LIVE!" I shouted, using as much of my voice as I had left.

"Julie lives!" she shouted, tossing her hair and turning her face up to the ceiling.

I pointed to myself. "LIVE!"

I went to the back of the line.

The voting dragged on for hours. When it was finally over, we were all exhausted and starving. Before we were allowed to leave, Patrice walked around the room with a mirror, pausing in front of each person.

"This is a mirror of your life," she said. "Every day, you vote for yourself to live or you vote for yourself to die. Tomorrow, what will your vote be?"

As she held the mirror up to my face, I saw myself for the first time in months. There was all this negative space where my cheeks and eyes used to be. Darkness was slowly swallowing me up.

It was well past midnight when we finished the game. We put the cafeteria tables and chairs back where they belonged, and they finally let us eat. In silence, we ate baked beans and hot dogs. I carefully drew lines of mustard and ketchup on my hotdog and ate it slowly. I thought about Rose jumping off the lifeboat and back onto the Titanic, of Jack telling her how stupid she was for doing that. I realized: Rose *wasn't* stupid. She was the opposite of stupid. She knew there was no lifeboat for Jack. She knew he would have to try to survive in the freezing water, and she didn't want to sit safely in a lifeboat and wait while Jack drowned. She didn't want to vote for herself to live if she couldn't do the same for someone she loved.

After the Lifeboat seminar, everyone walked around in a dream. The entire campus was silent; we marched in our heel-toe lines without saying a word. Even the girls who usually got in trouble for talking stayed quiet.

I had a dream that I was a third-class passenger on the Titanic. We weren't trapped behind locked gates like in the movie. We just got lost in the maze of staircases and corridors that seemed to take us sideways and forward, but never up. In the dream, someone grabbed my hand. I turned and saw Rose standing next to me, with her red wavy hair all undone and her blood-colored dress covered in glitter. The hem of her dress was heavy with saltwater.

"All you had to do was stay up on deck," I told her. "You could be floating safely in a lifeboat right now instead of trapped inside this sinking ship."

"Live," she said. "Die."

"Where is Jack?" I asked her.

"Die," she said. "Live." I realized those were the only words she could say.

"You'll live," I assured her. "Jack will die. But what about me?"

"Live. Die. Live."

A week passed. The fog finally lifted and things slowly got back to normal – or, what passed for normal at a place like Epiphany Lake. A new girl joined the Karma family. Her hair was corn-silk blond and she had a movie-star body. We all agreed there was something familiar about her face, but none of us could figure out who she was. It was Andrea who finally figured it out: the new girl was that hotel heiress who was in all the fashion magazines despite being kind of ugly. Andrea remembered that she'd been in trouble before, for shoplifting or something.

"I saw it on *Hard Copy*," Andrea said.

We got a new girl in our family too. She was thin too, but clearly anorexic. She'd arrived at Epiphany Lake with a headful of spiky, neon-pink hair. During her intake session, the staff shaved it all off. With her sunken eyes and shaved head, her resemblance to a concentration camp victim was striking; somebody nicknamed her "Treblinka."

One morning, during Treblinka's first week, we stood in line near The Shed. We'd been ordered to stand there and wait, but they didn't tell us why. I did the best I could to hide the fact that I was annoyed. *No sighing. No eye-rolling. No fidgeting. No looking around.*

"Excuse me," Treblinka said. "What are we waiting for?"

"No talking in line," the staff member said. "That's a Category 1 violation."

"A what?"

"You should have learned the rules by now. Stop talking."

"But —"

"Stop talking. Do you want to end up in there?" The staff pointed to The Shed. Just then, two male staffers came out of The Shed, each gripping a boy's arms. I recognized him. I remember watching two upper levels tackle that boy and lead him off to The Shed after he tried to run away.

Jesus Christ. Has he been in there this whole time? Six months? Then, I realized I wasn't sure what month it was.

He was thinner. And he was struggling against the mens' grip.

"Fuck you!" the boy shouted. "Fucking you, fucking pussies! Fucking cunts! Fucking pieces of shit!"

The men opened the door to a blue plastic Port-a-Potty and shoved him in. It rocked violently back and forth. It rattled each time he threw his body against the walls. His swearing was only slightly muffled by the plastic door.

Treblinka broke down in tears.

"You're going to clean all that up yourself if you tip this thing over," one of the men warned. But the rocking continued.

A radio crackled with a message that we could move on.

A few days later, a rumor went around that the boy in The Shed was gone, that Crandell and some other guy had taken the boy out of The Shed in the middle of the night and loaded him into an SUV. Nobody knew where he had gone, but the kids who'd been around the longest all seemed to agree: he must have gone to Mystic Bay.

"They threatened to send me there," Andrea told me. "They even told me they had already purchased the plane tickets. I promised to be good so they dropped it, but sometimes I'm afraid they're going to send me."

"What about that celebrity girl over in Karma? Do you think she'll be sent there? I heard her talking in their heel-toe line this morning."

"Looks like the staff is taking it easy on her," Andrea said.

"That's not fair," I said.

Andrea shrugged. "The Karma girls will take care of that."

Andrea was right. That night, the girls in Karma family cornered the heiress in their dormitory and all took turns beating her – all fourteen of them. We could hear the thudding of fists from our side of the cabin. I glanced over at Treblinka, who lay facing the wall, running her hand over her shaved head. I had this sudden urge to go over to the Karma side and join in the beat down. Andrea and I traded glances – I knew she was thinking the same thing.

We left our bunks and crossed the hall. When we opened the door, the heiress was on the floor, taking punches from a girl who looked like she played on the shot-put team.

"Can we take a turn?" I asked. The crowd of Karma girls parted, clearing a path for Andrea and me. The heiress was already bleeding from her mouth and nose. Her hair was tangled. She looked nothing like the sleek image I'd seen on magazine covers.

I thought of Treblinka's pink hair being swept into the trash. I thought of my mother saying "I'll cut your hair off myself," and remembered her coming after me with scissors. Who the fuck was this bitch, anyway? She got everything she wanted. Even here, people acted like she was special. I kicked her hard in the ribs. She coughed and I kicked her again.

I was jacked up on adrenaline. My legs flared like the Irish step dancers from *Riverdance*; I kicked her until she crawled away.

In the morning, Andrea, the girls from Karma and I all lost a week's worth of points for doling out prison justice to the princess.

It was worth it, I decided. *Live.*

It seemed like the snow would never melt. If I had known then just how painful sun and heat could be, I wouldn't have minded the winter so much. But at Epiphany Lake, every day was the same; the endless stretch of white didn't help.

I talked to my mother every other week. I told her everything the staff wanted her to hear, everything she wanted to hear. Each time we spoke I asked to talk to my dad, and each time I did she got angry. I never used the full twenty minutes.

Treblinka's hair grew back quickly. Her natural color was more like cinnamon. She ran her fingers through it constantly, as if she was surprised that it was there. She got in trouble every time staff caught her doing it. She didn't seem to get that she was on Level 1 and that meant there was *nothing* she couldn't do without getting permission.

She'll be on Level 1 forever, I thought.

I didn't see Julie much anymore, but I ran into her one evening in the cafeteria. While waiting in line for boiled bologna, Julie told me that she was a week shy of reaching Level 6. She would be graduating from the program soon.

"You'll get done soon too, as long as you keep your head down," she said in a low voice. "Remember: the only way out is through."

The only way out is through. The staff said that all the time. My mother even said it when I spoke to her on the phone. Were they brainwashing her, too?

Even though it still looked like Christmas at Epiphany Lake, kids at my old school were probably on spring break. I thought about LaKeisha. I wondered what she was doing now. Had she been in all the plays? Was she dominating Mr. Kyeong's class? Was she on the road to valedictorian?

I shook my head. I hadn't thought about LaKeisha in months. School plays. Valedictorians. Grade point averages. Spring break. None of that meant anything to me anymore.

What would Julie tell her friends when she got home? Would she tell them about staff restraining kids on the ground? Would she tell them about Lifeboat? About The Shed? Or would she say: "The program saved my life. Without it, I would be dead, insane or in jail."

Treblinka went a little crazy. One night, I had a dream I was in steerage on the Titanic, and I was jostled awake when it hit the iceberg. When I opened my eyes, the first thing I saw was the stain on the ceiling, and I heard Treblinka moaning on the bunk beneath me. I leaned over the edge and looked down: she was humping her mattress, her hips slamming down violently, over and over again. I grabbed my pillow and swung it into her face.

"Knock that off," I warned her. Masturbating was completely forbidden in our program. In fact, it was an automatic Category 5 violation. I could have ratted her out to the staff, but I didn't see the point. She'd been in the program almost two months and was nowhere close to moving off of Level 1.

The morning after the masturbation incident, she decided she was Gwen Stefani and started singing "I'm Just a Girl" while we stood in a heel-toe line. She mimicked Gwen Stefani's voice so well, I pictured her with cherry-red lipstick and a blond pompadour instead of chapped lips and fuzzy brown hair. Staff ordered her to stop singing, but she wouldn't stop.

"Haddonfield," staff said to me, "shut her up."

I didn't want to; I was enjoying Treblinka's performance. It was the most interesting thing that had happened in weeks. But I was just a few points shy of Level 5. That meant moving away from the Liberty/Karma cabin into one where I'd have access to a stereo and a VCR (no regular TV or radio, though.) I'd be able to walk across campus freely, without having to stand rigidly in a stupid fucking heel-toe line, without having some lame staff constantly babysitting me. I'd be able to go to sleep one whole hour later, and cook things like Spaghetti O's and Kraft macaroni and cheese in a little kitchen I shared with other girls, instead of eating cafeteria slop.

I cuffed Treblinka on the back of her neck and shoved her face into the dirt. But she didn't stop signing, even with clumps of earth and dead grass filling her mouth. I sat on her hip. She squirmed but kept on singing.

The staff crouched low and spoke into Treblinka's ear. "Do you want to go to The Shed?" she asked.

Treblinka went on singing.

"Stand her up," the staff said to me, "Take her to The Shed."

I gripped Treblinka's tricep. She yelped as my fingers dug into her flesh. She refused to walk, so my biceps burned as I held her up and led her off to The Shed, her feet dragging on the ground. She continued to sing, starting the song over each time she finished it. When I reached The Shed, my arms were aching, and I was sick of the sound of her voice, so I kicked the door open and threw her as hard as I could. She landed on the dirt floor and fell silent.

When I rejoined the line, Crandell pulled up in his pick-up truck. He turned up the radio.

"Dance party time!" he declared. "Dance, girls!"

Fourteen zombie-eyed girls shifted from foot to foot and twisted their hips while Crandell watched and laughed from the window of his truck. His car radio was playing the same song that Treblinka had been singing.

Was this real? Was this a dream? I pinched an inch of my own flesh between my thumb and forefinger.

5

I didn't make level 5.

To reach levels 5 and 6, you had to give a speech in front of a panel of upper-level students and staff, stating why you deserved to be promoted. I was supposed to talk about what I'd learned since I'd been at Epiphany Lake and how Epiphany Lake had changed me. In my speech, I used words like *responsibility, gratitude* and *visualization.*

When I was finished, the panel voted on whether to promote me or not. The vote had to be unanimous and one girl voted no. Her eyes glittered when she said it, and I could tell she didn't like me, which was odd because I had no idea who she was. But I knew instantly that she was one of those people who got through the program by constantly ratting out everyone else. Some people are like that – they enjoy saying mean things and getting other people in trouble. The program is the perfect place for them.

I wanted to go over to her and tell her to go fuck herself, to fall down a well, to die in a fire. I wanted to spit in her face and yank her hair and stomp on her instep. But I stood as still as possible, with my hands behind my back and my feet firmly planted. I froze my face so that none of my emotions would show on it. If I complained or protested or even frowned, I could get dropped back down to Level 3, or worse.

"Thank you for your consideration," I said.

The panel dismissed me and a staff member accompanied me back to my cabin. As I stepped inside, I inhaled the scent of mildew and dirty laundry. *Another month in Liberty*, I thought, sighing internally. *Another month at least.*

That night, before Shutdown, I described the girl who voted no to Andrea and asked her if she knew who the girl was.

"I think I know who you are talking about," Andrea whispered. "I think she used to be in the Tranquility family. But why do you care who she is? It's not like you can go talk to her."

"What if she's on the panel again the next time I try for my promotion?"

Andrea shrugged. "Why worry? She might graduate or get dropped."

I nodded in agreement but a strange feeling suddenly came over me. Maybe it didn't matter who was on the panel; maybe there was always someone – at least one person – on the panel who would vote no.

"What if…what if someone *told* her to vote no?"

"What are you talking about? Who would do that?"

"I don't know. Crandell?"

Andrea furrowed her brows. "You're getting paranoid."

"I guess," I said. But that night I lay awake, thoughts churning in my mind. *There's something else going on*, I thought. *There's something that goes on behind the scenes, and they don't want us to know.*

I closed my eyes and willed my brain to be quiet. But even as my thoughts died down, the hard knot of anxiety in my stomach grew.

Two days after I was denied my promotion, Treblinka was released from The Shed. She was even thinner than before, and she had red sores all over her hands. While in isolation, she dug holes in her skin with her fingernails, then picked at the scabs that formed.

As we stood in line on our way to breakfast, the staff radio crackled. *Third from the back. Category 5: self-harm.* It was Crandell's voice on the radio. He must have been somewhere nearby, but I couldn't see him. It was almost like he had an invisible watch tower that gave him a 360-degree view of the entire campus, twenty-four hours a day.

The staff pulled Treblinka out of line. She held up Treblinka's hand; a small rivulet of blood trickled from the scab she had picked.

"Don't you have any respect for your body?" the staff said. "Look, girls," she commanded all of us, "this is what happens when you don't treat your body like a temple. You end up looking like something that crawled out of a gutter." She turned to Treblinka. "Do you want to live under a bridge someday? Because if you don't shape up, that's where you're headed." She ordered Treblinka to get back in line.

At breakfast, Treblinka gobbled her oatmeal so quickly, it made me wonder what she ate – or didn't eat – while she was in The Shed.

I looked down at my own oatmeal. Today it was cooked properly. I added sugar and slowly stirred it. I wished I could add cinnamon, too. And apple slices.

On Level 5, I'd be able to eat cereal with milk. Not Lucky Charms or Count Chocula or anything fancy like that, but a bowl of Rice Chex with cold milk sounded amazing after eating oatmeal day in and day out.

I just had to get that promotion. I would have to prove that I was dedicated to the program, that I really believed in it, that it *had* changed me. If I did that, they would *have* to promote me.

I closed my eyes. What *did* I believe about the program? When I first arrived at Epiphany Lake, I thought the program was bullshit but realized I had to go along with it if I wanted to go home. Now I wasn't sure what I believed.

I opened my eyes and looked down at my hands. My fingernails were jagged and dirty because I never got a chance to clean and file them. (On Level 6 I'd gain the privilege of using a nail file.)

Before I came here, I cared about my grade point average. I cared about winning heats and becoming the swim team captain someday. I cared about going to a good college, making Mr. Kyeong proud and getting my mom's permission to sleep over at LaKeisha's house. Now all I cared about was going home.

Epiphany Lake has changed me, I thought, *but I don't know if it has made me into the person that they want me to be. I don't really know what they want.*

6

Treblinka couldn't stop picking at her hands. The staff duct taped oven mitts onto her hands and told her she'd go back The Shed if she took them off. She couldn't take them off even to go to the bathroom. They started to smell bad real fast, and I was convinced that she peed on those mitts on purpose.

She started telling weird stories in therapy too, and they all revolved around babies. Babies born with full sets of teeth. Babies strangled on the way out by their own umbilical cords. Babies sold out of Victorian nurseries. "In my grandmother's parish in Louisiana, there was a convent that sold babies. They told everyone that they were an orphanage but really they would buy babies from girls who were prostitutes or young unmarried girls and sell the babies to childless couples. The police caught on when the nuns started filling the convent with silk damask furniture. They planned to raid the convent, but someone tipped the nuns off and they all left in the middle of the night. When the police raided the convent, they found three babies writhing in their cribs, stewing in their own shit."

Everyone stared at Treblinka, waiting for her to go on. Her stories *were* more interesting than listening to girls cry with shame about that time they let some guy go to third base.

"We're here to talk about *you*," the therapist said, "not about nuns from ninety years ago. Why don't you tell a story from your life?"

"What kind of story? Oh, you mean like how I gave birth at the prom and left the baby in a Dumpster out back? You want to hear all about how a big blood stain spread all over my prom dress while I danced? Well, I would tell you that story if it had happened. But I've never done any of those things. I'm here because my dad wanted me to be a blond cheerleader. I dyed my hair pink and listened to Marilyn Manson. He was mad he couldn't make me be what he wanted."

The therapist frowned. "You know that's not the only reason you're here. If you want to succeed in this program you will have to start telling the truth."

"I am. You just don't want to hear it."

"Why would your parents send you here if they didn't think you were deeply troubled? If they didn't think you had done something wrong?"

Treblinka barred her chest with her crossed arms, the oven mitts sticking out from under her elbows like Mickey Mouse hands. "Because all they care about is what other people think."

She's so stupid, I thought. *All she has to do is tell the truth. She's so ungrateful. She'll stay on level 1 forever.*

Then, I remembered LaKeisha and the Marilyn Manson poster that hung above her bed. I remembered her combat boots and the black crushed velvet shawl she wore even in the heat of summer. Why was Treblinka here for listening to Marilyn Manson while LaKeisha was at home with her mom and dad?

"You need to learn some gratitude," the therapist said to Treblinka. "That's why you're all here, to learn gratitude."

"I'll be grateful when I'm out of here," Treblinka said.

The therapist smirked. "At the rate you're going, you won't be out of here for a long, long time."

From therapy, we went to lunch. As we stood in the chow line waiting for cold cheese sandwiches, Andrea whispered into my ear through gritted teeth, "If you sit next to Treblinka, I'll give you my Hershey bar."

"Why?"

"I can't stand sitting next to her. Those fucking oven mitts smell like Port Authority."

"What?"

"Port Authority. In New York City. Homeless men use it as a giant toilet."

"You're from New York?"

Andrea nodded. We weren't supposed to exchange contact information. That was a category 3 or 4 violation.

"So if I sit by her today I get your Hershey bar?"

"If you sit by her for the rest of the week."

"I'll sit by her indefinitely if you promise me all your Hershey bars."

Our whispering began to attract attention from a junior staff who glared at us while standing guard to make sure no one took more than one sandwich.

"Fine," Andrea growled, and we both stared straight ahead and pretended we hadn't been talking.

I waited for Treblinka to sit, and I took the seat next to her, guaranteeing Andrea at least one buffer. Andrea was right: those oven mitts did reek of piss. I pulled my shirt over my nose, took a deep breath and held it. The Wonder Bread flattened as I bit into it and the Kraft cheese was cold and rubbery, but I ate as fast as I could so I wouldn't have to breathe.

Treblinka's oven mitts got more disgusting every day. Not only were they thoroughly stained with piss but they were also starting to get crusty – and not just with food. Our entire dormitory stank thanks to those mitts – and with the nights starting to get warmer, the problem just got worse and worse.

I held my breath as I sat on my bunk, eating Andrea's Hershey bar. I mused about what we could do about the oven mitts. If we took them off for her, we'd all risk violations. We could get her sent to The Shed, but we'd have to set her up somehow, and I was too tired to come up with a plan. Maybe we could steal some bleach or detergent and just pour it on them…

The next day, in silent study hall, I wrote, "Steal bleach for T's stinky mitts" onto a scrap of paper which I shoved into a Bic pen and passed to Andrea.

In the front of the room, our "teacher" crunched on a bag of Doritos. My history textbook predicted that the Berlin Wall would never come down. I filled in the bubbles of a multiple choice test and raised my hand when I was finished. By the time the teacher noticed me, blood had drained from my hand. He nodded his approval, and I approached his desk to hand him my test. He checked off my answers, grunted and handed me the test for the next unit.

When I returned to my desk, the pen I'd passed to Andrea was lying in the crease of my textbook. I removed the endcap and extracted the slip of paper. Under my note, Andrea had written, "I'll do it."

That night, just before Shutdown, Andrea lifted her pillow to show me the can of lemon Lysol that she'd managed to pilfer. She winked, and we waited for the lights to go out.

As soon as our eyes adjusted to the darkness, we approached Treblinka's bed. She was already asleep. I held up Treblinka's mitted hands while Andrea generously sprayed the Lysol. The air thickened with the chemical lemon scent. Andrea tucked the Lysol back under her pillow and I climbed into my bunk.

7

One of Treblinka's oven mitts caught fire. I didn't know how she did it, but I figured she must have held the glove over the halogen light in the hallway and waited for it to ignite. She woke us all up with her screaming.

She stood in the hallway, holding up her flaming oven mitt, sparks flying as she waved it around. For a moment, she looked like a circus performer. I waited for her to hold the flame up to her mouth and breathe a cloud of fire. Instead, the sprinkler system rained down tepid water, extinguishing the glove and soaking all of us. Girls shrieked as their hair got wet. Two junior staff marched into the cabin and promptly hauled Treblinka away.

Her stunt cost her two weeks in The Shed. When they let her out, her bones showed a little more. She had a sort of a smile on her face though. It was barely there; I had to look hard to see it. But once I saw it I knew why it was there. Treblinka was at Epiphany Lake partly because of her eating disorder. In The Shed, staff fed her limited rations. I'd heard her speak in therapy about how hunger felt like a source of power to her. She'd talked about how she felt hungry and refused to eat, and when her hunger faded away, she knew she was strong.

"I'm not anorexic," she'd said. "I'm on hunger strike. I won't eat until my family learns to accept me. I won't eat until they stop trying to make me be like their friends' kids. I won't eat until there is equal justice for everyone."

The therapist told her she was stupid and self-involved.

Treblinka's power ran out quickly. During a fitness session, she was too weak to keep up. She collapsed on the ground, face down in the grass. Crandell bent over and screamed in her ear, telling her she was lazy, manipulative, weak and ugly.

I blocked out his voice as I counted my jumping jacks. I ignored the cramp in my left calf.

"PUSHUPS!" Crandell bellowed.

We dropped to the ground and cranked out pushups. We did them from the toes – if we did them from the knees, Crandell would say something about how feminists wanted equal treatment so all us lard-bags could do pushups from the toes like men.

As I did my pushups, I heard Treblinka crying. From the corner of my eye, I saw Crandell lifting her and forcing her into a pushup position. Each time he did, she collapsed and each time she collapsed he lifted her again.

"Come on!" he shouted. "Keep up!"

My shoulders burned and sweat dripped into my eyes. My heart pounded and blood rushed everywhere. My face felt hot. Crandell's shouting seemed far away.

It doesn't matter how many pushups or situps or jumping jacks they make me do, I thought. *I won't let them see how tired I am. I won't be like Treblinka.*

A few days later, Treblinka tried to run away during the fitness session. She was too weak to get very far, but Crandell still made me chase after her.

"Haddonfield," he said, digging the toe of his work boot into my ribs as I did pushups, "go get her."

I caught Treblinka around the waist and she tumbled to the ground.

I landed on top of her, and for a moment I was afraid she would break apart. She looked up at me, the sun hitting her face just enough to make the flecks of amber in her eyes glow.

"Grace," she whispered, "why do you do this? Why do you all do what they say? None of this is good. None of this helps us. There's no point to any of it. If we all just refused to do what they say, we could end all this."

"That won't happen," I hissed back. "Someone will rat you out if you try. And then you'll end up someplace worse than this. Is that what you want?"

"How could *any* place be worse than this?" tears formed in her eyes. I didn't know. I didn't want to know. Maybe there wasn't somewhere worse than this. Maybe it was something they made up to keep us in line. But why would I take that chance?

"If you want to leave, you have to do what they say. Work the program. The only way out is through."

She shook her head. "Not for me," she whispered. "Not for me."

Three weeks later, Treblinka left Epiphany Lake. Her parents had decided to pull her out of the program. When she left, the staff made us pretend she didn't exist.

"Goodbye, Grace," she said to me. I stared off into the distance, saying nothing.

"Oh my word," I heard Treblinka's mother say. "These girls look *terrible*."

I watched Treblinka and her parents disappear as they walked across the campus. I heard the sound of car doors slamming, an engine turning over and gravel crunching under tires.

I felt a strange feeling after Treblinka was gone. Then I realized: I missed her.

I wondered why.

8

Treblinka was gone from Epiphany Lake Academy, but she visited my dreams every night.

In one dream, Treblinka and I walked through a dusty red desert. She reached down, snatched a lizard, bit into it and offered it to me.

In another dream, we both had hair down to our waists. Hers was pink, mine was blue, and we both took turns braiding pearls into it. We put on velvet gowns and rode horses while she sang like Gwen Stefani.

I saw Treblinka in the halls of my old high school, reaching into a locker. She wore her ELA uniform and dirty socks. She pulled a coat out of the locker; it was crimson red and ankle length with a sable fur collar. She put on the coat and tied a belt around her waist, making the ugly uniform disappear. "Come on," she said to me. "We have to go home and get ready for the Snow Daze dance." Her voice echoed. Fluorescent lights made her shaved head gleam.

I heard Treblinka's voice calling me from The Shed. She wanted me to let her out. "Grace, please," she begged, over and over again. "I can't," I tried to say, but the words wouldn't come out.

I had a different dream almost every night, and they all ended the same way: I'd ask her to tell me her real name, and as soon as she opened her mouth, I woke up.

Of course, it didn't exactly help that the new girl in Treblinka's bunk was on "special care support" for some stupid thing that she'd done. "Special care support" was for kids who stopped taking their medication or took too much of it or swallowed somebody else's. Threatening suicide, cutting and even scratching a mosquito bite hard enough to break skin could land a kid on "special care support" too. "Special care support" meant that staff watched you even when you had to pee or take a shower. It also meant that a staff member came and shined a light in your eyes every half hour while you were trying to sleep. They said it was for 'safety,' but I never could figure out why.

Treblinka had been on "special care support" for a night before they put the oven mitts on her. Sleep deprivation didn't seem to bother her, so they took her off support and did the oven mitt thing instead.

Every time that flashlight went on, it pulled me out of my dreams. Then I'd hear somebody crying in the Karma dorm, and I wouldn't be able to get back to sleep.

Treblinka may not have needed sleep, but I sure as hell did. Three days of half sleep made me lose track of things. I kept losing points for stupid stuff, like forgetting my notebook in a classroom or failing to ask for permission before crossing into a room. Level 5 seemed like it was years away.

I got a violation for dozing off at breakfast. The lack of sleep and the droning of the boring self-help tapes we had to listen to at every meal made me so drowsy I couldn't keep my eyes open.

The sole path to greatness is to be one with the 'I am.' To ask too many questions is to stray from the path. To stay on the path, you must trust it wholeheartedly.

"If I weren't so tired, I would ask just what the fuck that means," I thought. "But I'm too tired to care. At least I'm not 'straying from the path.'"

I managed to get decent scores on the multiple choice tests I took for math and biology, but sitting through therapy without falling asleep was a chore. The new girl cried. Patrice yelled at her and told her to stop lying.

"Tell us the real reason you're here," Patrice barked. "You can't advance in this program if you're not honest."

I was desperate for a nap. "Could I train myself to sleep with my eyes open?" I wondered. "I bet I could. I could really make this program a breeze if I could do that. But how?"

"I *am* telling the truth!" the new girl wailed. "What am I supposed to say? Am I supposed to lie?" Her face was red and beaded with tears. "Fuck!" she shouted. Two men instantly tackled the girl and shoved her face into the carpet. She continued to cry while they twisted her arm and made her fingers touch the space between her shoulder blades. Patrice knelt on the floor and repeatedly asked, "are you ready to tell the truth?"

I shut my eyes. With Patrice and the two men busy with the new girl, I had the perfect chance to score a few moments of sleep. I actually did manage to sleep. I drifted off into a dream that let me float on a quiet, sunny lake where the water was bathtub warm.

The new girl sliced the room with a scream, shaking me out of my dream. I glanced across the circle and saw another girl with a new face. She was trembling and carefully dabbing at her eyes.

"You're not going to tell the truth? Last chance!" Patrice brayed. All the new girl could do was cry. "Ok," Patrice said to the men, "take her upstairs." The two men hoisted the new girl up and hauled her to the second floor.

We could still hear her screaming.

Two letters and a postcard came for me in the mail. One letter was from my mom. It was full of complaints about her clients.

"I don't know who these people think they are. They all want houses they can't afford," she wrote. "They think they deserve the finer things but won't pony up the money. I'm sorry, but if you want a house on Lake of the Isles with granite counter tops, hand-carved mahogany wainscoting and a wraparound porch, you have to pay for it. They just want to look at the houses. They don't intend to buy anything. They waste my time. But I can't say no to them because it might cost me a sale."

"Jesus, mother," I grumbled to myself as I sat in my bunk, reading. "Do you really think I give even the tiniest shit about mahogany fucking wainscoting? You get to drive around and look at fancy houses, and you think you have problems? Fuck you and fuck your clients."

The second letter was from my dad. "I'm becoming concerned," he wrote. "I've called the school a few times to arrange a time to visit you, but they keep telling me I can't. I just got off the phone with somebody named John Crandell. He ranted at me for forty-five minutes and said that if I visited you I'd derail your progress in the program. He sounded belligerent. It seemed very weird. When I spoke to your mother, she said the same thing about 'derailing your progress,' and that was even weirder. I'm starting to feel uncomfortable about this whole thing, but when we spoke on the phone you said everything was fine. Maybe I'm just paranoid. Grace, please write to me and let me know how you are doing."

I felt a lift of excitement when I read my dad's letter, but it only lasted two seconds. What could I possibly write? The staff read all of our mail and if I wrote about what really went on I'd get in trouble. Once, the staff made a girl rewrite her letter to her family because she wrote, "I miss you." The staff accused her of trying to manipulate her parents into bringing her home.

I'd have to think of some kind of code that I could use to write to my dad like Irina Ratushinskaya did when she wrote English words with Russian letters.

I set my dad's letter aside. I was too tired for code words.

I tucked the letters away, dropped down onto my pillow and shut my eyes. I slipped off into sleep. I met Treblinka in a diner where I found her standing next to a jukebox. The colored plastic around the outside of it was broken in several places and it didn't light up anymore, but the music still worked.

The jukebox played the No Doubt song that Treblinka got in trouble for singing. Treblinka sang along with Gwen Stefani and twirled, her blond ponytail and poodle skirt flaring. She reached toward me, her fingers splayed.

"Dance!" She said.

I looked down at her feet: dirty socks.

9

I stopped getting my period. I didn't notice at first. It hit me one morning during fitness training. A girl who had just arrived the night before said she'd just gotten her period and needed to get a pad, but Crandell wouldn't let her. She had no choice but to do hundreds of squats while a red stain bloomed on the crotch of her uniform slacks. I recognized the faint smell of rust and seawater and realized I hadn't smelled it in a long time. When was the last time I'd had my period? I couldn't remember. I remembered that nurse had given me a stack of pads. They were thick and kind of rough like they had been shipped from the Soviet Union or something. There was a blue coat and a scarf that matched hanging on a hook behind her. Was that the last time I'd had my period? In the winter? It was! I hadn't had my period since the first month after I got here.

The new girl was in front of me, but I could still hear her sniffling, trying to cry without anyone noticing.

It didn't work.

"Are you crying?" Crandell asked, his voice soft. "You're upset?"

She nodded.

I watched redness start at Crandell's hairline and continue down his face until he looked sunburned.

"Whose fault is that?" he shouted. "You should have known you were going to start shitting blood all over the place. You should have prepared."

The girl's crying wasn't quiet anymore.

"You know there are bears here," he said, gesturing to the thick pine woods beyond the cabins, "and wolves, too. They love the smell of blood. It attracts them. We'll have bears all over the place because of you. The only way to protect all these other kids is to let the bears eat you."

He leaned close to her with his mouth almost touching her ear. I saw her shudder.

"Which part do you think the bear will eat first?" He whispered, but it was loud enough for the rest of us to hear. He tugged on his groin.

Crandell did that sometimes. He'd get real close to a girl and then say something weird, like "do boys like how you smell when you're sweaty?" or "Does it hurt to do jumping jacks with big tits like that?" Then, he'd reach down, grab the crotch of his pants with four fingers and pull down like he was trying to fix a wedgie. His thumb would move back and forth over the fabric, slowly.

I wanted to barf. It was the same feeling I got whenever he told a girl that she "really needed a hug," and then held her for several minutes, his hand trailing up and down her back. He'd always shut his eyes and sigh a little. I was grateful that he never wanted to hug me.

Like everyone else at Epiphany Lake, I wanted to leave, so I did everything they told me to do and said everything they wanted me to say. Sometimes, if you say something often enough, you start to believe it. I started to think that I had done terrible things at home, that I deserved to be at Epiphany Lake and that the program was helping me.

But I still fucking hated Crandell. Especially when he did that crotch thing. I fantasized about swiping a knife from the kitchen so that the next time Crandell's meaty paw clamped onto his groin, I could jam the knife into his neck. I hoped that there *were* bears. I hoped that they would leap out of the darkness and use their fangs to tear away his flesh, starting with the spot where he had his hand.

Crandell punished all of us for the new girl's period problem. We had to do extra pushups, each of us counting off ten. By the time we got to the dining hall for breakfast, we barely had time to eat. I put extra sugar in my oatmeal that day.

In class, I circled answers on a multiple choice test on *Romeo and Juliet*. I had the Leonardo DiCaprio and Claire Danes version on VHS at home and watched it over and over – until my mother yanked the ribbon out because she got mad when I didn't pay attention to her while I was watching it.

I blinked hard and stared down at the test questions. I didn't want to think about my mother just then. The questions were easy, at least:

Q: Who kills Tybalt?
1. *Romeo*
2. *Benvolio*
3. *Juliet*
4. *None of the above*

Q: In which country does Romeo and Juliet take place?
1. *France*
2. *Italy*
3. *USA*
4. *England*

Q: Who wrote Romeo and Juliet?
1. *Claire Danes*
2. *Danielle Steel*
3. *Mark Twain*
4. *William Shakespeare*

I quickly circled all of the right answers and handed it in. The teacher, who was really a boy from Level 6, set aside the bag of Doritos he'd been crunching on and took my quiz, staining the page with the red Dorito flavoring powder that clung to his fingers. I'd never liked Doritos much, but suddenly I was ready to risk being thrown in The Shed in exchange for the whole bag.

As I waited for him to grade my test, I glanced out the window and saw Crandell's truck leaving campus.

The boy looked up from my quiz, his eyes narrowed. "You got 100%. Every question right."

"Yes, sir," I said.

"You cheat?"

"No, sir. I just know that play really well."

"Why? You some kind of Shakespeare geek?"

I shook my head. "I've just seen the movie several times."

He grinned with half of his mouth and gave me a nod which meant I could return to my seat. Before I did, he held the Dorito bag out to me.

"Want one?" he asked.

I nodded.

He took a single Dorito from the bag and placed it on the palm of my hand, and I held it like it was a butterfly. I sat down at my desk and put the chip into my mouth. I tasted salt and imitations of tomato, garlic and cheese. Underneath that, corn. The chip was supposed to taste like pizza. I held it on my tongue until it dissolved.

I breezed through quizzes for books I'd already read, like *Tom Sawyer* and *A Wrinkle in Time.* The boy didn't ask me if I'd cheated when I handed them in. He also didn't offer me any more chips.

Just before class ended, I saw Crandell's truck reappear. This time, the bed was loaded with gravel. Was that for the road?

A radio crackled. "We got a girl staring out the window in classroom D," the boy said into his radio. "She looks like she's making run plans."

"Write her up," said a voice on the other end.

I looked away from the window and saw the boy filling out a violation sheet. He got up, walked toward me and slapped the sheet on my desk.

"Cat 3," he said, grinning with his whole mouth this time. "You were looking out the window for a lot longer than 3 seconds. That was more like…12 seconds."

A category 3? I thought. *Oh, fuck. That's 150 demerits! Ten days' worth of points!*

I would never make Level 5.

10

I couldn't sleep. The cabin was hot. I twisted onto my side and stared out the window. I wanted to throw it open to let the cool breeze in, but the window was locked. Every window in the cabin was locked. They also each had little plastic boxes attached to them – motion sensors – that set off screeching alarms if anyone opened the window even a tiny bit. Some girl on the Karma side had tried it. None of us got any sleep that night, either.

I turned to my other side, but the bright rectangle at the front of the room made me turn away again. Every night, the light from the hall soaked through our doorway. We couldn't shut the light out because we didn't have a door, just hinges covered in cobwebs.

Through the window, I could see the faint outline of Crandell's truck and the heap of gravel in the back. He had made several trips into town, each time returning with more gravel. The day before, I watched three upper-level boys help Crandell unload the gravel, creating a huge pile in the middle of campus.

Maybe they're building a new cabin, I thought. *Just what we need.* There were so many kids at Epiphany Lake already. It seemed like every day there was at least one new kid. I didn't know where they all came from – we weren't allowed to exchange contact information – but some of them had Southern accents, and others had Pacific Coast tans that faded quickly after they arrived.

If this place gets overcrowded, will they start sending us somewhere else?

My stomach knotted. I squeezed my eyes shut.

In the morning, a dense fog rolled in off the lake. The air smelled like fire. A transport vehicle parked near the main building had its radio playing; it said there was a forest fire in Canada, just over the border. That was the first piece of news I'd heard in months. I couldn't believe it. What else had I missed? What happened with that guy who was trying to impeach President Clinton for sticking a cigar in that intern's coochie? How did that whole Kosovo thing turn out? Did Angela and Shawn get back together on *Boy Meets World*? What about the *Luanne* comic strip – did she finally get a boyfriend?

The questions stacked on top of each other, like colored bricks in a Tetris game. *When I get out of here, the world might be a totally different place. People will talk about things that happened, and it will sound like another language to me. They will look at me like I have extra heads.*

I was so busy thinking about the news blackout that I didn't even notice that Crandell wasn't leading us through our usual fitness routine. Instead, we stood in front of the gravel pile. A group of boys stood in front of it, too. They didn't look at us.

"You are all here to challenge yourselves," Crandell said. "You're all here to push your limits. Those of you who have been here for a while should notice that you've gotten stronger. Today, we'll put that to the test."

Three rows of shovels laid in the grass next to the gravel. Yesterday, the upper-level boys who unloaded the gravel had gloves on. I looked around for gloves that morning but didn't see any anywhere.

"You're going to work together to move this pile of gravel from here," he extended his arm and pointed to a spot several yards away, near the lake shore. "To there."

One by one, we each filled our shovels with gravel and carried it down to the spot that Crandell had pointed to. The first trip didn't seem so hard. When I reached the end, I dumped the gravel on the ground and patted it flat with the back of my shovel.

"What are you doing?" Crandell asked, startling me. Hadn't he just been standing by the gravel pile?

"I...aren't we making a path?"

Crandell grinned. His eyes and mouth were narrow slits in his face. I looked to see where his hands were; one rested on top of the radio clipped to his hip and the other one smoothed the thin hairs on the top of his balding head.

Thank God he's not doing that other thing, I thought.

"You take gravel from that pile and move it here until that pile becomes this pile."

I wanted to ask why, but instead, I said, "Yes, sir." I gripped the shovel and ran my thumb over a crevice where the wooden handle had cracked.

Moving the gravel took all day. My shoulders and thighs burned. The only sound was the constant scrape of metal on rock. Each time I plunged my shovel into the pile, I felt slivers of wood needling into my skin. Sweat trickled down my back and mosquitos swarmed around me. I had no choice but to let them bite me.

"My back hurts," one girl complained.

"You're using the wrong muscles," Crandell said in her ear. "Lift with your legs." He stroked her thigh, squeezing it all the way from her hip to her kneecap. My face burned. I wanted to take my shovel and swing it hard against Crandell's skull, showering the gravel pile with ruby droplets of blood.

Sure, I'd go to jail. But even jail would be better than this. At least those people in the orange jumpsuits spearing trash along the freeway don't get in trouble for swatting mosquitos.

Someone in front of me tripped and spilled gravel onto the ground in front of her. She landed on all fours and didn't get up. A young man – who had been in the program for years, graduated and stayed on as junior staff – motioned for me to go around her. As I walked away from them, I heard him shouting at her, something about 'accountability' and about how if she didn't complete this exercise, she would become a prostitute and die.

After a few hours, the second gravel pile was big enough to hide behind and catch a few seconds of rest. I tossed a load onto the pile, leaned against my shovel and looked across the lake. On the opposite shore, I could see a tiny flicker. Someone at that old farmhouse was having a bonfire.

A few minutes later, I returned with another load and found a boy behind the pile, stealing my trick.

"Your hands are bleeding," he whispered to me. I looked down and saw a rivulet of blood staining the handle. I glanced over at him. He wore one flip-flop and one dirty sock.

"You only have one shoe," I whispered back.

"Lost it," he said. "And I think I might lose a toenail!"

"Gross!"

He smiled, but his eyes still had that heavy-lidded, just-woke-up look – like a baby tipped back just far enough to make its eyes close halfway.

We've all got the heroin-chic look down pat, I thought. Teen Vogue *should do a photo shoot here.* Teen Vogue *fashion spread: The Untamable Teens of Epiphany Lake Academy Turn Tough Love into a Fashion Statement. Silly.* Vogue *would never come here. Our outfits are too ugly.*

My fingers ached. My arms shook as I carried the gravel. Crandell and the other people on staff shouted every time someone dropped even a little bit of gravel. My stomach rumbled; it was late afternoon, and we still hadn't eaten.

I dumped a load of gravel and went back to get more. On the way, I passed the one-shoe boy carrying his load. He stretched his lips into a smile when he saw me. I gave him one back and immediately heard a radio crackle. Had someone seen us make eye contact? I looked straight ahead and walked as fast as I could. I felt a rush of relief when I realized that radio crackle wasn't about me.

By the time we were finished moving the gravel, there were only a few of us who were still working. Everyone who had complained or dropped their load or cried had been sent off to write twenty-page essays on why they'd failed. They also had to stay in the program for an extra month.

Crandell decided that those of us who passed the test should get a reward, so we went into the dining hall and ate pizza in silence. The crust was a little scorched, but the cheese burning the roof of my mouth was the best thing I'd felt in months. I was sure it was the frozen kind with the plastic wrap on top and the round piece of cardboard on the bottom. We never had that at home. When my dad still lived with us, he always made it from scratch, and after he left, my mother preferred to have it delivered. Before Epiphany Lake, I considered frozen pizza to be poor-person pizza.

Even as I ate my slice, I knew once I was finished, I would crave it constantly.

Before I went to bed, I read a letter from my mother. She was mad at me for not answering her last one.

> *Why don't you understand that I need to feel loved? I cherish knowing that I'm loved and wanted and needed. But you never make me feel loved. Everything you do, everything you say tells me the opposite. Why can't you be the sweet little girl you were when you went off to kindergarten? Do you remember the blue dress you had with the pink flowers on it, and the white tights with the tiny red hearts? Do you remember standing at the bus stop, wearing that tag around your neck, waiting to go to school for the first time?*
>
> *Do you know how much Epiphany Lake Academy costs? I pay three thousand dollars a month. That's how much I love you. How will you show me that you love me?*

I folded her letter and looked down at my hands. Hundreds of tiny brown splinters speckled my skin. There were patches of naked skin where blisters had burst and worn away, blisters that had filled with blood and burst, and blisters filled with blood that just sat there: purple, painful, ugly.

"I love you too, mom," I said to myself. Then I went to sleep.

11

I picked the splinters out of my hands with my teeth. Angela, a new staff therapist, granted me permission to use tweezers, but we couldn't find any. It seemed odd to me; with all the makeup kits that the staff seized whenever new girls arrived at Epiphany Lake, there ought to have been a few sets of tweezers lying around somewhere.

"I might have a sewing kit," she said. "Maybe you could use a needle…" she stopped mid-sentence and got this look on her face like she'd turned onto the wrong street. I was pretty sure she was asking herself whether or not she'd get in trouble with Crandell for offering me a needle.

How much damage could I do with a sewing needle? I read in a book once about spies who assassinated enemies with just a tiny drop of super toxic poison on the tip of needle. But I had no idea what kind of poison they used. There were little blue bricks of D-Con rat poison in the corners of all the buildings at Epiphany Lake, but somehow jamming a needle into one and then sticking it into Crandell's flesh didn't seem like it would be all that effective.

"I'll try to get you an appointment," Angela said, but I told her not to bother. I was sure I'd end up just like Treblinka with oven mitts duct taped to my hands. Instead, I sat on my bunk before Shutdown and pressed my warm, wet teeth against the palm of my hand and worked the splinters out, one by one.

In the morning, my hand was covered with dried blood. The last of the blood blisters had split open in the middle of the night. I cleaned it as best I could, but it still felt sore. During our morning fitness routine, I balled up my hands into fists and pushed up on my knuckles so I wouldn't get dirt in the open wound.

"Are you showing off?" Crandell asked. "I've never seen a girl do pushups on her knuckles before."

"No sir," I replied, "I'm not showing off."

"All of you," he said, turning toward the rows of girls in pushup position, brows sweating and arms shaking, "should follow this young lady's example. Toughen up. Build character."

Praise? From Crandell? When someone you hate says something nice about you, how does it all add up? I tried to work it out in my head like an algebra equation, but it just didn't make any sense. I glanced over my shoulder and caught several pairs of eyes glaring at me. Crandell made all the other girls hate me. I hoped they wouldn't make me pay for it later.

As we finished the workout and lined up to go to breakfast, Crandell pulled me out of line. I felt like I'd just fallen through cracked ice. What had I done wrong? What was my punishment going to be?

"Your mother called," he said. "She's very upset that you haven't written to her."

I wanted to tell him that my mother's letters were annoying, and I hadn't felt like answering them.

"You see," he went on, "your mother thinks that we're not doing our job. She wants you to become a happy, healthy teen who is capable of expressing gratitude. She thinks if you're not writing to her, it means she's not getting her money's worth."

Great! I'll just keep not writing to her until she pulls me out of this hellhole.

"I would hate for this to affect your points," He said.

"What? How?" I scanned the list of rules in my mind. I could swear that there was nothing in there that said writing to my mother was a requirement, or that I'd lose points for not doing it.

If I wrote to my mother and told her how grateful I was, she'd keep me in the program. If I didn't write to her, I'd lose points and be stuck here longer while she made up her mind. And what if she decided not to pull me out after all? I would make level 5 soon. I didn't want to go backward.

The only way out is through.

"I'm sorry that I haven't been writing to my mother," I said. "I'll write to her tonight."

"Good," he said. "And of course you'll tell her about the progress you're making and how much you've grown as a person since you've been here."

"Yes, sir. Of course."

He squeezed my shoulder, and I resisted the urge not to jerk it away.

My chat with Crandell cost me time at breakfast, and I didn't get a chance to finish my oatmeal. I left the dining hall still feeling hungry.

At therapy, Angela noticed my hunger and slipped me a Nutrigrain bar. I ripped open the wrapper and shoved the whole thing into my mouth at once. The soft crust dissolved and left a coating of sweet, sticky raspberry filling on my tongue.

Therapy sessions with Angela were different from sessions led by Patrice or the other therapists. She never accused anyone of lying or not being 'real' enough. She didn't demand that girls confess to drugs, sex or arson like the others did. During Angela's sessions, nobody cried.

"It's a nice sunny day," Angela said. "Let's have our session outside." Immediately, my stomach crimped with nervousness, but I followed her and the other girls outside anyway. Angela led us to a spot of sun-warmed grass in view of the shimmering lake. The house on the other side of it looked as small as the nail on my pinky finger.

"It's hard to talk to our parents sometimes, isn't it?" Angela asked. Several girls nodded, quietly. "Are you ever afraid to talk to your parents?"

"I am," Andrea said.

"Tell me why."

"Because they get mad." Andrea rolled her eyes a little when she said it. Angela didn't take points off for that sort of thing.

"Why do you think they get mad?"

"They got mad because I quit basketball and got fat and smoked pot a few times," Andrea replied. She twisted her fingers together. She'd been doing that a lot lately; crossing and uncrossing her fingers.

"I'm not talking about what you did," Angela clarified, "I'm talking about what your parents felt inside that made them mad."

Several of the girls traded glances and waited for Angela to continue. I ran my hand over the soft grass and let the tips of the blades tickle my sore palm.

"Anger is a secondary emotion. There's almost always something else underneath it. It's like a thunderstorm: lightning is flashy and scary, but lightning doesn't happen without heat." Angela looked around the circle, examining each girl's face. When she got to me, her eyes lingered and she called my name.

"My mom was always mad," I said. "But I think...she was afraid."

"Afraid of what?" Angela asked.

"Afraid I'd make her look bad. I always had to wear the right clothes and fix my hair the right way because she was afraid I would embarrass her."

"Why was she afraid of that?"

I hesitated. Across the lake, two tiny points of red light appeared as the owner of the house backed a car into the driveway. "I don't know."

"She must feel awfully bad about herself," Angela said, "to carry around that much fear."

Tears welled up in my eyes, and I hugged my knees to my chest. The other girls ignored me, but they moved to make room for Angela as she came over to sit next to me. She put her arm around my shoulders, and I began to sob. I buried my face into my knees to muffle the sound.

"It's your mom's problem, not yours," Angela whispered.

But I wasn't really crying about my mother. I felt Angela's fingers gently kneading my shoulder like it was a set of piano keys and cried harder. I felt the weight of her head land softly on my other shoulder and cried harder. I remember the sewing needle she offered me and cried harder. Everything about Angela filled me with sorrow because I knew she would either become like the other staff therapists or leave Epiphany Lake altogether.

Angela gave me high scores for sharing in therapy and wrote a note to the other staff saying that I'd experienced a major breakthrough.

That night, I fulfilled my promise to write to my mother.

> *Dear Mom,*
>
> *I'm sorry I didn't write sooner. We have been working hard, and I am often very tired at night. But I promise to write more often. Things are great here. We have a new staff therapist, Angela, who has helped me understand some things about myself and my relationship with you. I hope you know that you don't need to be afraid that I'll embarrass you anymore.*
>
> *Later,*
>
> *Grace*

The next day, I made Level 5.

12

Level 5 changed everything.

I moved out of the cramped, 15-bunk 'Liberty' cabin and into one across campus where I shared a bedroom with just two other girls. The new cabin wasn't much nicer than the old one; it had fluorescent lights, gray linoleum floors and metal folding chairs in the kitchen. However, it did have a TV and a VCR. There were no rabbit ears for the TV, so all we could watch were the videos stacked on the bookshelf. Every last one was G-rated, movies like *The Sandlot, Beethoven* and *The Mighty Ducks*. We had a cassette player, too (no radio) and a few tapes, but they were all people I'd never heard of. I popped a tape labeled *Peter Frampton – Baby I Love Your Way* into the tape deck. I listened to about fifteen seconds of it before I mashed the stop button.

"Yeah, those tapes are awful," said Rosie, one of my new roommates. "We never play them."

The best part of the new cabin, though, was the kitchen. The pantry was stocked with boxes of pasta, Kraft Mac & Cheese, canned tomatoes, tuna, corn, peas, Wonder Bread, peanut butter and a few canned soups. For breakfast, we had cornflakes and milk.

Level 5 also meant I could wear my hair however I wanted and put makeup on, but I didn't care about that as much as the other girls did. At home, I never wore makeup and never did much to my hair other than that time I let LaKeisha put blue dye in it. The part I cared about was "Trust Status" which meant I was allowed to leave campus once a week.

On Trust Status, you could walk into town and go to work for a few hours. The boys did odd jobs for people in town, like mowing lawns and cleaning gutters. The girls worked in the antique shop, mopping floors, dusting shelves, bubble-wrapping customers' purchases and making sure that kids didn't break anything.

We didn't get paid for the work we did. It was supposed to teach us the satisfaction of doing a job well, or something like that.

On my first night in the new cabin, I cooked dinner. All six of us were supposed to take turns cooking, and the newest person always went right to the top of the order. I turned on the electric stove and waited for the coil to glow. I filled a beat up saucepan with water and set it on the burner. In the pantry, I found a can of Cream of Mushroom soup, some canned mushrooms and tuna. I opened a box of spaghetti noodles and broke them into smaller pieces and then dropped them in the boiling water. I mixed the soup, mushrooms, tuna and cooked noodles in a Pyrex dish.

Before I slid it into the oven, I paused. Something was missing. I thought back to my grandmother's kitchen, where I'd watched her make this many times. She always crumbled potato chips and sprinkled them on top. They turned golden brown in the oven. We didn't have any potato chips, but I was sure we had to have something to add that extra crunch. I spotted the box of cornflakes and quickly poured out a handful, careful not to take too much. I crumbled the cornflakes in my hands.

Thirty minutes later, I took the bubbling hotdish out of the oven. The other girls sat down at the table, and I served them all before serving myself. Two of the girls were sweaty from their walk back to town.

"This is so good!" Rosie said as she shoveled noodles into her mouth. "I vote for Grace to do *all* of our cooking."

One of the sweaty girls frowned and shook her head. "We can't do that. The rules say everybody takes turns. We have to stick to the rules."

"But how would anyone know?" Rosie asked, her mouth still full of food.

"Patrice," said Sweaty Girl Two. "Patrice always finds things out. Plus you never know when she's going to do one of her surprise inspections."

Surprise inspections? Patrice? My heart sank a little.

"So…what's your name?" Sweaty Girl One asked.

"Grace," I replied.

"When are you going to town?"

"Day after tomorrow."

"Let me give you some advice," she said. She held her fork in her hand and pointed the tines at me. "You better make sure that store is clean. The old lady who owns it can't see all that well anymore, and you don't want Crandell or Patrice showing up there and telling you that you missed a spot."

"Ok," I said. "Thanks."

"Oh, and one other thing: if you ask nicely, she'll let you make calls on the phone in her office, and she won't say anything to Crandell."

My stomach coiled into a corkscrew. I shot a glare across the table at her. That last part had to be a lie. She was trying to set me up so she could rat me out and earn the last few points she needed to push her toward the finish line. I decided right then and there that I strongly disliked Sweaty Girl One.

"I don't really have anyone to call," I retorted. Her lips made a hard line.

After we finished eating and washed the dishes, we sat on the floor by the TV and watched *Heavyweights*, a movie about a bunch of chubby boys whose parents ship them off to a fat camp. Their parents tell them that it will be just like summer camp only with a little more exercise, but it turns out to be rundown and run by an evil personal trainer.

Nobody said anything during the movie. Nobody said anything after. We took turns in the bathroom and went to sleep.

Unlike the Liberty cabin, this one didn't have open bedroom doors and hallway lights that leaked into the room. Here it was dark and still like it was supposed to be in the country.

One thing was the same, however: the muffled crying. At Epiphany Lake, crying was as much a part of the nocturnal symphony as crickets and tree frogs.

I pretended that the crying came from wolves howling in the distance and fell asleep.

13

As soon as I moved into the new cabin, things started to get weird on campus. But I didn't really notice at first. I was on Trust Status, and I could walk into town.

On my first day off campus, I ate a bowl of cereal with a splash of milk. I made a peanut butter sandwich to take with me. I washed and put away the bowl and silverware I'd used. Then I left.

I exited the Epiphany Lake gates for the first time since last fall. I hadn't been on the other side of those gates in eight months.

I had an urge to run to the end of the gravel driveway, but I knew if I did that I risked someone seeing me. They'd think I was running away.

I walked along the road toward town. When I reached the point where I couldn't see the Epiphany Lake cabins through the trees any more, I felt like an invisible backpack full of dictionaries dropped from my shoulders. I took a deep breath and for the first time, noticed the clean smell of pine.

A little bell tinkled as I walked through the door of the antique shop. An older woman stood behind the counter. She looked at me over the top of her glasses.

"You're from the school?" she asked. I nodded.

"Can you run a vacuum?"

"Of course I can."

Without another word, she led me to a supply closet where an old dusty vacuum cleaner sat in the dark. It was heavy.

"It's old," she said. "They made them a lot sturdier back then."

It had an old-fashioned cord – the kind with rayon braid wrapped around it. Near the plug, the braiding was slightly frayed. I remembered something that a science teacher had once told me, that electrical cords were covered to keep the electricity from escaping. A frayed cord could shock me.

I decided not to mention it to the old lady though. If she told the school I'd complained, they might decide I was being uncooperative. Besides, if I got electrical burns, I'd get to go to the hospital and stay away from Epiphany Lake for a few days.

As I ran the noisy old machine over the dull carpet, I fantasized about all the ways I could get injured while in town and how much time I could spend in the hospital as a result. I imagined lying in a clean hospital bed with crisp linens, watching TV, sipping orange juice, letting nurses massage my shoulders.

I turned off the vacuum cleaner. I thought she would go around and thoroughly inspect every inch of carpet, but she simply glanced around and told me I did a good job. She looked back at the newspaper she was reading while I stood, waiting for orders.

Finally, she looked up. "Yes?"

"Is there anything else I can help you with?"

She rolled her eyes and sighed a little. "There's really not that much to do here. Why don't you read a book? You saw where the books are, right?"

Read a book? I hadn't read a book, other than a text book, in months. The moment she said it, I knew I desperately wanted to sink into a book, but I was afraid. What if this was a test? What if I accepted her offer and she told Crandell?

"Are you sure? I could dust the shelves, or clean the display case, or empty the trash cans –"

"Just go read a book!" she snapped. I walked away from the counter, confused.

I scanned the bookshelves. A book with a worn, cloth-covered spine had *The Black Stallion* printed on it in faded ink. I took it from the shelf, sat down on the floor and began to read.

When I was nearly four chapters in, the old lady came to talk to me.

"I didn't mean to get ornery with you earlier," she told me. "It's just that I've managed this place alone for nearly fifty years. I've never needed help."

"Then, why –"

"Do you know much of the history of the town?"

I shook my head.

"This was a logging town. Loggers started coming here in the 1850s and some years later they built the town. That's the way we made our living for a long time. But then the industry dried up. Nobody had any work. Then that school opened up. The hired a lot of people in town. Everyone's doing better because of it. One day that man who runs it – Crenshaw? Clemens?"

"Crandell."

"Crandell, right. Anyway, he came and he explained to me that part of his program was to get the kids working. Give them a taste of the real world, see what it's like to work hard and be productive. He said there were plenty of jobs for boys in town but not so many for the girls. He wanted to know could they work here. I told them I didn't need help and that he should ask the people at the café, but he said he didn't think the café was a good fit for his students." She made a spitting sound and rolled her eyes. "One day the owner of that café came in here and told me that Crandell had asked him and he'd said no. He said those jobs are for his friends' kids. He didn't want them to wind up taking home less in tips because they had to split shifts with girls from the school. Crandell said something like, 'oh, I don't want my girls to get paid.' The owner got mad and threw Crandell out."

Confusion zig-zagged through my mind. I hated this lady for thinking that Epiphany Lake was a good thing but at the same time, I liked her for letting me sit on the floor and read. I loved the café owner for throwing Crandell out, even though he was someone I'd never met. I wondered what they served at the café and suddenly craved a grilled cheese sandwich.

` For the rest of my shift at the store, I sat and read. Twice, the little bell above the door jingled and both times I leapt up and hid the book, thinking it might be Crandell. Both times it was some stranger, shopping for old porcelain dishes. The second time I jumped up, the old lady shot me a knowing look.

I ate my peanut butter sandwich on the way back to campus. A voice in my head whispered, "run away." It seemed like it would be easy. No one was on the road. No one could see. I could just pick a direction and take off. But I didn't. I knew I'd either get lost in the woods and starve or get caught and be sent back. And after that, what? Mystic Bay? I had made it to Level 5, a better place to live and a few hours to sit and read every week. I could make it to the finish line. I could make it out in time to start the fall semester at my old school. If I ran away, I'd have to start the program over again.

The risk wasn't worth it. I picked up my invisible backpack full of dictionaries and walked back through the Epiphany Lake gates.

The weirdness started that night.

I was sleeping more soundly than I had in a long time, but the blast of an alarm woke me up. My roommates stood around the window in the kitchen. Several beams of light searched the dark. Flashlights.

"Somebody busted out of one of the boys' cabins!" Rosie exclaimed. We watched until all but two of the flashlights flicked off. Then we heard the sound of truck doors slamming. The engine rumbled as the truck sped off toward town.

The alarm stopped shrieking.

I wondered which cabin the sound came from. The alarm was so loud, it sounded like it was right above my head. In the morning, the story spread throughout campus faster than fire on spilled gasoline. The men who drove the truck into town came back empty-handed. The boy got away.

His escape wasn't exactly a success yet. Someone from town could see him and bring him back. A state trooper might find him walking by the road. But if he managed to make it far enough south without anyone catching him, he might just make it.

"Who was he, anyway?" I asked Rosie. She had run into one of the other boys on the walk back from town. He said he knew the runaway, and told Rosie what he looked like.

The description sounded familiar. Then it hit me: it was the boy I'd talked to behind the gravel pile. I felt chills.

Therapy with Angela was weird, too. She sat silently while we took our seats in the circle of chairs. The stern expression on her face looked like something she'd practiced in the mirror. She wanted us to talk about sex.

"I'm a virgin," Rosie said, in a voice that was almost haughty.

"No shit," Sweaty Girl Two said, disguising her insult with a fake cough.

"You're not being real, Rosie," Angela said. "Tell the truth."

As soon as the words left her lips, Angela burst into tears. We all traded glances. The only emotion we were accustomed to seeing from the staff was rage.

"I can't do this!" Angela cried, her voice barely audible. She ran from the room. I looked down at my feet. That was the last we'd see of her. I was sure of it.

Other weird things: there were so many kids on campus that fights broke out at least once a day. To deter fights, Crandell introduced "5-point Restraint." Anyone who fought would be forced facedown onto the ground and have five staff members restraining their arms, legs and neck. One boy begged to be released. He said he couldn't breathe. Patrice, who was kneeling on his shoulder, brought her face very close to his and told him to stop being manipulative.

"If you can talk, you can breathe," she screeched.

They sat on him until his lips turned blue.

Crandell also invented a new punishment for swearing. "Some of you just can't seem to help yourselves," he said. "From now on, if we hear you using foul language, your mouth will be duct-taped shut for a full day."

Soon after, I watched the lines of lower levels that marched across campus and counted all the kids with strips of silver plastered to their mouths. Every single one of them stared at their feet when they walked.

There was also a very small boy who couldn't have been older than 12 who was forced to wear a bra on the outside of his shirt, and a girl who had to carry a baby doll around all day. She was not allowed to set it down or let it go for any reason. No matter where she was or what she was doing, she had to hold that rubber baby in one of her arms. By the end of the day, she was in tears. Her arms ached.

It doesn't matter anyway, I told myself. I'll be out of here soon.

14

The boy I spoke to behind the gravel pit didn't come back. He'd done it. He'd evaded the staff, police and anyone else who might have been able to recognize him as a runaway and bring him back to camp. He could have been anywhere, but I pictured him wandering the streets of Minneapolis, on Lake Street, hungry and panhandling for change – but free. If a cop picked him up, he might go to juvie. If a judge said to him, "You can go back to Epiphany Lake or you can go to jail," he'd choose jail.

Crandell was pissed. Gravel Pit Boy's escape made him look bad. It also inspired other kids to run. None of them were as fast or as clever as Gravel Pit Boy. They were all caught and brought back to camp. Crandell made up another new rule: anyone who ran away would have to wear a bright orange shirt. Soon, there were a half dozen kids walking around in orange shirts. The message: you won't get away, so don't even try.

One morning, I watched a line of lower-level boys walk by, and I noticed that one was wearing an orange shirt and had duct tape over his mouth. The cornflakes I'd just eaten churned in my stomach. I swallowed hard. Fortunately, it was my day to work at the store. I walked fast toward the end of the driveway, eager to get to town, where I wouldn't have to see any more boys with double punishments.

The old lady acknowledged me with a nod when I arrived at the store. Without a word, I went straight to the closet and lugged the vacuum cleaner out of it. When I finished my work, I went to the bookshelves to find a new book to read. I'd finished *The Black Stallion* in one sitting the last time I was here. I found a copy of *A Wrinkle in Time* sandwiched between *The Electric Koolaid Acid Test* and *What a Young Wife Ought to Know*.

"That's one of my favorites," the old lady said approvingly when she saw what I was reading. Rain struck the storefront glass and glowed green with reflections from the only stoplight in town. The rain and screech of the printing calculator that the old lady used to add up receipts were the only sounds.

At first, I didn't care all that much about Mrs. Who, Mrs. Whatsit and Mrs. Which, but I kept reading, and before I knew it, I'd followed the teenage heroine, Meg, and her brother Charles Wallace, to the dark planet Camazotz. On Camazotz, every house looked the same. All the children came out at the exact same time and bounced the exact same ball. I read the description over and over. It made me shiver. I knew what it was supposed to be about – suburbs and conformity. But to me, it was about Epiphany Lake.

Hours passed. I finished the book and started reading it again from the beginning. The old lady said something to me, and I looked up. She tapped her watch. It was time for me to head back to Epiphany Lake.

"You don't want to be late," she said.

I slid the book back into the space that I'd taken it from.

"Take it with you," the old lady offered. "You can have it."

I shook my head. "I can't," I said.

The rain extracted perfume from the pine trees that lined the road as I walked back from town. I bowed my head and crossed my arms against my chest. The rain struck the back of my neck. For a summer day, it was chilly. Why did this school have to be way up north? Our cabin was sure to fill with mosquitos as soon as the sun went down.

Rain drops came down a little harder, and I wished my sweatshirt had a hood. The school didn't issue hooded sweatshirts. They were afraid kids would choke themselves with the strings. But I was on Trust Status. Didn't that mean I deserved a hood?

The dirt road to Epiphany Lake was pure mud and sucked gleefully at my heels with each step I took.

When I reached the cabin, my feet were covered with mud and my sweatshirt was soaked through. I took my shoes off before I went inside; I didn't want to risk getting snitched on by one of the Sweaty Girls for tracking mud into the cabin.

The sharp smell of tomatoes filled the cabin as I stepped inside in my stocking feet. Rosie was at the stove, stirring a pot of tomato soup she'd improvised out of a can of canned tomatoes and corn. A stack of cold cheese sandwiches sat on a plate next to the stove.

"I'd grill them," Rosie said, "but I always burned grilled cheese. I'm not in the mood to get bitched at by the Princess Twins."

"They won't burn if you keep the heat lower," I said.

She turned and looked at me, almost smiling. "Do you want to grill them?"

"Ok," I said. "Just let me change out of my shirt."

I hung my wet shirt to drip-dry in the bathroom and fished a frying pan out of the cupboard beneath the sink. I scraped a thin layer of butter over the outsides of each sandwich and cooked them gently until they turned golden brown on the outside and the cheese wilted like a fainting actress. Rosie watched as I flipped one over and butter hissed softly against the hot pan.

"You make that look so easy," she said.

I shrugged. "The bread will burn faster than the cheese will melt. You just have to have patience."

"Look at me," she said, grasping the roll of fat above the waistband of her pants with her free hand, "Does it look like I have patience when it comes to food?"

I laughed. Rosie laughed. Sweaty Girl One walked in out of the rain, her hair plastered to her forehead. She stopped to glare at us before she went to her room to change.

Rosie's tomato soup was a little bland because she forgot to put salt in it, but we all ate it in silence, slowly savoring our grilled cheese sandwiches.

"Why is it," Sweaty Girl Two asked, "that when they make these in the cafeteria they're black on the outside and cold on the inside?"

"Because they don't care," I said, without thinking. I glanced at Sweaty Girl One, but her eyes were closed as she chewed her sandwich.

When we were finished, Sweaty Girls One and Two washed dishes while Rosie and I sat at the kitchen table. Rosie complained about the stack of moldy books we had arranged on the floor next to our VHS tapes.

"*Goosebumps? Sweet Valley High? Saddle Club?* I read those in 4th grade! Would it really be so bad if they let us read *Number the Stars?* Or *Walk Two Moons?* Or *A Wrinkle in Time?*"

"I just read that!" I exclaimed. "At the antique store."

Sweaty Girl One turned around from the sink, a dripping sponge clenched in her fist.

"What do you mean," she asked, "you read a book at the store?"

Every muscle in my body tensed, starting with my toes and all the way up to my jaw. That's when I knew I'd made the biggest mistake of my life.

15

Crandell's office had a weird smell. I tried to figure out what it was. It was like grass clippings and cinnamon with something else thrown in. Burnt leaves? Rotting pumpkins? Leaky coconuts?

I played this game as I waited for Crandell to come in. It seemed like I'd been waiting for hours, though it had only been a few minutes. It all happened so fast: Sweaty Girl One waited until Crandell made his nightly rounds. He came around each night to the upper-level cabins to make sure we were all accounted for before lights out.

"Grace read a contraband book," she said. "She read *A Wrinkled Sheet.*"

"*A Wrinkle in Time*," I said, quietly.

Crandell looked at me. "My office. Seven-thirty tomorrow morning." Then he turned and walked out. That night, I didn't sleep at all.

Crandell walked in and shut the door behind him. My heart began to race as he sat at the desk across from me.

"You've been here for a long time," he said. "You're almost on level 6. Another few months and you'll be out of here. At the rate you've been going, I'd say you'd be home in six weeks, maybe five."

My arm began to shake. I gripped the chair so Crandell wouldn't see.

"That's correct, sir," I said.

"What have you learned since you have been here?"

"I've learned that I have to own up to what I've done. I've learned how to be the daughter my mother wants me to be."

"Have you?" he asked. He sat back in his chair. "Are you going to own up to this?" He tossed the copy of *A Wrinkle in Time* at me.

"I read it," I said. "The woman at the store gave me permission to read it."

"So if she gave you permission to shoot up heroin, you would do it?"

I crossed my legs under the chair. "I don't understand. I'm on Trust Status. I thought we were allowed to read on Trust Status."

He sat up and folded his hands on the desk. "You are. But does that mean you're entitled to read anything you want?"

"But there's no list. There's no list of books we're not allowed to read."

"You see? You're not owning up to what you did."

"We have books in the cabin. *The Baby Sitters' Club* and *Sweet Valley High* and *Goosebumps.* There's even a novel-version of *Jurassic Park* on our shelf. How was I supposed to know *A Wrinkle in Time* wasn't allowed?"

Crandell smiled. "If you had really learned something here, you would know the answer to that, wouldn't you?"

I felt as if I had just crashed through thin ice.

"I think you should be here a bit longer. That's why I'm dropping you back to level one."

My entire body shook. I wanted to get up and throw my chair at him. Level one?! I would have to be here *another* eight months! I wouldn't be able to leave until I'd been here for more than a year? Just for reading a book?

A line from one of my mother's letters scrolled through my mind: *I pay 3,000 dollars a month for you to be there.*

Three thousand dollars per month times eight months was twenty-four thousand dollars. Three thousand dollars times sixteen months was forty-eight thousand dollars. There were almost five hundred kids at Epiphany Lake. Five hundred times forty-eight thousand…that number was in the millions.

"This is all about money," I said. "The longer we stay, the more money you make."

Crandell's expression darkened like an apple rotting in time-lapse.

"You've learned nothing," he said. "You're the same ungrateful brat you were when you came in here. This program isn't for fakes. This program isn't for people who want to skate on through. This program is for people who want to grow up and change and be decent humans. You are going to sit on level one until you take responsibility. Until you admit what a worthless, manipulative, lying little cunt you are. I oughta make you suck my dick. Nasty little whore."

I heard a zipping sound.

"You're back on level one, effective immediately."

His face was red and he was starting to grunt.

"I'm rubbing my dick right now," he said, "Do you want to see it?"

I shook my head. "What for? I know what cocktail wieners look like."

"Get the fuck out of here!" he shouted.

The woman who had strip-searched me on my first day at Epiphany Lake was waiting for me outside of Crandell's office. She grabbed me roughly by the arm and slapped a handcuff onto my wrist.

"New policy," she said. "Kids who get dropped are liable to run away."

No shit. I thought.

She led me back to the Karma cabin. I cried with every step.

16

Life back on Level 1:

    I needed permission to stand.

    Permission to sit.

    Permission to put on chapstick.

    Permission to cross in and out of rooms.

    Permission to speak.

    I couldn't have sugar on my oatmeal anymore. I couldn't wear my hair in anything but a ponytail. I couldn't go anywhere alone. I couldn't talk to any of the other girls on Level 1, girls who had just arrived, girls who looked scared, girls who cried all night long.

    I'd followed every one of their stupid rules, and look where it got me. Was I supposed to kiss all of their asses just so I could have sugar again in three months? *Fuck that,* I thought, *and fuck them.*

    A week after my demotion, I received a letter from my mother.

    I am VERY disappointed, Grace. Why would you throw away so much progress? I am sure it's because being a loving daughter to me is just too much for you. I am paying so much money to help you unlearn your selfishness. I am grateful that this program is refusing to send back a low-quality result. I'm willing to pay whatever I have to in order to get you back. Your father isn't contributing a cent to this. I should have shipped you off to live with him after he left. Commit yourself to this program. Take it to heart this time. The only way out is through.

    I ripped it up and threw it away. I didn't answer it. Instead, I wrote to my father:

Dad,

You asked me how I am doing here at Epiphany Lake. Do you remember the dog that our neighbors had? My life is a lot like the one that dog had — before they came and took him away. Also, do you remember that place on the corner, across from the funeral home, that makes the spaghetti that comes with huge meatballs and crunchy garlic bread? I remember the times when mom was busy working and you took me there to eat. You would give me quarters so I could pick out songs on the jukebox. We'd have cherry phosphates and ice cream sundaes and on the way home, we'd rent a video. Remember?

Sometimes I wonder if I'll ever have cherry phosphates again…

As I sealed my letter into an envelope, I thought of Irina Ratushinskaya, writing letters to her husband, using Russian letters to write English words so the censors at the Gulag wouldn't know what she was up to.

Send me cucumber seeds, she wrote.

If my dad answered my letter about the dog and cherry phosphates, I never received it. The child services people came around again, which meant half the girls in our cabin had to spend a day in the woods, while the other half had to take apart their bunks. This time, it was my turn to disassemble bunks.

With a flathead screwdriver in hand, I worked to remove the middle bunk out of each three-tier bunk bed, reducing the total from 15 to 10. We crammed the bunks into a closet and pretended to dust while the child services people walked through. We got to work putting the bunks back in as soon as they left.

I hid my screwdriver in my pillowcase and waited for nightfall.

That night, after shutdown, I stared at the ceiling. Gravel Pit Boy had escaped, and he'd never been caught. He could be anywhere. His parents could have sent him straight back into a program the minute he got home, but he hadn't come back here. And that was enough for me.

When I was sure everyone else was asleep, I slipped out of my bunk, screwdriver in hand. I crept along the wall until I felt the electrical socket. I wrapped my sleeve around my hand and jammed the screwdriver in. I recoiled from the jolt just as the hallway lights snapped off. I crept out into the dark hallway toward the front door. I opened it a crack and hesitated a second; the alarms didn't sound.

I ran as fast as I could, with nothing but hazy moonlight to guide me down to the lake. The smell of pine needles stung my nose. Thistles pierced my bare feet, but I ignored the pain. The sound of water gently lapping the shore grew louder and louder. An owl's hoot echoed across the lake. I felt the chilly water lick my toes and dove in.

17

Lily pads tangled around my neck. I felt their delicate stems snap as I pushed forward. The water was warmer than I had expected. I could tell from the way it smelled that it was clear, not murky like most lakes. It was too dark to see anything. Aside from the stars, the moon and the piss-colored lamps in front of the main lodge, there was very little light.

I kicked as hard as I could kick without splashing too much. I didn't want to make any noise. It had been so long since the last time I'd used my body this way. My shoulders ached. I swallowed too much air and could feel it pressing against my collarbone. My sweatshirt became a concrete sack that wanted to drag me down to the bottom of the lake. Somewhere in between the shores, I shimmied out of it.

Behind me, I heard the crunch of tires on gravel. I glanced over my shoulder and saw the headlights of a transport vehicle. I held my breath and ducked underwater. I waited. I wouldn't risk getting caught in their brights. Even underwater I could hear the kid crying. It sounded like a small boy.

Heat rose in my chest. *Fuck Epiphany Lake*, I thought. *Fuck that kid's parents*. After the transport vehicle turned and drove back out to the main road, I gritted my teeth and punished the water with my kicks. I ignored the burn I felt in my shoulders as I stroked, barely stopping to breathe. I picked up speed.

The first thing I would do once I reached shore would be to find some place safe, somewhere to hide. I would sleep during the day and wait for nightfall. I'd find a way to get to Minneapolis with the stars as my guide. My plan had just one flaw: this was summer in the far north, where the sun burned until almost midnight. I couldn't wait that long.

It's ok, I told myself. I would figure it out somehow.

The letter I wrote to my dad would beat me home. I was sure of that. By the time I got there, he would know everything and find a way to make sure I could stay with him. Tomorrow, I would stow away on a train, walk through the woods, hitchhike with a trucker — anything to put three-hundred miles between me and the nightmare I'd been living for the past eight months.

The shore was close but not as close as it seemed. I paused and treaded water, struggling to get my bearings in the blackness. I had an urge to close my eyes and drift off to sleep and let the water do whatever it wanted with me. If I drowned, Epiphany Lake Academy might have to shut down. But it might not, and then they'd think they go to me. If I drowned, they'd claim it as a win. They only way for me to win was to successfully escape.

I told myself I needed to stop thinking about how far I still had to go and just keep swimming. I counted my strokes. *One, two, three, four, five, breathe, one two three four five, breathe…*

I could feel the lakebed slowly rising, higher and higher until I could touch the bottom with my feet. As I walked out of the water, my legs shook. I stumbled once I reached the shore, landing hands and knees in the sand.

I walked with my hands out in front of me like a police officer directing traffic, gesturing for cars to stop. Finally, I felt something: a wooden wall. I patted my palms against it until I discovered a small metal handle. I grabbed it and pulled. I stepped inside the wooden structure and pulled the door closed behind me, softly.

It was an outhouse; I could tell by the stench. I sat down and shut my eyes. A cob-webbed stack of toilet paper served as my pillow. I imagined the lake rising higher and higher until it swept Epiphany Lake Academy away.

18

"What the hell?" a male voice said, startling me awake. The outhouse door was open. Blinding sun burned the edges of his large silhouette.

"No! I won't go back!" I shrieked. I clamped my hands onto the walls and made my body rigid.

"Take it easy," he said. "Did you run away from that shithole across the lake?"

I nodded.

"Come out of there. That school must be a really nasty place if you'd rather sleep in an outhouse than stay there."

With the sun at his back, I couldn't see his face, but I could tell he had long hair.

I was hungry and wanted a shower, but I wasn't ready to trust this guy just yet. He could have been pretending to understand how bad Epiphany Lake was just to get me to come out, only to tackle me, hogtie me and take me straight back to hell.

"Who are you?" I asked.

"I'm Anders. This is my aunt's house. I've been out fishing since five."

"How old are you?"

"I'm 22. You look like you're 110."

I laughed. He reached for my hand. I reached back. His hand was large, strong, but a little cold.

"Normally, I'd say I'm sorry that my hands smell like fish, but you spent the night in an outhouse, so the fish smell is an upgrade." He held up a stringer of crappies. Their scales glistened in the sunlight. "You've gotta be hungry. I bought some sticky buns on my drive up yesterday. I think there's one or two left."

My stomach rumbled. The last thing I'd eaten was the hot dog soup they'd started serving in the cafeteria. The broth was clear except for a few tiny specks of fat and it didn't taste like much. Unnaturally pink slices of hot dog bobbed in it. They were lukewarm when I bit into them.

Cracked acorn shells bit into my feet as Anders led me to the house. I tripped over an exposed tree root. As Anders helped me up, I saw tiny white daisies, no bigger than my thumbnail. They were everywhere.

I followed Anders into the kitchen. A woman stood at the stove, her back to us. Without turning around, she said, "Anders, how many times do I have to tell you, fillet your fish before you bring them into my house?"

Her voice sounded familiar. She turned around and my bones locked. She was the woman from the bookstore in town. My heart pounded so loudly I could hear every blood cell rushing through my ears. I knew I was wrong to trust this guy. I turned to run, but he caught me around the waist with his arm.

"Easy! Nobody's sending you back there. Right, Aunt Jackie?"

She pursed her lips. Behind her, a coffee pot percolated on the stove. I could see the hot brown liquid leaping into the glass knob.

"Come on, Aunt Jackie. Just last night you were saying you didn't like what's going on over there."

"I don't. And I don't much like that Crandell, either. A couple of weeks ago, he came into my store and started carrying on. He said he'd heard that I was lax with the girls and that I wasn't fully on board with the program. Something about him just rubbed me the wrong way, and I told him I was done."

The smell of coffee filled the room. Anders was still holding onto my hand.

"Why don't I just drive her back to the city tonight?"

Jackie shook her head. "If you get pulled over you could get charged with kidnapping. Remember what happened with that Wetterling kid? People will think this is like that and go nuts."

Anders looked down at me. I noticed how green his eyes were, like sunlight shining through maple leaves. He looked a little bit like Daniel Johns from the band Silverchair.

"So I just won't get pulled over. I never get pulled over anyway. I'm a good driver," he said.

Jackie pressed the heels of her hands into her eyes and groaned. "They're probably looking for her, Anders! They'll probably start pulling over *anybody* who drives down the main road."

I started to shake. Anders squeezed my hand. "Then what *can* we do?"

Jackie looked at me. "I bet you'd like a shower," she said. "And some breakfast."

I nodded. I knew she wanted to get me out of the room so she could talk to Anders alone, but I hadn't had a decent shower in months. The hot water and steam felt good, and the thick soapy lather quickly turned a dark gray color as it gathered up the grime I missed during my three-minute showers at Epiphany Lake. It didn't stop me from shaking.

Why did I have to sleep in that outhouse? Why didn't I just keep going? I could have made it farther away. How did Gravel Pit Boy do it? If only he could have left behind a map for me to follow.

I worked shampoo into my hair and scrubbed hard. These people could go on all they wanted about how they hated the program and Crandell, but they'd send me back. They'd send me back just to keep themselves out of trouble.

After my shower, I put on the clean clothes that Jackie had laid out for me. In the kitchen, breakfast was waiting for me. Jackie's scrambled eggs were fluffy and slightly sweet from the cream she whipped into them. Her hashbrowns had a golden crunch on top and a creamy center. Steam rose from them every time I dug into them with my fork.

"There's more if you want it," Jackie said. "I can see it's been a while since you've had a decent meal."

I ate more. I felt better than I had in a very long time.

"Anders and I discussed it. While I think it's too risky for him to drive you back to the city, I also don't want to send you back. We've placed a call to the Sheriff's office. They're sending over an officer who will help us sort all this out."

"Ok," I said. My throat tingled. Maybe this would turn out better than I thought. Maybe I would not only get to go home but convince the Sheriff to go see what's really going on at Epiphany Lake. Maybe he'd shut the place down.

As I sat waiting for the officer to arrive, I began to daydream about all the things I would do once I got home. I would go straight to my dad's house and watch reruns of *Full House, Boy Meets World, Step by Step, Family Matters* and *Sabrina the Teenage Witch*. My dad and I would order pizza. I would call LaKeisha. I would get on my bike and ride wherever I wanted.

I heard a car approach and my heart raced with excitement. A police officer would arrive in less than a minute and help me get home.

But when I heard the crunch of approaching tires, I had a sudden feeling that something was wrong. My breakfast rose in my throat. I swallowed hard and squeezed my eyes shut. *That's the police officer's car,* I said to myself, willing myself to be calm. It wasn't. I recognized the low rumbling sound of a vehicle too big to be a police car. I opened my eyes and through the window, I saw the truck creeping past the row of trees that marked the edge of Jackie's property. I wanted to run. I thought Jackie and Anders wanted to help but they lied — they called Epiphany Lake, not the Sheriff, and now I would have no choice but to go back.

"You bitch! You lied to me! You called him! You fucking bitch!" I screamed as I jumped out of my chair, my voice reaching octaves I never thought possible.

"Lower your voice, young lady. And besides, what are you talking about?" Jackie asked.

The truck reached the end of the row of trees and turned the corner, slowly inching into Jackie's driveway. I flashed back to the night when Gravel Pit Boy ran away. I could hear the alarms blasting and the rumble of that same truck racing away from campus, its menacing white headlights slicing through the night.

Through the windshield, I saw his face. The face of the person I hated most in the world. He fixed his eyes on me and we stayed locked in a stare down as the truck came to a stop, and he turned off the engine. His glower slowly curled into a sneer.

"What's *he* doing here?" Jackie asked. No one said a word.

"I want to throw up," I said, and my mouth filled with bile. I swallowed it down. I wanted to vomit all over Crandell. I wanted to drown him in vomit. I wanted to kick him in the head until his eyes exploded and then puke on him until his nose and mouth were completely coated and he choked to death. I wanted to stomp on his crotch until everything was flat and useless like a popped balloon. I wanted to drop a lit match onto his body — onto my flammable vomit – wanted to watch him combust.

The truck door opened and Crandell's legs swung out. I could see his beer belly and the radio he had holstered to his belt. I braced my trembling hands against the table. The china and silverware rattled like that scene in *Titanic* just after the ship hits the iceberg. My heart beat louder and faster than it ever had since I'd been alive. I peed, wetting the clean gray sweatpants that Jackie had laid out for me.

I lunged toward Anders, forgetting about the kitchen table that stood between us. One of the leaves collapsed, causing Jackie's china to drop straight onto the floor and shatter. Jackie said something about the shards of china on the floor and my bare feet but none of her words registered as I rushed to Anders' side, ignoring the bits of china biting into my feet. I clamped my hand onto Anders' forearm. His muscles tensed under my fingers. I looked up into his cobalt blue eyes. "Please," I begged him, squeezing his arm. "Don't let him take me back there."

He gave me a silent nod, and I let go of his arm. I noticed the white impressions on his skin where my fingers had gripped him, and the little pink half-moons where my nails had dug in.

Crandell waltzed into the kitchen and stood with his legs apart, a hand on each hip.

"I'll thank you to *knock* before entering my house, Mr. Crandell," Jackie said, her voice cool as slate. Crandell grinned. My face burned with hatred.

"I'm so sorry to trouble you," he said, using a sugary tone I'd never heard before. "But this young lady is in my care, and I need to return her to where she belongs."

"You're not taking her anywhere," Anders declared. "We called the Sheriff's office. They won't let you take her."

I searched for fear or alarm in Crandell's face, but his grin stayed fixed in place. I felt a hard knot form in my stomach. *The police will help. They have to. It's their job.* I repeated that in my mind over and over again, but Crandell's grin made shivers zap my spine. I knitted my shoulders together, but the shivers didn't stop.

Finally, a police officer arrived. The officer strode into the kitchen. When he saw me, he looked disappointed and tired. "Crandell, are you ever going to quit torturing those kids?" the officer asked with a sigh.

Bile rose in my throat again along with cold waves of anxiety and dread. The police *knew?* They knew how we were treated and it still went on?

"Get the girl's parents on the phone," the officer said. "She's not going back to the school unless the parents say it's ok."

I gave the officer my dad's number. He dialed and held the phone to his ear, but after letting it ring he set it back on the cradle. "There's no answer," he said. He asked if I knew my dad's work number, but I couldn't remember it. Maybe my mom would understand. Maybe I could convince her to let me come home.

The officer dialed my home number. In a calm voice, he explained the situation. Crandell reached for the phone, but the officer gave him a hard shove. He handed the phone to me.

"Mom?"

"Grace," my mom said, disappointment ringing in her voice. "Our decision to send you to that school is *final*. You're not coming home until you finish your program. That's the deal."

I looked at Crandell. He glowered at me, but with the police officer there, he couldn't stop me from telling the truth.

"Mom, it's a *scam*. They dropped me so I'd have to stay in the program longer. They just want to get more money out of you."

Anders shot Crandell an angry look.

"Stop it, Grace. You're just trying to manipulate me so you can come home. Just work your program, and you'll be fine."

I could hear the clatter of dishes on my mom's end of the line. She was loading the dishwasher. A jazz station was playing in the background.

"Mom, I *did* work the program! I was on level five and then they dropped me back to level one just because I read a book. The dorms are crowded, and they feed us hot dog soup because it's the cheapest way to stretch their supply. It's all about money."

On the other end of the line, my mom sucked her teeth and sighed. "Enough, Grace. This lying is exactly why you're there in the first place. Work your program, behave, do as you're told. Be someone who won't embarrass me. When you learn to do all those things, you can come home."

"Mom," I pushed the word through a flood of tears. "Mom, I'll be good, I promise! Please let me come home! Please, mom! I'll do whatever you say!"

"Nice try," she said and hung up the phone.

The officer gently pried the phone from my fingers. I put my head on the table and let the loud, ugly sobs tumble out of me.

The officer hung up the phone. I felt Anders' hand on my back.

"You're not taking her," Anders said.

"I'm sorry," the officer said. "There's really nothing I can do. Her mom wants her to go back to the school."

Crandell smiled. He clamped his hand around my wrist. Anders threw a punch at Crandell, but the officer held Anders back. Anders shouted as Crandell dragged me to his truck. Once inside, he wrapped a zip tie around my wrists to bind them together.

Crandell called the officer over. Through his open window, he handed the officer a ten-dollar bill. The officer flicked it back at him. It landed on the floor, under the brake.

"You're lucky the Sheriff likes you," the officer said. Had the Sheriff tipped off Crandell? Did Jackie know that the Sheriff would do that?

I watched the police car drive away. As Crandell drove back to the Academy, he fixed his glare on me.

"You little cunt," he spat, "that was the biggest fucking mistake you could make," he said. "But it'll be your last. I guaran-fucking-tee it."

He tossed a wad of fabric at me. "By the way, this washed up on shore this morning." It was my sweatshirt. It was still damp. "When I saw that I figured you'd try to swim across. You led me right to you. I think you wanted me to find you." He tugged at his crotch.

He turned toward me and grinned just like he did in Jackie's kitchen. "You're not as smart as you think you are," he said through clenched teeth. "Not by half. I'm going to show you just how soft your brain really is."

My stomach twisted. Bile rose in my throat again and flooded my mouth. I kept my lips shut tight and swallowed hard. *Is this what you wanted, Mom? What do you think he's going to do to me? This is supposed to make me love you? Why do I deserve this?*

When the big ugly bunkhouses came into view, I suddenly felt relieved. At least I wouldn't have to be alone with Crandell anymore. Crandell gripped my arms so tight it hurt. When he took me to the Shed, I didn't resist. He threw me onto the dirt floor.

An hour later, Crandall left and locked the door behind him. My ribs ached fiercely and my mouth was full of blood. My vagina burned and bled, but not from my period. I laid down on the dirt floor until I felt numb. I vomited in the corner and the smell filled the room. Slowly, I scratched the packed dirt with my fingernails until I had made a hole big enough to bury the vomit.

My hands were black. I rubbed them on my face.

A spider crept up the wall. I followed it with my eyes and noticed that someone had etched a poem into the paint.

Your mother hates you
Your Dad regrets you
Your friends forget you
And Crandell rapes you.

I ran my fingers over it. I wanted to know how long it had been here. Treblinka could have written it, or Andrea, or some girl who had been here in 1996 when Epiphany Lake first opened.

I leaned against the wall and shut my eyes. Just as I began to feel drowsy, I felt the spider crawling on the back of my neck. Even though it made my skin jump, I let it walk all over me until it lost interest and wandered away.

I spent two weeks in the Shed. Or maybe three. I lost track of time. But it all came to an end in the middle of the night when Crandell opened the door and two men came in. Another pair of handcuffs, another strange van, another secret destination.

But I knew exactly where I was going.

19

The first thing I noticed when I walked out of Las Americas International was the heat. It was like walking through syrup. Even though the humidity made me sweaty and sticky, the heat felt nice after being in so many cold places. Cold vans, cold airports, cold jets. The Shed always got very cold at night, no matter how warm it had been during the day.

On the eight-hour flight out of Minneapolis, all I could think about was Crandell. I could still smell the burnt-grease stench that filled the tiny room when he unzipped his pants and shoved his crotch into my face. I could still feel something tearing inside me as he grunted on top of me. I fantasized about kicking him in the chest with both feet and slamming my fist into his face until blood leaked out of his skull. I punched the seat back in front of me and cried so much that the flight attendant came around and slipped me a few doll-sized bottles of vodka. I swallowed their contents and felt it burn my throat as I closed my eyes and finally fell into a light sleep.

By the time the plane landed, I felt as if someone had kicked me in the head. In the baggage claim, I saw a young woman waving a handwritten sign that said 'HADDENFELD' on it. I realized it was supposed to be Haddonfield, my last name. I could have said it wasn't me. I could have said, "I'm not Haddenfeld" and it would have been true. I could have walked right past her and slipped away into the streets of Santo Domingo. I could have found a way to get by, even if it meant letting men pay me to do things. (After what Crandell did, I figured that if I at least got paid, it wouldn't be so bad.) I could have had a very different life. I could have run again.

But I didn't.

I introduced myself to the woman and followed her away from the airport. She looked like she wasn't that much older than I was — eighteen or twenty at most. She informed me that her car had broken down on the way to the airport and that we'd have to wait for someone to drive down and pick us up. We climbed onto a crowded bus and rode toward the center of the city. She found a little cafe and said something in Spanish to the waitress, who returned a few minutes later with a plate of half-moons of fried dough and a pitcher of pineapple juice. The waitress left. My stomach rumbled. I could smell the ground beef and onion stuffed inside the little pies.

The woman gave me permission to eat, and I nearly ate one of the *pastelitos* whole, the meat juice and fat flooding my mouth. It was the best thing I had tasted in a long time. I knew I wouldn't taste anything this good again for months. Maybe even years. The woman told me that she had recently graduated from Mystic Bay and had stayed on to work as a member of staff.

Bachata music floated on the air from somewhere inside the cafe. I watched cars and buses and motorcycles criss-cross the streets haphazardly and wondered whether this country had any traffic laws at all. I pretended I was having some kind of vacation, a fun day in an otherwise normal life. As long as I sat at that cafe, sipping cold pineapple juice and watching traffic, I could pretend that this was where I was supposed to be.

Three hours later, the van arrived. The driver was a boy who was a little bit older that me. I knew right away that he was an upper level; he could be trusted to drive because he would be going home soon. There's no point in joyriding when the real joy is leaving.

People riding motorcycles buzzed in front of us like swarms of bees.

Not one of them wore a helmet. One of the bikers carried three lengths of pipe over his left shoulder as he drove. For several blocks on our way out of town, we drove behind a truck piled impossibly high with sacks of rice. I wondered what would happen if the cords holding the sacks in place gave way and all the sacks came tumbling out. Our van would probably be crushed and catch fire. I would be the sole survivor - set free by an avalanche of rice.

We drove through a neighborhood of pretty colonial houses with curving verandas, ornate bell towers and magenta vines of bougainvillea exploding over pastel-colored walls. There were old stone buildings streaked with gray from centuries of rain. I tried to think of a word to describe them. Majestic? Sad? Was there a word that meant both?

The grand buildings gave way to rows of tidy shotgun-style houses, all painted in bright blue, yellow, green and pink hues. I watched as a small boy came running out of one of them, chasing after a small brown and white dog.

Traffic slowed just before we reached Santo Domingo's city limit. Up ahead, on the opposite side of the road, I saw a pickup truck with a man standing up in the back. His fingers curled around the top of the frame. As we crawled past the truck, I saw that its tailgate was down and the man was bracing something with his feet: a shiny white casket. He straddled it and gripped it with his ankles so it wouldn't go sliding out onto the road.

I wondered who was in the casket. It must have been for someone important, or at least, someone important to the man standing in the back of the truck. It was a little bit funny that they found cords to keep the rice sacks secure, but none for a single casket. What if the driver had to hit the brakes? The guy would go flying and then they would need *another casket* and *another* person to keep it in place with his ankles. I imagined a long line of trucks, all with caskets in the back, all braking at once, catapulting them into the air and directly into the next casket in line.

The traffic let up just as we passed rows of ramshackle houses made of pieces of rusted corrugated metal, patched together to form walls and roofs. A dirt path connected them.

Once we were out of the city and there was nothing to see but green hills and sugar cane fields, a sense of dread began to creep in.

Mystic Bay.

The last stop. The worst place. The scariest punishment.

When my flight from Minneapolis to Miami took off, I felt relieved. I felt the way I did when I was eleven-years-old and had to get a tooth filled. I felt anxious right up until my appointment when suddenly, all the fear melted away because the terrible thing would soon be over.

I changed planes in Miami, and the bright blue ocean made me forget where I was going. But now, all this green made my chest feel tight again. The groves of trees were so thick they made the hills seem shadowy and dark. And something about the sugar cane, with its bright green fluttering fronds on top of tall, gray stalks made me shiver.

What was I going to do? Working the program didn't work. Running away didn't work. Maybe there was nothing I could do now but wait.

I closed my eyes for a while.

The van shuddered as we drove over a rough, gravelly road. My stomach sank like I'd swallowed a sack of marbles. *This is it. I just know it.*

I opened my eyes and at first, they hurt from something glowing white-hot in the sun. Then my eyes adjusted. There was a tall white fence with a metal gate. Beyond it, a white building. It looked like it had been a hotel once with a series of verandas surrounding a courtyard. But the verandas were all covered with white metal bars. The lowest level of the building that looked like it was the only one that wasn't closed in, but as the van drew closer I saw a row of boys in brown jumpsuits standing on the ground level behind a set of thin black lines.

It was a barbed wire fence. Curls of barbed wire also decorated the roof.

Last chance to run.

This place probably had a Shed too. Or something worse. Something much worse.

The metal gate swung open just as the driver parked the van. I got out. It felt good to stand and stretch after so many hours of sitting. The woman led me through the gate and it immediately slammed shut behind me.

A strange tree stood in the center of the courtyard. It had gray bark, twisted limbs and little green apples that dangled from its branches. Apples littered the ground beneath it, untouched even by insects. A handwritten sign posted next to the tree read, *"¡¡No tocar! ¡¡¡Manzanillas venenosas! ¡¡¡Peligro!"* I hadn't studied Spanish, but I figured out what the sign meant: Don't touch. Poisonous apples.

"That's a manchineel tree," the woman explained. "It's completely toxic. Even if you just stand under it while it rains, you'll get burns on your skin. It's a category 5 if you touch it or try to eat the apples."

I didn't ask her why someone would do that in the first place. I already knew the answer.

She led me into the building. It was dark and eerily quiet except for the occasional crackle of walkie-talkies. There was a smell too; it reminded me of the outhouse I slept in after running away from Epiphany Lake. It grew stronger as we passed one of the bathrooms.

"The plumbing is a bit finicky sometimes." She said.

Finicky? That was a word for cat food commercials, not for talking about plumbing.

She opened a door to a room that wasn't much bigger than a closet. It had one slatted window that let in a few, thinly-sliced beams of light but not much in terms of a view of the outside. The woman unhooked something on the wall, and a board with a thin mattress on it slammed into place with a loud crack.

"For the rest of today and tonight, you'll be in here. Tomorrow, you start the program. Someone will be by to bring you dinner in a couple of hours, and again to take you to the bathroom. Any questions?"

I shook my head. I also didn't tell her I kind of needed to pee after that three-hour drive. She left and locked the door behind her. I climbed up onto the mattress, squeezed my thighs together and threw an elbow over my eyes.

A scream echoed through the corridor followed by the sound of running feet.

I knew one thing: in the morning, I would definitely *not* be starting the program.

20

I woke up to the sound of someone banging on my door and shouting in Spanish. The door swung open. A large woman with a graying black pony tail and a blouse that was too tight continued her tirade. I couldn't understand the words, but I quickly figured out what she wanted me to do. I slipped down off the thin mattress and folded the bed back into the wall. I put on my new uniform—a brown jumpsuit—and flip-flops that were three sizes too big.

The woman led me down the hall. The bars on the windows cast shadows on the floor that stretched all the way to the opposite wall. We turned a corner, and there was a girl lying crumpled on the floor, crying, with two men standing over her.

"I want to go home," she cried. "I want to go home."

I wondered how long she had been here.

We walked down a dark staircase. It was the only part of the building so far that was cool. I followed her as she led me along the lower level, which was just a narrow strip of concrete next to the building, enclosed by the barbed wire fence. I looked up at the top of the fence, at the way it angled toward the building, to keep us in. The fence looked like it was eight feet high.

Finally, we passed a series of doors. The woman opened one. A group of girls was inside, cleaning in silence.

"This your family," the woman said. "Is called 'Challenger' family."

Challenger? Wasn't that the name of a rocket that blew up?

"You call me Senora Mondragon." She pronounced each syllable slowly, and I got the feeling that pronouncing her name wrong was a Category 1, at least.

Sra. Mondragon popped her head into the room. "*Chicas!*" She shouted. "*Hagan fila!*" The girls quickly lined up and moved aside so Sra. Mondragon could step in and scrutinize their cleaning job. Over her shoulder, I managed to get a brief glimpse into the room. It had no windows so it was pretty dark, but I did notice that there didn't seem to be any bunks. Just things that looked like nets, folded and hanging on the walls.

Sra. Mondragon unholstered her radio and rattled off a rapid-fire message. Static crackled as she waited for a response. She gave the girls permission to cross out of the room, and I fell in line behind them.

We marched into a concrete courtyard that probably once had fountains and plants and lounge chairs in it but now was just a grubby square with clothes lines strung across it. A few boys' t-shirts hung stiffly, waiting for a breeze that never came.

Sra. Mondragon made us do our fitness routine in the courtyard. She shouted out the exercises she wanted us to do, and we had to keep doing them until she called out another one.

"Sit-ups!"

"Jumping jacks!"

"Pushups!"

"Squats!"

"Plank!"

My thighs, abs and shoulders all burned while the sun seared my back. My arms shook. Sweat dripped from my forehead. I counted the drops. I was sure I'd never held a plank for this long before. I didn't know if it was the heat, the long trip, the weeks in the Shed or what, but it seemed like Sra. Mondragon was an even tougher drill sergeant than Crandell.

Well, at least she wouldn't play with her dick the whole time.

Two floors up, a boy broke the silence by barking through the bars, his voice echoing down at us.

"Woof! Work it, ladies! Woof, woof!"

The bars rattled. I glanced up in time to see two male staffers pulling the boy away from the bars. They hoisted him into the air and threw him against the wall. I stopped watching when one of them men flattened the boy out and sat on him. I could hear him trying to say something. It sounded like 'I can't breathe.'

I went back to counting my sweat drops.

At Mystic Bay, they didn't blast self-help tapes during breakfast, lunch and dinner, like they did at Epiphany Lake. I learned later that this was because someone had left the cassette tapes out in the sun, and they all melted and the man in charge was too cheap to order more.

Without the droning voices, the lunchroom was quiet, but in a way, the silence was worse than the tapes. Here, quiet wasn't really quiet. It was just space in between screams.

Breakfast was flavorless mush. Plantains, boiled and mashed. I ate it fast so I wouldn't have to taste it.

The rest of the daily schedule wasn't that different from Epiphany Lake. School work, therapy, more school work, dinner, silent free time, bed.

In therapy, the girl next to me bit her bottom lip until it started to bleed, then pulled it into her mouth and sucked. She repeated the process four times. She had big, blue doll eyes and curly blonde hair. When she drew her lip into her mouth, she looked like a baby.

My eyes felt hot. I didn't know if it was her huge eyes or the way her mouth turned down at the corners when she sucked on herself but watching her made me feel like crying. Then, I remembered Treblinka, how she got in trouble for picking scabs on her hands.

Treblinka is lucky they never sent her here, I thought. *If she'd ended up here, she would have picked every last bit of skin off her hands.*

I pictured thin, bald Treblinka with red, throbbing raw-beef hands while the rest of her bony frame curled up like a dried spider. I shivered, and I started to cry. I hid my face and prayed the therapist didn't notice.

Nobody talked. I understood why: we'd already talked. We'd already confessed. We' already cried. It didn't get us anywhere but here.

Instead, the therapist talked. She told us we were whores. Ungrateful brats. She said she knew what we all wanted: to be back home, "letting boys put their hands up your skirts, drinking alcohol and shooting drain cleaner into your veins."

Drain cleaner?

"You all need to wake up and realize how lucky you are to be here. If you weren't here, you'd be dead. This program is the only thing standing between you and dying in an alley."

I stared at her shoes while she ranted. They were shiny and black. Surrounded by flip-flops on dirty feet, her shoes made her look like she belonged in one of those commercials for feeding orphans for thirty cents a day.

"I want to hear you all say how grateful you are to be here," she said. "I want to hear you all say that this place is saving your life."

Nobody said a word.

"Don't *any* of you want to finish this program?"

I already almost did, I thought.

"You," she said. I glanced up and realized she was talking to me. "Aren't you grateful that this program is saving your life?"

"I'm grateful that this program is saving my life," I parroted.

She didn't think I meant it. She made me say it again.

"I'm grateful that this program is saving my life," I said, again. Was that robotic voice really mine? She glared. She made me repeat it again. And again. I repeated it so many times I began to cry out of frustration.

Satisfied, the therapist moved on to someone else. I looked over at the girl next to me. Her inside-out lip had swollen to twice its original size. Something about her shiny, purple engorged flesh reminded me of

Crandell, the way his thing flopped around as he stood up to put his pants back on.

I grabbed two fistfuls of my hair and pulled, hard. Every time Crandell flashed in my mind, I fantasized about clawing trenches into his face or ripping open his jugular vein with my teeth. I wanted to flip him, like a judo artist would, onto his back and stomp on his groin with all my weight.

You stupid bitch, I said to myself, *why the fuck didn't you fight him? Why did you let him do that to you?*

I wanted to scream. I filled my lungs with air and pushed it out as hard as I could, shrieking, "I AM GRATEFUL TO THIS PROGRAM FOR SAVING MY LIFE!"

In the afternoon, during the hottest part of the day, we worked outside. Sra. Mondragon made me pick vines off of one of the barbed wire fences. The thin, green tendrils wound themselves around so tightly, picking off every last bit of vine seemed to take forever.

The toilets here don't work, I thought, *but there are never* any *vines on the fences!* It seemed like the sort of thing that should have been funny, but I didn't laugh, not even in my head.

I'm not even doing this to earn points, I thought. *I'm just doing it to stay out of Mystic Bay's version of the Shed.*

I knew Mystic Bay had something they used for kids who wouldn't do what they were told. But so far, I hadn't seen anything that looked like an isolation room. I shivered. Everything here was worse than Epiphany Lake. That meant iso had to be worse, too. I didn't want to know what iso was like here. *You won't have to find out,* I told myself, but a gnawing in my stomach told me I was wrong.

Am I really here? I thought. Maybe I was dreaming. Maybe I was in someone else's dream. When Sra. Mondragon turned her back, I wrapped my hand around the wire fence and felt the barb prick my skin. The wire was hot from baking in the sun.

Dreams don't burn. They don't pierce.

Sra. Mondragon whirled around, and I let go of the fence and pretended I'd been picking vines the whole time.

Sun seared the back of my neck. Sweat pooled under the collar of my jumpsuit. Sra. Mondragon walked over to inspect my work. She reached for her radio, and I felt as if I'd been splashed with ice water. Had I missed a vine? What would my punishment be?

When I didn't hear the radio crackle, I looked at Sra. Mondragon just as she cracked it against the side of my face. The hard plastic ripped the skin under my eye and made me bleed.

"What did I do?" I asked, pressing my fingers against my throbbing head.

She smiled. "Nothing," she said. "*Absolutamente nada.*"

My eye swelled shut. I got in trouble for touching the sticky gash where blood was slowly drying. With only one good eye, I had a hard time walking straight and bumped into walls. I got in trouble for that, too. By the end of my first day at Mystic Bay, my points total was a double-digit negative.

I didn't think there was a level lower than 1. But there I was.

21

The nets on the walls in our dorm room were made of coarse rope and had hard knots that dug into my spine and the back of my head. I wasn't allowed to have a pillow; at Mystic Bay you had to 'earn' the right to a pillow.

No one in my room had one.

Every hour, flashlights swept the room. I quickly learned to listen for the shuffling steps and the scrape of the key in the lock so I'd know exactly when to shut my eyes and pretend to be asleep. Then I'd wait for the beam to hit my eyelids before I opened them again.

The flashlights, the knots, and my sore, swollen eye all chased sleep away.

I did sleep a little, just before dawn. I had a dream that overnight, the vines near the fences grew thick and lush, completely covering the barbs. I climbed to freedom on soft leaves.

My dream ended when one of the guards came and opened the door and caused it to bang against the wall. We had ten minutes to get up, get dressed, fold our rope hammocks and sweep the floor. When the guard returned, we lined up while he inspected the room.

He pointed to one of the hammocks. He wanted to know whose it was. All but one of the hammocks were hanging straight with spreader bars parallel to the floor. My heart raced. That wasn't *my* hammock was it? I suddenly couldn't remember which one I'd slept in.

A tiny, dark-skinned girl in line ahead of me raised a bird-like hand.

I could see it trembling. "That is my hammock, sir." Her accent sounded French. I remembered that I'd studied French back home. If I were still there, I'd be in French II. I wasn't sure what month it was, but I knew that at some point, my sophomore year started.

"You lazy girl," the guard growled. "You think because your *papi* has money you're a *princesa?* Do you want to wear the crown?"

The girl immediately started sobbing and a chill galloped down my spine. *What the fuck is the crown?*

"Fix it," he ordered. Then, he spat, "*Haitiana.*"

The girl walked over to the wall and tried to straighten her hammock, but the guard kept shaking his head. It looked perfectly straight to me, but he stood over her and made her hang it and re-hang it over and over again.

With his back turned, I took the opportunity to touch my eye. It hurt even worse and it felt hot. When I pressed on it I could tell that it was full of liquid—blood or pus or something. I wished I could see it in a mirror.

When the hammock was finally straight enough, the guard spun the girl around by her shoulders and shoved her back into line.

Asshole, I thought.

We marched out of our room and into the fitness yard. The guard introduced himself as Jorge Ramon Trujillo. He stood with a strange grin on his face as if he was waiting for us to catch on to something.

"You ignorant Americans probably don't know what the name Trujillo means to Dominicans. I am not a descendent of Generalissimo Rafael Trujillo, but I will punish you if you cannot say *perejil* correctly. *Perejil* is a Spanish word for parsley."

He looked straight at the small dark girl when he said that last part. My head swam. Crowns? Parsley? Generalissimo? Maybe they wanted us to feel like we were always walking around with one eye shut.

"Sra. Mondragon called in sick today. She probably picked up something from you *huerfanos*. Normally, I stay on the boys' side. But today I get to have more fun—it's easier to make girls cry."

For a split second, I was grateful for swollen lids because they prevented me from rolling my eyes.

Sr. Trujillo's workout was hard, but not that much worse than Sra. Mondragon's. At one point, while I was doing pushups, I felt a large, rough hand grab me by the back of my neck and pull me to my feet. I panicked. What had I done wrong?

"What is that all over your face?" Sr. Trujillo asked. He thought I had vomited, but I touched the gash under my eye and realized it had burst and that pus was leaking down my cheek. He sucked his teeth in disgust and let go of me.

"Get back down," he said, and I finished my set of pushups.

As he walked away, I felt a rush of relief. That was the first time in my life I'd ever been grateful for pus.

When the workout was over, the little dark girl smoothed her hair with her hands as we stood in line. As I watched her do it, I felt all the muscles in my back tense up as I waited for what I knew would come next.

Sr. Trujillo walked toward her in silence and didn't stop until his face was inches from hers. "What are you doing? Making yourself pretty for a ball? You did not have permission to fix your hair."

The girl trembled.

"You're being a *princesa* again aren't you?"

She shook her head.

A grin spread across Sr. Trujillo's face. He held his radio up to his mouth. "Bring the crown," he said, still smiling.

Moments later, one of the junior staffers came out to the yard carrying a weird contraption that looked sort of like the leafy crowns Greek statues wear. The staffer was wearing thick gardening gloves. She placed it on the girl's head, and I got a chance to see it up close. It was made of chicken wire cut into a narrow strip and had bright green leaves stuffed in it, secured with twist ties. The leaves looked just like the ones on the tree in the courtyard — the one we weren't supposed to touch.

Sr. Trujillo crossed his arms and nodded as if he was admiring some kind of art.

The girl had tears silently streaming down her face.

That night, after wearing the crown for an entire day, the girl's forehead was completely covered with red, angry blisters. I shuddered hard when I saw them. I could tell her skin was burning from whatever was in those leaves. She also had little cuts from the chicken wire. She set up her hammock and crawled into it, her back turned to the rest of us.

The last hour of the day was the only time when we were allowed to talk.

"I'm Annie," said a girl with a thick Southern drawl. "I got kicked out of a Baptist school in Missouri for using a butt paddle on a teacher's face. How about you?"

I hesitated. We weren't supposed to tell 'war stories' or brag about anything bad we'd done in the past.

"I ran away," I told her.

She nodded but didn't say anything else. Footsteps on the pavement outside the door made us lower our voices so the night watch guard wouldn't hear us.

"What about her?" I asked Annie, with a nod toward the girl who'd worn the crown.

"That's Seraphine. Jorge picks on her because she's Haitian."

"What?"

"They hate Haitians here. Kind of like how people back home hate Mexicans."

I glanced over at Seraphine. Her shoulders were shaking. A distant scream came from the boys' side of the facility.

"She doesn't speak any English," Annie continued. "She doesn't seem to know much Spanish, either, so she's had trouble understanding the rules. Sophie," Annie pointed to an Asian girl with a thick black ponytail, "figured out that she speaks French and tried to translate for her. Sophie caught hell for that. First rule of Mystic Bay: don't help nobody."

I nodded. I was familiar with that rule. I couldn't stop thinking about the way Jorge had looked at Seraphine. His lip curled the same way Crandell's did when he described the punishment he was about to dole out to me. He had the same narrow, piggy eyes, too.

"I wonder what he does to her," I mused.

Annie furrowed her brow. "You see what he does to her."

"No, I mean, when nobody's looking."

"Like what?"

I shrugged and looked down at my feet. "I don't know."

Annie pushed her finger into the hollow spot under my collarbone. "Yes, you do."

"I'm just saying…the way he picks on her. He probably does more than pick on her. I think he fucks her."

"He's fucking her?"

"There was a guy at my last school who used to fuck people," I mumbled. I was still looking at my feet.

"He fuck you?"

I nodded, my eyes trained on the sandals that were too big to run away in. I could feel my eyes start to burn, but I gritted my teeth to keep from crying.

"Was it big?" Annie put her hand by her crotch and pantomimed a huge dick.

"Stop," I laughed. I punched her in the shoulder. "We'll get a category 3."

"You didn't say what school you came from," Annie said. "Nobody ends up here unless they got kicked out of somewhere else first."

"Epiphany Lake," I replied. "In Minnesota."

She cocked her head to the side. "I didn't know they had tough schools up there. I thought sure you were gonna say you came from some outfit in Montana or Utah. Oh, well, it doesn't matter much. There's no place worse than this."

I looked over at Seraphine again. She was sitting up, and it looked like she had more blisters than before. Her face seemed to be swelling up like her skin wanted to run away from the poison.

I shuddered again.

22

By day three, I was already starting to zone out. My body learned the routine. In the morning, I cleaned before inspection. I stood in formation. I ate small portions of flavorless food. I exercised. I sat in therapy. I marched.

But my mind went somewhere else. Paris, where pink blossoms showered me as I walked along some cobblestone street. China, where I shopped for colorful silk fans. Spain, where I learned to dance wearing a dress covered in blood-red ruffles.

Other kids were zoning out, too. I could tell by their eyes. At Epiphany Lake, some kids got that 'heroin-chic' look; black and empty like a store that's closed. At Mystic Bay, everyone had that look, only it was much worse. It reminded me of pictures I'd seen of men who'd fought in wars, in a book my dad kept on the shelf when he still lived with us. The men's faces were caked with dirt and from underneath their helmets, they stared at nothing. I remembered telling my dad I thought the men looked scary.

"Combat fatigue," he explained. "That's a look people get when they've seen and done terrible things."

By now, I had learned all of the other girls' reasons for being here. There were two girls at Mystic Bay because they suffered from 'homosexual perversions,' one girl who had been caught with methamphetamine, and three girls with "Oppositional Defiant Disorder."

Sophie, the Asian girl who lived in the dorm with Annie, Seraphine and me, was born in Korea and had been adopted by white parents. She told her mother that she was interested in tracking down her birth parents. Her mother burst into tears, wailing that Sophie didn't love her. She made Sophie promise to stop trying to find her Korean family. Then, when she found a Seoul travel guide that Sophie had checked out from the library in her room, she announced that Sophie would be finishing high school at Mystic Bay. Whenever we had to go around the circle and "own up to" whatever it was that we had done, Sophie had to say that she was "ungrateful and disrespectful."

Seraphine was the only one whose story I didn't know. With her, every "therapy" session was the same. The therapist would order her to speak, Seraphine would answer in French, the therapist would yell at her and then radio Jorge to come and take her away.

Seraphine's eyes were the emptiest of them all.

23

One night, toward the end of my first week, I lay awake, unable to sleep. At dinner, they had served us boiled chicken legs with little bristles that poked out of the gray skin. They were quills—leftover bits of feather that remained after the chicken had been plucked. I ate mine as fast as I could so I wouldn't have to taste the bland meat or feel the quills on my tongue.

Annie refused to eat hers. She picked up a gray chicken leg and whipped it like she was playing fastpitch softball. It hit one of the junior staff in the face.

At Mystic Bay, junior staff kids who were so brainwashed that instead of getting the hell off the island once they'd finished the program, they stayed on as staff. This one was a girl not much older than Annie or me, and I could tell right off that Annie was stronger. When the girl grabbed Annie's hair, Annie grabbed onto her arm, yanked it down and sank her teeth into the girl's flesh. Suddenly, five grown men surrounded Annie and slammed her onto the floor. She disappeared underneath them as they all sat on different parts of her body, pinning her completely. Her screams were the only thing that let me know she wasn't suffocating.

Just as they hauled Annie away, Seraphine vomited her dinner back onto her plate. Jorge appeared—as if out of nowhere—and shoved a spoon into her hand. I turned away and gritted my teeth as Seraphine ate her own vomit. I was afraid if I watched, I'd end up having to eat mine, too.

Seraphine threw up again and refused to eat her twice-vomited food, so Jorge hauled her away, too.

A few hours later, I lay awake in a room with two empty hammocks. I had no idea where Annie and Seraphine were, and all I could think about were those little quills. I imagined them poking holes in my stomach and intestines. I imagined them boring right through my esophagus and poking holes in my heart, lungs and kidneys. I would die and my autopsy would say, "Death by hundreds of tiny holes."

A guard unlocked the door and swept the room with his flashlight. I shut my eyes before the beam of light hit my face.

The hourly sweeps didn't make sleep any easier. I began to wonder whether death by a hundred tiny holes would be such a terrible thing.

In the morning, Annie and Seraphine were both back with our group. Annie had a red scrape on the side of her face. Seraphine's eyes were red, puffy and jellied over. At first, I just thought it meant she had been crying but when I looked closer, I noticed a splotch on her cheek and welts on her ear. She smelled like some kind of chemical. Did they pepper spray her?

At breakfast, our group had to wait in a long line behind everyone else. When we finally did get our food, there wasn't any hot oatmeal or even flavorless mashed plantain left. All we got were bowls of leftover rice floating in cold milk.

"No hot food," the cook said. She stood behind the table where the food was laid out, her hands on her hips. "Senor Jorge say, you not eat food last night, you eat cold food today."

This was *so* unfair! I *ate* my nasty spiky chicken! I got almost no sleep because I thought I would die from it. I didn't refuse my food, I didn't barf—I was just being punished because I sat with people who did. And I never got to choose who I sat with!

I sulked as I ate my rice. The rice was slightly dry from being refrigerated and some of it was hard; it was the stuff they'd scraped off of the bottom of the pot the night before. Little specks of cooking oil floated to the surface of the milk. It mostly just tasted bland. I ate it as fast as I could.

For lunch, we got a watery pile of semi-mashed black beans and stale bread. Dinner was cold mashed plantains and more gray, spiky chicken. I glanced at Annie, then at Seraphine. *You two had better fucking eat that chicken*, I thought. I was afraid that if they didn't, we'd all have to eat these gross cold meals again tomorrow. I exhaled with relief when I saw them both nibbling their chicken.

I looked down at my own plate. I imagined that the chicken was golden brown from frying in hot fat, crispy and salty on the outside, and juicy on the inside. I pretended that the plantain mush was mashed potatoes smothered in dark, peppery turkey gravy. My trick worked.

My trick worked. The food actually did taste a little bit better.

24

A boy moaned and cried, waking me during the dark early morning hours. He cried the way a newborn would—with no control, no attempt to be quieter, just letting out every bit of sound that his body could make. It reminded me of something I'd learned about while working on an 8th grade history project. What was that thing that Irish women did at wakes, that thing that's a combination of wailing and singing?

Keening.

The boy was keening.

I strained to listen. His voice wasn't carrying from the boys' side of the facility. It was coming from somewhere else. It came from beyond the central courtyard where we washed our clothes in cold water and dirty buckets. It came from the part of Mystic Bay that was furthest away from the front gates—the part I had yet to see.

I shivered. It had to be bad, whatever it was. I remembered the Shed at Epiphany Lake with its cold dirt floor and bleach fumes. I remembered the etchings on the wall by the hard wooden plank that served as a bed.

ELA is hell.

Freedom.

Let me go.

It doesn't matter what it's like because you're not going to end up there, I told myself, but I didn't feel any better.

A beam of light hit my eyes. I didn't close them fast enough.

The next day, I stood in line with the sun beating down on the back of my neck, listening to Senora Mondragon's radio crackle as she gave a headcount. I had not slept more than four hours a night since I'd arrived at Mystic Bay, and I felt like I was surrounded in fog that never lifted.

During the morning workout, I felt like I was drowning. After the first thirty jumping jacks I wanted to collapse, but I knew I couldn't stop. I forced myself to keep going even though my chest burned, and I could barely catch air.

Senora Mondragon ordered us to get down on the ground to do pushups. My shoulders burned. I couldn't breathe. This had never happened to me before. I'd always been able to get through the workouts even when they were grueling. At Epiphany Lake, it had been my job to chase after runaways because I wasn't soft and out of shape like the other girls. At home, I was a Varsity swimmer. Now, I could barely do thirty pushups. What was wrong with me? What was happening?

I panicked.

I gasped for air and then collapsed onto the grass, a sweet, tingly feeling of near-sleep washing over me.

The next thing I knew, Senora Mondragon was screaming into my ear. Her shrill voice stabbed my eardrum and rattled my skull.

"You are worthless! You are useless trash living a pointless life! You are an ungrateful bitch! You'll amount to nothing. Men will put their *pingas* in you and retarded babies will crawl out of your diseased *toto*."

She kicked me sharply in the ribs. I didn't mean to cry out in pain.

"*Llorona*," she hissed and kicked me again. Shame curdled in my throat. I didn't need a translator to tell me what *llorona* meant: crybaby. No one had ever called me a crybaby before. But I couldn't make it through the workout, so maybe it was true. I was a weak, soft crybaby.

No. I wasn't a crybaby. I *wasn't.*

I gathered my strength, tightening my abs and raising myself up into a pushup position. I lowered my body and pushed up, once…twice…satisfied that her words and kicks had motivated me, Senora Mondragon walked away and found someone else to scream at.

When the workout was over, I heard a ringing in my ear and my ribs ached. The gash under my eye still hadn't fully healed. I wondered what my mother would think if she could see me. There was no way she would let me stand next to her at one of her cocktail parties in my brown jumpsuit and scabbed face.

Then I realized I had not received a single letter from her since leaving the United States.

25

After a month of near-sleepless nights, the world around me began to blur. I was sleepy and dizzy. I could *feel* the black circles under my eyes. Random phrases bounced around in my skull, echoing until I thought I'd go crazy, snippets of conversations or TV laugh tracks playing on constant loops. I bumped into things while walking in heel-toe lines and zoned out in therapy. This must be what it feels like to be drunk, I thought.

I was confused and forgetful, constantly losing points for leaving my notebook in a classroom or staring out the window for too long. I'd never get out of Mystic Bay—at least, not until I turned eighteen.

At some point, I had turned fifteen. *Three more birthdays and out.*

Every night at shutdown I was sure I'd sleep soundly. At some point, my body would have to be exhausted enough to just knock out completely, right? But one sleepless night bled into the next, and it seemed the less I slept, the harder it was for sleep to come.

The other kids had a word for what I was feeling: Mystic Brain.

It was thanks to a severe case of Mystic Brain that I ended up in the dog cages for the first time.

One hot, syrupy afternoon, our therapist made us re-enact our "crimes." The therapist brought Jorge over to be our "scene partner." I watched other girls simulate blow jobs while Jorge sat in the chair with his legs spread wide, the girl's heads bobbing up and down next to his crotch. At one point, Jorge grabbed the back of a girl's head and pressed her face against his fly. When he let go of her, she was crying. Jorge laughed.

Another re-enacted her heroin use by stabbing herself with a pen while Jorge pretended to be her dealer. "Pay me the money you owe me or suck my cock," he roared.

How does this help us? I wondered, dreamily.

The therapist shoved a finger at me. It was my turn. She asked me what I would re-enact and I froze.

"I don't know," I muttered.

"Yes you do," the therapist hissed, her lurid green eyes narrowed.

"I don't," I shook my head. I heard my dad's voice in my head: *your eyes look like two pee-holes in the snow.* He used to say that to my mom when she had dark circles from staying out too late at the bar. I'd been hearing his voice saying that in my head for two days straight.

"You slut," she hissed again. "You had sex with your teacher."

I swam in confusion.

"You already admitted it," she said, "There's no point in lying about it now."

Through my Mystic Brain-haze, I flashed back to another therapy circle: the false confession I gave at Epiphany Lake. The lie I told about having sex with Mr. Kyeong.

"I had sex with my teacher," I parroted, my voice sounding like an old computer.

Suddenly, Jorge was standing over me, a grin stretched across his face. I laid down on the floor and shut my eyes. I felt Jorge's weight on top of me, suffocating me in the sticky heat. I felt him grinding his hips into me and his hot breath behind my ear. In a flash, I was back in the Shed at Epiphany Lake with Crandell on top of me, red-faced and panting as he jackhammered his dick into me.

I screamed and bucked Jorge off of me, flailing my legs wildly, kicking him in the ribs and chest.

The next thing I knew, I was face down on the floor with Jorge sitting on my back. I continued to scream, even as Jorge shouted at me to calm down. Two other men came into the room and the three of them carried me out and down a dark hallway that opened into a blinding light.

I'd never been to this part of Mystic Bay before. It was a sun-baked concrete slab with a dozen chain-link cages in the middle of it. I saw seven other kids lying facedown and spread-eagle in dog cages, their chins burning on the hot concrete.

I heard metal hinges squeal as Jorge opened one of the cages. The two other men threw me into it. I landed chest-first on the blistering pavement. The fall knocked the wind out of me. My lungs took too long to reinflate. The cobalt sky melted and swirled around, trying to swallow me. The chainlink rattled as it slammed shut.

I spent hours under the melting sky, feeling the sun burn through my skin, layer after layer, my brown jumpsuit providing no protection at all. My chin was scorched and raw.

"Look on the bright side," I heard my mother say, "you might have a scar, but you'll never grow ugly black chin hairs like your grandmother does."

Die, I thought. *Die die die.*

When the sun set, it sucked all the blue out of the sky. Black silhouettes of palm fronds sliced into the savage orange that was left behind. The hinges on my cage door creaked. Someone dropped a metal plate onto the concrete.

Dinner.

Watery, flavorless beans and stale bread.

I closed my eyes and imagined that slices of spicy Cajun sausage, bright green peppers and juicy shreds of chicken made the bland beans into a spicy jambalaya. I ate it all as fast as I could and slid the empty plate under the gap between the chain link door and the concrete.

That night under hot, sparking stars, I slept soundly for the first time in weeks.

In the morning, Senora Mondragon came and let me out of my cage. I rejoined the Challenger family. At breakfast, Annie stood in front of me in the heel-toe line. She wound her hand behind her back and handed me a note with a small green spear wrapped in it. I shoved it into my pocket without looking at it.

Later, I unfolded the note:

This is aloe. Split it apart and use the goo inside on your sunburn. It helps.

Annie could've gotten a category 4 violation for doing this for me. I felt like crying; I bit my lip so I wouldn't.

That night, back in my hammock, I waited for the guard to complete his first round before opening the aloe branch and spreading the sticky gel on my skin. The feeling of hot oil spluttering on my skin stopped immediately.

I felt a warm rush of gratitude for Annie. Why had she decided to be so nice to me, I wondered. Then I realized it was because she was seventeen.

One more birthday and out.

26

After two months in Mystic Bay, I could see all of my ribs and there was a half-moon indentation between my hip bones. My brown jumpsuit was loose and baggy. My breasts were gone.

Some girls *wanted* to look like this. They lived in plush suburban houses and had plenty of food in the fridge that wasn't watery flavorless beans and they refused to eat any of it so they could make themselves look like this.

I hated them.

I fantasized about food all the time, and not just at dinner when I was trying to pretend my plate of bland slop was actually a tasty dish. I fantasized about omelets crammed full of steamed broccoli and bacon, of buttermilk biscuits covered in honey, pancakes bursting with tart, oversized blueberries. I remembered old commercials and played them over and over in my head: swirling chocolate, ribbons of frosting decorating flaky golden strudel, hamburgers sizzling on a griddle, dewy tomatoes tumbling out of nowhere.

Stringy pizza cheese. Salty tomato sauce. Pepperoni curled into crispy little cups.

Steaming pasta winding around a fork. Mushroomy Stroganoff over chewy egg noodles.

Egg rolls from the Vietnamese place on Johnson Street—sweet pork stuffing wrapped in crackling rice paper.

Soon I moved on from the food I remembered to the food I created in my mind. I imagined opening a can of tuna and mixing in mayonnaise and black pepper. I reached into the refrigerator and opened a jar of tiny, crunchy dill pickles. I chopped them up and mixed them in, then spread the tuna on soft white bread.

I wasn't the only one who thought about food. Annie told me she spent every day dreaming about Little Caesar's Pizza.

"We had it all the time," she said. "My mom would leave a note on the fridge, telling me to order dinner for my brother and me. She did that whenever she had to work late. She worked late most days."

"What about your dad?" I asked her.

"Business trips," she said, curling her fingers into quotation marks. "That's his code word for his visits to St. Louis. Where his mistress lives."

Annie was from Missouri. Her parents were strict Baptists who sent Annie and her sisters to Bible study after school every day. When they found out that she had been skipping Bible study to smoke weed in a basement full of greasy-haired boys, they shipped her off to a religious school hidden away in the Missouri Ozarks. Surrounded by sandstone ridges, the school was nearly impossible to escape. The rocks were too slippery to climb and too high up from the ground. Each cabin had a poster on the door warning the girls that if they tried to leave school grounds, coyotes, bobcats and black bears awaited them in the wilderness.

"Mistress? Doesn't that go against one of the commandments?"

"Sure does. I said to my dad: why do I need to study the Bible when you clearly have no idea what's in it? That's Missouri for you. Girls wearing 'purity' rings gave blowjobs in the boys' locker room. One day, she's outside Planned Parenthood protesting the killing of babies and the next days she's inside with a hose shoved up her twat. You know where those girls are? They're at the mall right now. The only difference between them and me is I refused to pretend I was all pious."

I understood what Annie meant. I knew I wasn't what my mother wanted me to be: a shining mirror of perfection that she could see herself in. I never tried to be that, because I knew no matter what I did, she would still see her own reflection, and she never liked what she saw.

"You know," Annie said, changing the subject, "there's a graveyard here."

"You're lying," I replied. I had a notebook open on my lap. I pretended to journal in it.

"In the 1950s, before Castro's revolution, there were all kinds of rich American families living in Cuba. They lived in grand hotels, and sometimes their daughters got too friendly with the staff if you know what I mean."

I rolled my eyes. "Of course I know what you mean. What does that have to do with this place?"

"Shut up and let me tell my story." She pinched the fat — or what was left of it — under my triceps. I smacked her hand away. "Anyway, in the 50s, this was a home for girls who were pregnant. Their families sent them here to have their babies."

"So?"

"So do you think they had babies with them when they went back to Havana?"

"What are you saying?"

"Jesus, are you thick?" She asked. I karate-chopped her hand as she reached for another pinch. "They came here for *abortions*. Or whatever you call an abortion when you kill a baby after it's born."

"No way," I shook my head, "This is a Catholic country isn't it?"

"So? Didn't I just say that Baptist and Evangelical girls give blowjobs and get abortions?"

"Fine," I said, closing my notebook, "So where's the graveyard?"

Annie leaned in and whispered: "Under the dog cages."

I turned and stared at her.

"They buried all the babies back there. There used to be a bunch of wooden crosses back there, but they rotted away. When this company bought the place, they poured concrete over the graveyard and put the dog cages in."

I wasn't sure I believed Annie, but I wasn't sure that I disbelieved her either. If I'd showed up here pregnant with Crandell's kid, would they have let me go home with a swollen belly? Or a baby?

They wouldn't. I was sure of that.

I shivered. I hadn't had a period in a long time. That meant I couldn't possibly be pregnant. Right?

"You're not," Annie said.

"What?" I shivered again. How had Annie been able to read my mind?

"Pregnant. You would know if you were. Before you got here, there was a girl who was pregnant. Not very far along. She threw up one morning while in line for breakfast and they made her lie face down in her puke all day. It went on like that every day for a week. Finally, one day she didn't get out of bed. They found her half-unconscious, soaked in blood. She looked like a shark had eaten the center of her. She never came back after that."

Annie peeled the foil away from a blue stick of gum. She snapped it in two and gave one half to me. The spearmint flavor burned my tongue. I savored the feeling. I didn't ask Annie how she managed to get ahold of this bit of contraband.

She pulled the cap off a Bic pen and wrote on the paper side of the gum wrapper. She passed it to me.

Jorge knocked that girl up. I saw him fucking her once. Now he's moved on to someone else, she wrote. I looked up at her, and followed her gaze across the room. Seraphine. I got a twisting feeling in my stomach. Jorge was always telling her how ugly she was. Men were weird. Weird and gross.

A few days earlier, Jorge had pinned Seraphine to the ground and sawed her hair off with a pocket knife. He was angry because she had braided her hair without permission. I was confused. I thought that once we reached a certain level we could wear our hair *down*; I didn't remember anything in the rules about braids.

Seraphine sobbed as he sheared her braids off one by one and piled them on the ground next to her. They looked like licorice whips to me. I was so hungry.

The nicks Jorge had made in Seraphine's scalp were healing slowly. Even so, she looked beautiful with her hair cut off. She looked like that model I'd seen in my mom's *Vogue* magazines, the one with the great smile and impossibly long legs. Alek….Alek Wek? Was that her name?

The scene replayed itself in my mind as I watched Seraphine dozing in her hammock. We had all just stood there watching while Jorge sat on her and hacked off her hair. But if I'd tried to stop him, it would've meant a trip to the dog cages. I had to watch out for myself; fuck anyone who would judge me for that.

"You gotta take care of you," Annie said. "That's the only way anyone gets out of here in one piece."

"Quit reading my mind," I said, folding her note into a tiny square.

Seraphine wasn't the only one who had to put up with perverted shit from the staff. We were segregated from the boys, but that didn't stop information from filtering through the walls and fences. A flimsy partition in one of the hallways was one place where girls and boys could trade information, so long as staff on either side weren't looking.

The other place was the dog cages. They didn't bother to separate us when they tossed us in and locked us up. When the tides came in, the waves on the not-too-distant shore provided cover for whispered conversations between cages. That's how Annie found out about the boy who'd been forced to strip while a schlubby male staffer hosed him down with icy water and scrubbed him with a toilet brush until his nuts were raw and bleeding.

We also heard rumors that the therapist on the boys' side liked to make them jerk each other off; if they couldn't get hard, he sent them to the cages. A female staffer got fired after Sra. Mondragon found out that she was having sex with four different boys. That staffer was a Level 6.

She'd graduated the program and stayed on as an employee.

I wondered how that would look on a resume:

Mystic Bay

Middle of Nowhere, Dominican Republic

Junior Staff

Helped troubled teens turn their lives around using a variety of techniques including:

- Screaming
- Hitting
- Starving
- Restraining
- Humping

Special skills: Screaming, yelling, making boys cry.

I pictured that staffer in a Dairy Queen uniform, screaming insults at customers lined up behind the counter.

I smiled.

Then I thought about Dairy Queen. Sweet, snow-white ice cream under ribbons of thick fudge and haloes of crushed pineapple.

"What are you thinking about?" Annie asked.

"Dairy Queen," I said.

She moaned and let her eyes roll back in her head. "I used to cut school on really hot afternoons and make my boyfriend buy me cherry-dipped cones. That first bite—cracking that sweet coating with my teeth—that was the best feeling."

"Are you guys talking about Dairy Queen?" asked Sophie, shadows pooling in her sunken cheeks. "Did you ever have one of those Mister Misty things? I love those. I used to get the lime ones. It gets so hot here, I fantasize about lime Mister Misty's all the time!"

Annie glanced over at Seraphine, who appeared to be dozing. "Do you suppose they have Dairy Queens in Haiti?" she asked.

Sophie nudged Seraphine awake and put the question to her.

Seraphine opened her eyes and shook her head in response to the question. "En Haïti, nous avons un dessert appelé blancmange. C'est un jello de noix de coco aux cerises et mangues. Si doux et frais."

Sophie translated: "She says in Haiti they have a dessert called 'blancmange' that's a coconut jello with cherries."

"Sounds good to me," Annie said.

Footsteps scraped against the pavement outside our door. We immediately stopped talking and went back to being dead-eyed robots.

I climbed into my hammock and shut my eyes. I imagined tasting Seraphine's dessert. I fell asleep imagining how it would taste: sweet and cool.

27

It was hard to keep track of time. At Epiphany Lake, I could tell by the changing seasons, but at Mystic Bay, the seasons didn't seem to change much. There was only bright, hot sun or heavy rain. A glimpse at the calendar on Sra. Mondragon's desk told me I'd been at Mystic Bay for four months.

I'd been in the program for a year.

That same week, Seraphine disappeared.

On a steamy, cloudy afternoon, before Seraphine vanished, Sra. Mondragon announced that a hurricane was minutes away from making landfall, and herded us over to the boys' side. As we crossed through the courtyard, we passed the big green tree we weren't supposed to touch. Seraphine scooped up two of the small green apples and shoved them into her mouth.

"You're eating!" Sra. Mondragon hissed at Seraphine. Her face was so thin, I could see all the muscles in her jaw. "How dare you eat when you're not authorized to!"

Seraphine's eyes blazed, black with defiance. A strange feeling rose up in my chest. Pride? Excitement? Admiration?

"Give it to me," Sra. Mondragon said, her hand outstretched, waiting for Seraphine to hand over a package of stolen candy. The sound of the waves crashing on the shore grew louder. We didn't have much time; the hurricane was almost here.

Seraphine showed Sra. Mondragon two empty palms. She swallowed and smiled. Sra. Mondragon looked stunned, her slack jaw frozen in place. She held her radio up to her lips and yelled into it, her voice barely audible over the rising winds.

Two men came running out into the courtyard just as Seraphine dropped to her knees and vomited, spewing undigested bits of green apple all over the place. The men restrained her and shoved her face into her vomit.

Wind tore glossy green leaves from the tree and shook the barbed wire fences. "Inside!" Sra. Mondragon shouted. We filed into a hallway that led to the boys' dorms. A few minutes later, the two men followed. Seraphine wasn't with them.

We climbed a dark stairway up to the second floor. From the veranda, I could see into the courtyard. Seraphine was still there, lying facedown under the tree, catching raindrops in the palm of her hand.

"She wouldn't get up," one of the men told Sra. Mondragon. "We had to leave her."

The storm lasted a few hours. Once she was certain it had passed, Sra. Mondragon led us back to our side. As I walked down the dark stairway, anxiety gripped me. I help my breath as we stepped out into the courtyard. A shiver rattled my spine.

Seraphine was gone.

I had a million questions about what happened to Seraphine, but I couldn't ask them. The staff made it a Category 5 violation to talk about her. You could lose all your points and be sent to the dog cages just for saying her name out loud.

That didn't stop the questions from churning around in my head.

Finally, two nights after her disappearance, I couldn't take it any more. I scribbled a note on one of Annie's contraband gum wrappers:

Is Seraphine dead?

Annie shrugged. She took the wrapper and pen from me, then handed them back.

Hospital? she had written under my question.

How can we find out? I wrote.

Annie put her hand on my thigh and shook her head. I bit back tears. I knew Annie was right. Hunting for answers would only make things worse.

Let's just assume she ran away right after the storm let up and leave it at that, Annie wrote. I nodded in agreement.

Even so, I struggled to get to sleep. I couldn't stop picturing Seraphine the way I saw her from the boys' veranda, face down on the pavement, brown jumpsuit soaked through. I focused on her hand, the one that was turned skyward. She was moving her fingers on that hand, so at least I could be certain that she was alive then.

Wasn't she?

Had I really seen her fingers move? Or was my mind making things up?

I forced myself to imagine Seraphine running away, running down the muddy road, running through the jungle, running all the way back to Port Au Prince.

It didn't help. No matter how hard I tried to steer my mind toward Seraphine's escape, it always veered back to that courtyard scene.

Maybe it was just the wind making her fingers move.

Two weeks after Seraphine vanished, the staff announced a change to the program. The higher-ups in the program didn't like what kids like Annie and me were doing; they called it "sitting." To encourage us to work our programs instead of waiting out the clock, they started a thing called an "exit plan." If you turned eighteen without finishing the program, you could either stay in until you did finish or take the "exit plan" which was fifty bucks and a bus ticket.

I couldn't believe it. They'd found a way to keep people in the program past the age of eighteen.

"They think I'm scared to take my fifty bucks and go make a life? Ha!" Annie laughed. "After this hole, I can survive anything. That includes never returning to the United States or seeing my family again. Shit, maybe I will take a boat to Cuba and apply for asylum."

"There's a thought."

"Really! It would be great PR for Castro. He'd be like, 'the excesses of capitalism turn Americans against their own children!' He'll be all over it."

"In that case, why don't we all go? Right now?"

Annie unwrapped a stick of gum. "Let's put a message in a bottle," she suggested. "Then maybe some guerilla fighters will come rescue us." She paused. "What?" she asked me.

"Maybe we could send a fax," I suggested, suddenly feverish with the thought of leaving this place.

"They have fax machines in Cuba?" Annie raised an eyebrow.

"There's got to be a Cuban embassy in Santo Domingo," I continued, ignoring her. "Maybe if we get a message to them—"

Annie punched my ribs. Our newest bunkmate, a program convert who'd recently transferred from a school that had been closed down, was staring at us. I shot a glare right back at her. *Go ahead, you little rat-faced bitch,* I thought. *Tell on me for making run plans.*

A few minutes later, that's exactly what happened. The night time guard came to tell us it was time for Shutdown and Rat Face piped right up. The guard spoke into his radio and within seconds two more guards arrived to haul Annie and me out to the cages.

Stars scattered across a cloudless sky so black it made them seem close enough to touch. The concrete floor of the dog cage was hot from baking in the sun all day. The rain that started a few minutes after the guard locked the gate was hot, too, but after it stopped a cool breeze came in off the ocean and chilled every inch of my body.

I shivered hard.

"*Deja de moverte,*" a guard hissed. I heard the snap of an electric current. Seconds later, a jolt passed through my body, like someone had jabbed me with a thousand scalding needles. I couldn't help it; I started to cry.

"*Callate*," the guard said, louder this time, his voice sounding like a steel shovel hitting cement, "shut up."

He hit me with another jolt. I felt the current race all the way up my spine, raising the hair at the nape of my neck. I bit the inside of my lip hard to keep from crying out loud but tears still leaked from my eyes. I saw a flash of Seraphine lying face down under the poisonous tree and another wave of tears erupted from the pit of my stomach. The spot on my hip where the cattle prongs had touched pulsed and throbbed. I wanted nothing more than to put ice on it.

I wish I could fall asleep and just not wake up, I thought.

But sleep didn't come. Somewhere in the dark courtyard, Annie was getting shocks of her own. I could hear her yelping and swearing. My stomach ached from hunger. I remembered a lesson from sixth grade geography. We each had to pick a country and write a report on it. I did mine on Japan and got points off for saying that their food sounded gross. LaKeisha did her report on Cuba and got an a-plus for making *dulce de leche* at home and bringing it in for the whole class to try. I told her later I thought it was unfair; Japanese desserts were made out of *beans* for God's sake.

As I lay twitching in my cage, I remembered that *dulce de leche*. It was smooth and sticky and sweet with that burnt flavor that is created when sugar turns to caramel.

I shut my eyes and played a movie in my head of sugar boiling and changing colors. I watched the liquid pour into pans to cool and be cut into squares. I dipped the caramels in chocolate, topped them with salt, rolled them in coconut. I decorated them with tiny marzipan flowers and thin slices of candied lemon peel. I covered them in chopped almonds and ate them three at a time.

I bit into a caramel and pulled it away from my face, watching a thick strand of caramel stretch stretch stretch without breaking once.

28

My electrical burns from the cattle prod took forever to heal. Annie's were even worse. Her skin blistered with infection. She didn't bother showing it to any of the staff because she knew they wouldn't do anything. She just gritted her teeth and plowed her way through the daily motions of Mystic Bay, even when she spiked a fever. I managed to sneak into the little closet where they kept all the "meds" and swiped a small packet of Advil and a tube of antibiotic cream. I knew it wouldn't be enough to help Annie's infection, but at least it made her feel a little bit better.

Her eighteenth birthday was coming up soon. Every time I thought about it I felt a bowling ball of sadness swell up in my abdomen. With Annie gone, I'd be all alone.

Annie figured out how she was going to use her exit plan. "I'll cash in the plane ticket," she said, "and use the money to rent myself a little place in Santo Domingo. I'll get a job as a waitress. I bet there are lots of places that need someone who speaks English. Maybe I can work at a resort."

She turned and looked at me. Her blue eyes had sunk deep into her head.

"You could come live with me," she said. Something that almost resembled a spark shone in her eyes. "When you get out of here."

"In three years?"

"You might get out sooner," she said.

"How? By working the program? I tried that. It didn't work."

"You'll think of something," she said.

A week and a half later, Annie was gone. I sank into a fog, trudging through each boring day that was no different from the last. I began to doubt whether I'd be able to hold out until my eighteenth birthday and take an exit plan like Annie did. Maybe I would have to play the game again and work the program even if I didn't believe in it. Or maybe I'd have to make myself believe it. The kids who believed were the ones who ascended quickly.

But I didn't *want* to believe.

A month after Annie left, a familiar face appeared at Mystic Bay. I couldn't believe my eyes.

Julie?

She'd put on weight since the last time I'd seen her and she looked better, but her eyes were red and raw, as if she'd been crying for hours. We traded glances as she passed me in the corridor. If she recognized me, I couldn't tell.

The next thing I knew, there was a lot of screaming and guards shouting. I turned just in time to see three large men tackle Julie. They bound her hands with plastic ties and hoisted her off the ground. She bled from her chin, shrieking as they hauled her off to the dog cages.

That night, the guards brought Julie into our section. She sat on the hammock that had been Annie's and stared at the wall. A sticky, violet scab covered her chin.

"Julie," I said to her. "Do you remember me?"

She raised her eyes slowly. I noticed that her left eye had a fading bruise, one that was three or four days old.

"Minnesota," was all she said.

"Right. You finished the program there. You graduated. You were done. All levels completed. How did you end up *here*?"

"I don't know," she said drowsily, "After I finished the program, my dad kept saying if I didn't get along with his girlfriend I'd have to do the program again. I didn't fight with her. I stayed in my room. But a week before their wedding, she called it off, said she wanted a man she didn't have to share with anyone. The next thing I knew, my dad said I had to do the program again."

"That's messed up," Sophie said.

Julie looked at me, her eyes covered in a wet glaze. "I don't know what I did wrong," she said. "He wouldn't say." Julie lightly felt her scab with her finger tips. It was swollen. I could see the pus gathering under it. "How did you end up here?" she asked me.

"I ran away and Crandell caught me."

"Crandell," she repeated, then said, "He's so gross."

"Tell me about it," I grumbled.

Julie leaned close to me and whispered, "He rubbed his penis against my butt once."

"Oh, how terrible," I said with mock concern, "He *rubbed* you? Big fucking deal. Let me tell you what he did to me. After I ran away, he threw me into the shed. Then he kicked me in my ribs. I was in too much pain to stop him when he took my pants off. Then he took *his* pants off. He made me lick him. It smelled like scorched butter. Then he shoved it inside me and grunted like a retarded donkey until he was finished.

"I wonder who else he did that to? Remember Treblinka? I bet he raped her. And that girl with the movie star parents, I bet he raped her, too. So how did you get away with not having Crandell's dick in you? Julie, you made it all the way through Epiphany Lake without getting dropped once."

Julie wouldn't look at me. She backed away but I stayed close to her until I had her cornered against the wall.

"You actually finished and got to leave. You were special. We were all supposed to be like you."

Julie squeezed her eyes shut. I remembered the night we played the Titanic game, when I told Julie to live.

"And now you're *here*. Special ones aren't supposed to end up here. It doesn't make any sense, Julie. None of this makes any sense."

Tears bubbled from my eyes, but none of the girls made any attempt to comfort me, because they heard the footsteps of the guard approaching. They knew they'd all be punished if the guards caught them doing anything other than pretending I didn't exist.

I climbed into my hammock and turned my back to everyone.

Two days later, Julie and I still hadn't spoken. I felt a sorry ache in my chest every time I thought about the way I'd gone off on her. I kept thinking back to Epiphany Lake, when she told me I'd never get out of there if I didn't tell the staff what they wanted to hear. She had tried to help me.

Not that it really mattered.

Julie hardly ate anything at breakfast. Jorge noticed her barely-touched oatmeal and asked her why she wasn't hungry but didn't say anything else. I glared at him. After the way he'd treated Annie and Seraphine for refusing to eat, I couldn't figure out why he was letting Julie getting away with it.

Julie's face was white except for the violet scab on her chin. Yellowish liquid oozed out from underneath it. She looked feverish and shaky. When we reached the exercise yard, she collapsed before the workout even started. Sra. Mondragon started in on her, shouting and kicking her in the ribs.

"She's sick you stupid bitch!" I felt lightheaded, shocked that those words had come from me. "She's not faking. She's not lazy. She's not a brat. She is fucking sick and needs a doctor."

"Do you want to go back to the dog cages?" Sra. Mondragon snarled.

"Go ahead and put me back there. I don't give a fuck."

She took her radio off of her belt, and I thought she was going to call someone to come take me away, but instead she clubbed me, bashing the heavy casing against my head just above my right ear. Everything went black.

When I came to, the stars were out. I'd missed a whole day.

A week passed. Sra. Mondragon visited. She gripped the chain link and rattled my cage. She said I could come out, then and there, if I would just apologize to her.

I said nothing.

Another week passed. Sra. Mondragon offered me the same deal. Again, I said nothing.

Then, the rain started. I didn't apologize after three days in the rain. On the fourth day, when I didn't apologize, Sra. Mondragon dragged me out of my cage and made me follow her to the main courtyard. She made me stand under the tree, next to the sign that said *Venenosa! No tocar!*

Hours later, I had blisters all over my skin, and I felt like I'd been swimming in paint thinner.

I didn't apologize.

When the blisters broke open while I lay in the sun, I didn't apologize. When a guard shocked me with the cattle prod because I was too uncomfortable to hold still, I didn't apologize.

Eventually, they stopped paying any attention to me. They brought me watery beans and took me to the bathroom twice a day. But they didn't care whether I'd learned my lesson, or was ready to get out of the cage.

"She can just stay there as long as her mother pays the bills," I heard one guard say to the other. I stopped counting the days and moved into a world that I created in my mind.

I replayed *Titanic* in my mind and cast myself as Rose, rewriting the script to suit me. In my version, Rose did not meet Jack while attempting to hurl herself off the back of the ship. Instead, I imagined myself in beaded silk, creeping down a dark staircase to the third-class deck, on a mission to find a girl who would be willing to slither into Cal's bed and create a terrific scandal in exchange for a generous sum of money. How horrified everyone would be if mother tried to force me to marry him after such a scene! I found a Parisian hooker who assured me she could humiliate Cal. I handed her the money and turned around; there was Jack, entranced by my beauty and my cunning plan.

The hooker held up her end of the bargain, allowing me to catch her in bed with Cal and loudly announcing my incredulity to the entire first class deck. In a fit of shame, Cal threw himself overboard and mother took to her bed. Jack and I spent the whole last day of the Titanic's journey having sex in the huge bed that had once belonged to Cal.

When the ship hit the ice, we tore my state room apart, looking for anything that would float and we cobbled together a makeshift raft. Instead of staying on the ship until it pulled us into icy water, we carried our raft to the head of the ship, to where the water was already over the top of the rails, and set it afloat. We sat on our raft, dry and cuddled together for warmth, until the Carpathia came to bring us home.

We docked safely in New York City, got married, moved to Brooklyn and opened a tiny cafe on the beach. Jack drew portraits for people on the boardwalk while I cooked fried fish and Irish stew. Comfort food to welcome home any third-class lost souls who managed to wash up on the shore.

I replayed this fantasy over and over, adding new twists, characters and recipes. Instead of Rose, I was a cook in the third-class dining room. When the ice hit, I refused to leave my crewmates even though Jack managed to secure a lifeboat for me. In this version, I died and he survived to tell his grandson my story. In another version, there was a horse on board, like in *The Black Stallion*. Jack and I followed it to safety as it swam through the choppy waters. Alone on an island, Jack figured out how to build a fire with just bits of flint, and I cooked fish we caught over open flames. We rode on the horse's back through the misty surf.

While we waited for the Carpathia, we were hungry. So hungry we no longer felt hungry. So hungry we stopped feeling hungry and then felt hungry again. At least I wasn't alone. At least I had Jack.

I had Jack until the air crackled with radio static or cattle prod shocks.

I am not here. I am on a raft in the North Atlantic. I am holding Jack. We're waiting for the Carpathia. We can see its lights. We navigate by our own stars.

I had no idea how long I'd been in my cage. My fantasies and food cravings became more like mirages or hallucinations. They seemed real, and they filled long stretches of time. One night, they tossed a boy into the cage next to mine. During a brief window of time, when the guard was doing something other than watching us, the boy whispered to me.

"Tell me: how do you do it?"

"Do what?"

"Stay out here for so long? For so many days in a row?"

How long had it been? I wanted to ask him but I was afraid to know the answer.

"You're, like, so hard," he said. "You're a legend to everyone in there," he jerked his thumb slightly, indicating the main school building.

"Just before is worse," I said, but I heard the guard's footsteps, so I couldn't say anymore.

He left his cage the next morning.

Carpathia.

Car - pa - thi - a.

The syllables played in my mind on a constant loop, like something I'd repeated in church a thousand times without ever knowing what it actually meant.

Car.

Pa.

Thi.

A.

I forgot what the word meant. A woman? A ship? A town in ancient Rome?

Car.

Pa.

Thi.

A.

Maybe it meant "seize the day," like in that Robin Williams movie with the kid who shoots himself because he can't do Shakespeare. Good thing that kid never had to come to a place like this.

Car.

Pa.

Thi.

A.

Car payment. Am I sixteen yet? I turned fifteen at Epiphany Lake. But I don't know what month it is or how long it's been since I got here.

Car.

Pa.

Thi.

The metal hinges on the cage door squealed. Sra. Mondragon stood there, holding the door open.

"Haddonfield," she said to me. "Get up."

I stared at her, waiting for some sort of explanation, but she just stood there, staring at me. I felt dizzy as I peeled my body off the hot concrete. My knees wobbled, and I caught myself against the chain link. I waited for some sort of punishment, but Sra. Mondragon just stood there, saying nothing. When I'd steadied myself, she led me back into the main building. The dim hallway felt cold, and it took a long time for my eyes to adjust.

I followed her to the main entrance, where I saw the figures of two men. With the courtyard sunlight to their backs, all I could see were their silhouettes. Was I being shipped off again? I wondered what could possibly be worse than Mystic Bay, but was afraid to make a list.

"Grace?"

The familiar voice stopped me cold.

"Dad?"

I stepped closer and saw his face clearly.

"What the fuck have you done to my kid?" he shouted. "She looks like she just got out of Auschwitz."

"I encourage you not to pull her out now," the man said. He was young-ish and tan. I didn't know who he was. "Our program is carefully calibrated. If she leaves now, there's no telling what the damage might be."

"Come on, Grace," Dad said to me, "let's go." He took hold of my wrist and did a double take, like he was surprised by how much smaller it was.

"Sir," the man said as my dad led me out to the courtyard.

"Save it," Dad said, without breaking his stride. "We're leaving."

We walked through the courtyard, past the *venenosa* tree with its toxic leaves and apples, past the row of staffers' cars, through the main gate. I turned and watched the gate close, the rambling white building blurring behind the black wrought iron bars. A shiver rattled my spine.

We got into a car and drove away. I watched Mystic Bay disappear in the side view mirror. I could hear my dad talking to me, but his words burned up in the air before they could reach me. The cane fields we passed melted into a thick wall of green.

In my mind, I was still at sea, on a raft, watching for the rails of a ship silhouetted against the breaking dawn.

Book 3

Last Day of School

1

Anesthesia is a heavy blanket. I am not asleep or awake, just drifting on a tingly cloud. In spite of it, I can still feel the pain. A wide stripe of blistered, throbbing, flame-bitten flesh stretches from my wrist to my elbow, like an opera glove. It's still hot. I wish I could pack it in ice.

I can hear people talking. Doctors, mostly. They talk about numbers. Milliliters of this. Grams of that. Percentages and rates. Third-degree, extensive tissue damage, concerned about circulation, more surgeries. It's like I've fallen asleep watching "ER."

I hear my dad. He doesn't talk to me because he knows it would annoy me. None of that cooing or "hey honey, I'm here" shit. He knows I hate that. I hear him talking to the doctors, though. He tells them he was on the phone with me just before the accident. They ask him questions but he doesn't know the answers to all of them.

He's telling them I smoke too much and am under a lot of stress. He doesn't tell them why.

Sometime later, the itching starts. The itching is almost worse than the pain. It's like being stabbed with needles or splashed with hot oil. There's no relief at all. I just have to grit my teeth and wait. The doctors say it's a good sign. It's a normal part of the healing process. My body isn't rejecting the skin graft. I'll recover.

Still, the itching. I haven't felt an itch this bad since Mystic Bay when I had a constant sunburn from baking all day in the dog cages. At least this time, the itching isn't all over and I don't have to wear a uniform made of cheap fabric that chafes the burns.

Another day passes. I'm not on as many drugs. I sit up in bed, eating Jello and watching reruns of *The Nanny* with my dad.

"Thanks for not calling her," I say, and that's all either of us says on the subject of my mom.

On the day I'm discharged, the doctors give me several prescriptions, a schedule of follow-up appointments, a detailed list of care instructions and a timeframe for returning to normal activities.

Dad drives me home. On the way, we stop at CVS. I sit in the car while he goes inside to get my prescriptions. He comes back with a large paper bag full of pill bottles and a giant lollipop.

"The doctors should have given you one," he says.

I laugh, though it's more like a snort. Laughing takes too much energy.

I peel back the cellophane and let the lollipop touch my tongue. I taste a burst of artificial fruit. I gnaw on it all the way home.

2

Just hours after leaving Mystic Bay, our flight touched down in Minneapolis. It was late spring there. I counted backwards; it was fall when I left Epiphany Lake. That meant I had spent six or seven months at Mystic Bay. 15 months total in the program. My sixteenth birthday had come and gone and so had most of my sophomore year.

Dad had an apartment on Aldrich in the top floor of an old house that had been converted to a duplex. I had a room of my own. A bed with brand new blankets and sheets. A shelf lined with books. A radio. A small TV. Fresh towels. A window that looked down onto the street below and a wooden fire escape.

I showered. The hot water and steam caressed my skin; I could almost feel all my pores opening at once. I scrubbed away the burnt skin that was peeling away from my arms and cleaned the dirt from under all of my fingernails. A clump of my hair came out in my hands when I went to wash it. My legs and armpits were covered with thick hair. The one thing my dad didn't have for me was a razor, but I wasn't sure I cared. I held a brand new bar of Irish Spring in my hand and held it under water until the cool scent flooded the room. I rubbed the pearly white lather all over my skin and watched it turn dark gray.

I got out when the water started to run cold. I wrapped myself in a soft towel and used another to dry my face, hair, and legs. I put on fresh clothes.

Dad had just come home with takeout from a Vietnamese restaurant on Hennepin Avenue.

"Feel better?" He asked.

I nodded. I stood by the kitchen table, waiting for permission to sit. Dad pulled my chair out for me.

"*Pour vous, madame,*" he said.

I waited for permission to eat.

"Grace, why aren't you eating?" He asked as he handed me an egg roll. I bit into the crisp, flaky wrapper. I felt the delicate cellophane noodles in the filling snap. The pork tasted sweet. I licked the oil from my fingertips.

That night, Dad said, "Sleep as late as you need to, Grace."

I burrowed under the covers and fell into a deep sleep, but during the night, I awoke with a start. Sweat gathered on the back of my neck and my heart raced. I glanced around in the dark, waiting for a flashlight beam to sweep the room. When my eyes adjusted, I noticed the shelf full of books and the small TV. I exhaled slowly, but I couldn't stop shaking.

I grabbed the little TV, turned it on with the volume on low, and burrowed under the covers, watching re-runs of *Rhoda* and *The Bob Newhart Show* until I finally managed to sleep again.

3

Two days after my release from Hennepin County Medical Center, my drugs have worn off. My burn throbs and itches constantly around the edges. I pace back and forth in my apartment to distract myself from the sensations. I'm anxious and bored. I grit my teeth and turn on the radio, changing the station every few minutes.

I'm supposed to be resting, but I feel like going for a run, or climbing onto the back of a thoroughbred, or getting in my car and just flooring it, paying no attention to the exit signs on the freeway.

I log onto the Epiphany Lake website. My name is still on it. I clear my cache and check the site again. My name is still on it.

I call my dad.

"My name is still on there," I say.

"I know," he says, "Sam is working on it."

"It's been almost three weeks."

"Grace, you shouldn't be worrying about this right now. You need to relax and focus on your recovery."

"What about work? What did Sam say about my job?"

"Grace…"

"Are they firing me? Did you tell them I don't care about Worker's Comp—that I just want my job back?"

"Grace, you are putting too much stress on yourself. This stress is going to make your healing take longer."

"Dad —"

"Gracious, take it easy. Read a book, watch a movie or take a nap. Forget about all this other stuff. It's not important right now."

"To me it is."

"Yeah, well, nothing is going to be resolved today or even by the end of the week. You know lawyers. Everything takes forever with them. You need to put this out of your mind for now and relax."

I promise Dad I will and hang up the phone. I paw through my DVD collection and open a random case. I put the movie on but I don't watch it. I go back to pacing while the theme from *The Godfather* fills the apartment.

I grab my phone and scroll through my emails. I find the one from the writer who wanted to interview me. I find her phone number under the signature line and call. Voicemail clicks on.

"This is Grace Haddonfield, chef at Saveur de Vie. If you still want to interview me, give me a call back. Let's set up a meeting."

Finally, I stop pacing. I order spinach in coconut curry and mango custard from a Nepali restaurant in Uptown. I settle onto the couch and pull a blanket up to my neck. I watch Michael Corleone explain Luca Brasi's negotiation techniques to Kay Adams.

I meet the writer, Gail, at the Daisy Chain Cafe. I chose this place because it's the only coffee shop I know of that also serves alcohol in the morning. I get there early and order a shot of whiskey to steady my nerves. Then I order a coffee and wait.

Gail arrives a few minutes later. She's wearing a black hooded sweatshirt and no makeup. I relax a little as she takes the seat across the table from me.

"I'm so glad you called," she says. "Everyone wants to know what happened. You know, with your arm."

"Well…"

"But we don't have to talk about that just yet. Why don't we start with what inspired you to become a chef?"

"Look, I'll answer any question you want, but I called this meeting because I need to set the record straight."

She leans in slightly and waits.

I fidget. My cheeks are flaming from the whiskey. "There's this school. Up north. Epiphany Lake Academy." I sip my coffee. My hand trembles a little, and I spill some on my hand. I let it run backward, staining my wrist.

"They put my name on their website saying that I went there."

I pause. Gail furrows her brow. Through the window behind her, I see a bus pull up across the street. It waits for someone to get on, then takes off, on its way downtown.

"And, did you go there?"

"Yes."

"So?"

I let out a long, slow breath. "They are claiming me as a success story. And I'm not one."

"But you're an amazing chef. Sounds successful to me."

"No, I mean, I am not *their* success story. That school…" I don't even know where to begin. "Epiphany Lake is a school for 'troubled teens.' They call it a 'therapeutic boarding school' but it's really a…"

"Like a reform school?"

"Yes," I nod. "Exactly." Then something inside me crumbles and the words rush to the surface. I tell her everything: the lockdown bunkhouses, the levels system, the Shed. Crandell grunting as he raped me on the Shed's cold dirt floor. Being taken in the middle of the night, first to Epiphany Lake and then to Mystic Bay. Seraphine disappearing during the hurricane. The countless days I spent lying face down on hot concrete.

I tell her about how I sometimes feel like I live entirely in the past, how that period in my life never really ended, how I think about it almost every day.

Gail's eyes shimmer. "Wow," she says.

"Yeah," I say. "I just wanted to make people understand that if I am successful it is *not* because of Epiphany Lake, or Crandell, or Mystic Bay or any of those fuckers."

Gail nods. The light on her tape recorder blinks. She writes something in a notebook. Behind me, a latte steamer hisses.

"I guess that's why I was always trying to get myself fired."

"What do you mean?" Gail asks.

"I put weird stuff on the menu, like pig snouts, because I secretly wanted to get fired. I mean, I didn't want to get fired, but…you know."

"Sure, I get what you're saying. But one thing I don't get is if you were trying to get fired, why didn't you just make *gross* food?"

I drain the last of my coffee and set the cup down. "I could never do that. Serving people bad food is a form of torture. At Mystic Bay, we had to eat boiled chicken with the feathers still in it. Bad food is a line I won't cross. For any reason."

Gail smiles a little and writes furiously in her notebook. "There's so much talk these days about ethical food. You know, sustainable sourcing, farm-to-table, local, organic, yadda yadda yadda. This is the first time I've heard anyone mention the *taste* of food as an ethical issue."

I shrug. "I hadn't thought of it like that. I just think it's wrong to serve bad food."

"So what happened the day of the fire?"

I stare into my coffee cup. "My dad called. He told me about my name being on Epiphany Lake's website. I can't really describe what happened after that call. I remember feeling very cold. I kind of went outside of myself. Next thing I remember is being in the hospital."

"Wow…" she says. "What a story. I do have one more question."

"Shoot."

"Is it a religious school? The name sounds religious, but nothing you've described suggests that it is."

I shake my head. "It's secular. The 'epiphany' you're supposed to have is that you're a terrible, ungrateful brat and that you have to change your ways."

"Jesus," she mutters. "Before we go, can you tell our readers what they can expect to see on the menu at Saveur de Vie?"

"Oh…well, I was thinking of getting back to basics. Adding a few classic Brittany-style dishes to the menu like steamed artichokes and mussels with French fries. That's *if* they let me go back to work. That's sort of…in question…right now."

Gail squeezes my wrist. Her hand is warm and dry. "They'd be crazy not to." Three days later, the article goes live.

How Chef Grace Haddonfield Survived an Abusive Boarding School and Became a Culinary Star

4

Dad took Mom to court and argued that he should have full custody. Dad's lawyer showed the judge pictures my dad had taken of Mystic Bay, of the barbed wire, the metal bars, me in my jumpsuit.

"It is unconscionable that any parent would pay to have their child live in conditions that are worse than those of most American prisons. This young woman has more than earned the right to decide how she wants to spend her time and with whom."

I told the judge I wanted to stay with my dad. My mother's lawyer protested, but the judge ignored him and spoke directly to my mother: "Frankly, ma'am, I don't understand why you are fighting to get your daughter back into your house after you went to such lengths to get her out of it. If I allow her to live with you, I fear it may only be a matter of time before she is quietly sent away again. I'm ruling in favor of the parent who has truly demonstrated that he wants to be one."

Mom made a big show of crying and trying to hug me, but Dad and I just walked out of the courtroom. That was the first time I felt like I knew what my life was going to be: I was going to live with my dad and finish school. No more heel-toe lines, self-help tapes, hammocks or isolation sheds. No more being told I was the most selfish kid alive. No more screaming, no more crying.

At least, not while I was awake.

5

The first person to call me after the article goes live is Jess.

"Why didn't you tell me?" There's disco playing in the background. She's calling from the gym. Suddenly, I wish I could be there, at the gym, freezing my toes on the foam mat instead of laid up at home waiting for my new skin to come to the surface.

"I was afraid you wouldn't believe me." I dab aloe gel onto my arm. The new skin is bright pink and shiny.

"Man, of course I would have believed that shit! Don't you think my folks threatened to ship me off when they first found out I was gay? I know about those schools."

In the background, on Jess's end of the line, I hear someone say, "Are you talking to Grace? Tell her we miss her!"

Fuck, I think to myself. *I'm going to cry.*

"Man," Jess mutters, "I'm so sorry you had to go through that shit."

"Thanks," is the only reply I manage to squeak out before an ugly sob escapes my throat.

"So what's next?" she asks.

"What are you talking about?"

"We're going to confront them, right? We're going to drive up there and set all the kids free?"

"Yeah, right," I laugh. I picture driving up to Epiphany Lake in Jess's noisy old GTO, blowing past the "Keep Out" signs on the driveway.

Some staffer would be there to turn us away at the gate, but we'd fight our way past them. Crandell would saunter out of his hole, his gut hanging over his belt, red-faced and sweating. He'd demand to know who had invaded his domain. Jess would get him in a rear-naked choke and bring him down to the ground where I would stomp on his crotch until he passed out. I would snatch the keys from his belt and unlock every door on campus, starting with the door to the Shed.

"You know what?" I say. "Let's do it."

On Survivors of the Shadows, the link to Gail's article has over 100 comments. So often, our stories are hushed up, swept under the rug, hidden in plain sight. Even though there are thousands of us, no one believes us, so whenever one person's story gets some attention, or a school we've never heard of goes down in flames, we know it's a win for all of us.

In my living room, I sit at my computer while the morning sun streams through the windows and warms my face. A half-moon of lemon floats in a steamy mug full of Prince of Wales tea. I sip the mild, amber liquid as I click on my SOS inbox which is full of private messages from other survivors.

NOLAJack: I'm so fucking proud of you. You were very brave to tell your story like that. It's so great to see you kicking ass. By the way, I hope you didn't read the comments on that article. There are a couple of industry shills calling you a liar in the comments section. The journalist believed you though, and so will a lot of the people who read it. That's what counts!

Unicorn203: Hey I don't think we've met, but I was at Epiphany Lake in '96 what a shithole. Crandell can suck it!

AndyAndy: Remember me? I used to be Andrea. I go by Andy now. Man, you were so badass for running away and swimming all the way across the fucking lake! You scared Crandell shitless because after that, it was a cat 5 just to look at the lake or to mention your name. But everybody knew about it. You were our hero and you still are!

BisousFromParis: Sorry for my English. I go to Mystic Bay with you. I want you to know I not die. In storm, they leave me outside and I run away. I walk all the way back to Haiti and tell police. They help close down Mystic Bay. I live in Paris now with husband and daughters. We own little dress shop. If you come in Paris, please visit me! Gros bisou, Seraphine.

The message from Seraphine nearly makes my heart stop. My hands tremble as I type my response.

Seraphine,

Je suis très heureux savoir que tu est bien vivant. J'espère que pourrons nous rencontrer bientôt à Paris. Tes filles sont trop belles!

Almost immediately, I receive a response:

Tu parle français! Génial! Rends-moi visite et écris-moi souvent!

I think back to that day, when Seraphine lay face down in the rain under the manchineel tree in the path of the hurricane. For fifteen years, I've seen Seraphine lying on the concrete and, after the storm lifted, the empty spot that she had vanished from. Now I can see her waiting for all of the guards to go inside, picking herself up and dashing toward the gate in sandals that were too big for her petite feet. I see her running through the heat and humidity, her skin seared by manchineel venom, her brown jumpsuit soaked with sweat. I remember the fire in her eyes when she sank her teeth into the poison apple. Jorge's *princesa* became a rebellious Snow White, eating the apple to spite the wicked and waiting for the kiss of rain to wake her from sleep.

Tears roll down my face. Seraphine and Treblinka and I—we all defied them, and we all survived. If they beat us harder, it was only because they couldn't break us. Even though I haven't heard from Treblinka in years and I can't remember her real name, and even though Seraphine is thousands of miles away, I feel like they are all in the room with me.

As I dry my eyes, I think of Jess. I realize the reason I've been drawn to her all along: she's defiant too. *We're a family of misfits,* Jess once said. She was half right. We're a family, but we're not misfits. There's a lot of us, and we fit right in.

6

Dad got me a tutor who worked with me all through the summer so I'd be able to start my junior year on time. When I wasn't studying, I was cooking. Early one morning, I woke up from a dream and couldn't get back to sleep. I went to the fridge to find something to drink, but the only thing I could find was a half-empty pack of bacon.

One by one, I took the limp strips of bacon out of the pack and laid them gently in a frying pan. I turned on the heat and watched the opaque white fat slowly turn translucent. The flat strips rippled as they bubbled in hot grease. I removed the strips to a paper towel to drain, and I noticed that the fat left in the pan was the color of amber. Too pretty to throw away. I poured it into a small jar and tucked it into the fridge.

"I'm sorry," I said as my dad entered the kitchen, his eyelids droopy and his hair pointing in three different directions. "Did I wake you?"

He nodded and picked up a bacon strip. I watched him bite into it.

"That," he said, "is the best bacon I have ever had."

A few hours later, I went to the library to check out cookbooks and then to the grocery store with cash that Dad had given me. I bought a brisket, fresh dill, heavy cream, a pound of white button mushrooms and egg noodles. For hours, I slow-roasted the brisket. When it was cooked and tender, I let it rest while I cooked the mushrooms and a diced onion in some of the broth that had cooked off the meat. Then, I sliced the meat and added it to the mushrooms, slowly mixing in the heavy cream and sprinkling in fresh dill. Gradually, the meat juice and the cream transformed into a thick, silky gravy. I drained the egg noodles just as Dad returned home from work. We ate our Beef Stroganoff in silence.

From then on, I did all the grocery shopping and cooking for my dad and me.

In September, I started my 11th-grade year at South High, the school where I had almost completed one semester of 9th grade before two kidnappers came in the middle of the night to take me away.

South High was a flat brick building. The first two floors had no windows. The halls were well-lit, but when I stepped inside after being out in the bright sun, they seemed dark at first. Banners commemorating state championships for various sports hung from the ceiling. Kids spilled out in every direction, carrying backpacks, duffle bags, instrument cases and skateboards. There were no lines. Boys and girls traded glances. Laughter seemed to echo all throughout the hallway. I watched a pair of girls squeal and rush to hug each other, reunited after the long summer.

I shuddered. The walls seemed to melt and swirl around. It made my head hurt. *Be quiet*, I wanted to tell them all. *They'll punish us all. We'll all have to do burpees in the sun until we vomit.*

I felt faint. A boy in a soccer jersey asked me if I was ok. When he touched me, I panicked and tried to run, but there were too many kids in the hall. The lights slowly went out. When they came back up, I was in the nurse's office, holding an ice pack to my forehead.

"Feeling any better?" the nurse asked. "First days can be rough." She handed me a Dixie cup full of water.

"Can I call my Dad?" I asked. She nodded and handed me the phone. I punched his work number into the plastic keys. I let the cord twist around my fingers while I waited for it to ring. When my dad came on the line, I explained what was going on.

"Grace," he said, "those things are *normal*. That's how school is *supposed* to be. No one is going to get hauled off to a cage for talking in the hallway."

"You promise?"

ELIZABETH SOWDEN

"If that happens, they'll have to deal with me."

I hung up the phone and finished my water. I held onto the Dixie cup, unsure what to do with it. The nurse extended her hand and took the cup. I walked out.

Later that day, I ran into Mr. Kyeong in the hall. He was standing outside his class room, adjusting a poster on the wall. A blast of ice ran up my spine. I was sure he knew about the story I'd told about him at Epiphany Lake, the one about us having sex. I was sure he'd be angry if he saw me. I hurried past.

"Grace!"

I turned. Mr. Kyeong had notice me. I froze. He walked toward me.

"It's so great to see you!" he said. His hand landed gently on my shoulder. I tried to not to flinch. "Will you be in my American Lit class next semester?"

"Yes," I said, barely managing to cough out the word.

"Great!" he said, and then ducked back into his classroom. I found my classroom for American History and slid into a seat in the back.

How was it possible that Mr. Kyeong didn't know? How was it possible that my mom didn't turn the whole thing into a media circus with her at the center of it? She was convinced that I had slept with my teacher and that was the reason I deserved to be sent away. Yet, somehow, the whole sordid story had stopped with her?

I sat in class until the bell rang, then went to my next one.

At lunchtime, I wandered around outside. Kids sat in the grass, clustered in groups. I spotted LaKeisha. She was wearing a pink dress and a pink headband that matched. She covered her mouth when she laughed at something a boy said. I didn't walk over to her. Instead, I flattened myself against the wall, the school's bricks pulsing with late-summer heat.

"You want a smoke?" asked a kid with green hair.

"What?" I asked. I pictured him in a brown jumpsuit, his cheeks stained with tears because all of his neon hair had been shaved off.

"It will help you calm down," he said. He held out the pack. One cigarette stuck out above the others. I took hold of it between my thumb and forefinger and eased it out of the pack. He took a yellow plastic lighter out of his pocket and rolled the metal wheel. The flame merged with the end of the cigarette, giving its end and orange glow. I hesitated. The kid nodded. I noticed his eyes were brown. I inhaled and immediately coughed out most of the smoke. Still, the boy was right. I did feel calmer. I took another drag.

"The little store on Cedar will sell them to you without asking to see ID," he said.

That afternoon, I skipped 6th hour and found the little store on Cedar Avenue. I bought two packs of American Spirit cigarettes. When I got home, I opened my bedroom window and crawled out onto the fire escape where I sat in the sun and smoked. If mom caught me doing this, she'd send me back to Mystic Bay. But Dad, he wouldn't do that, not after getting me out of there.

When I saw my Dad's car approaching, I stubbed out my cigarette and stuffed it into a small crack in the floorboards.

I learned the truth about the Mr. Kyeong story a few weeks later. I still had a key to my mother's house, and I went over there one afternoon after school to pick up a few things I'd left behind. While I was there, I decided to slip into her office and log onto her computer. It was a Gateway that took up nearly all the space on her desk, and she had left it on. She'd left her email account open, too. I searched for Crandell's name and found several emails. I found one dated January 3rd, 1999— two months after I arrived at Epiphany Lake.

The subject line read: Your Daughter's Confession

Mrs. Haddonfield,

I encourage you not to go to the authorities with this information. There will have to be an investigation and that will

disrupt your daughter's therapy. I think we can agree that her therapy is the most important thing. We don't want a bunch of detectives and lawyers up here. They would just get in the way. Call me ASAP if you need more convincing.
  John Crandell
  Owner
  Epiphany Lake Academy

That's why Mr. Kyeong didn't seem to know anything about the story I'd told—because he didn't. My mother had followed Crandell's instructions and let the story stop with her. I scrolled down to see the message that my mother had written to Crandell.

Mr. Crandell,
  I am incensed at that teacher for his statutory rape of my daughter.

A hard shudder rattled my spine. The words *statutory rape* on the glowing computer screen made the sound of Crandell's hog-like grunting echo in my mind. I wrapped my arms around my chest and kept on reading.

I am going to take this matter to the police, and then I am going to sue the school district for allowing this to happen. Thank you for getting my daughter to come clean about all of her lies. I cannot tell you how much better I feel knowing that I have been right all along.

Below that, there it was:
Everything I'd said about Mr. Kyeong, neatly typed in Courier New and cut-and-pasted into a 5-page email. As I scanned through the details—most of which I had forgotten—of my made-up affair with Mr.

Kyeong, I wondered how my mother could actually believe any of them. Did she really think I had sex with Mr. Kyeong on his desk in the middle of the school day? Or that he performed oral sex on me in an abandoned house at 7 o'clock in the morning?

I cannot tell you how much better it makes me feel to know I was right...

I printed out the email and carefully tucked it into a folder and zipped it into my backpack. I was about to leave, but instead, I scrolled down further in my mother's inbox. I found another email, dated August 1998.

Re: Help With Teen Daughter
Dear Mrs. Haddonfield,

Thank you for your inquiry! Epiphany Lake Academy is a therapeutic boarding school dedicated to helping young people turn their lives around. We can certainly help your daughter learn how to express gratitude and help her remember how great it is to be a loving child to her parents.

We can take her at any time. We recommend that you do not tell her about this ahead of time as she might try to run away. Instead, please follow up with American Transport Services and schedule a pick-up. ATS is a separate entity from us and will charge an additional fee. However it is very affordable.

When you are ready to start your daughter on this journey, call us back with your credit card handy and we will take care of the rest.

Looking forward to working with your family!
Sincerely,
John Crandell.

August. I hadn't even met Mr. Kyeong in August. I had started early morning swim practices, but I hadn't yet started school. This was three and a half months before the cop brought me home from the abandoned house, before mom forced the school to take me out of Mr. Kyeong's class. Before the scissors, before the hair dye. Before all of it.

She was going to send me away anyway. But if it was never about Mr. Kyeong, then what was it about?

I left my mother's computer on, with Crandell's email up on the screen. Then I tossed my key on to the kitchen table and walked out.

7

"You're sure you want to do this?" My dad asks when I tell him about my plan to revisit Epiphany Lake with Jess.

"You think it's a bad idea?" We're sitting on the same roof where I used to smoke cigarettes after waking up from nightmares. Dad opens a bag of Twizzlers and hands me one.

"Not at all," he says. "I just think it could be tough on you. I want to make sure you have thought it through."

I bite into the chewy black rope, savoring the fake anise flavor. "Other people have done it. They said it helped them a lot." I neglect to mention that most of the stories I've heard from people who visited their old schools featured weedy, crumbling buildings—schools that had long been shut down and abandoned. Still, I knew it was something I needed to do.

The sun is setting, layering the sky with soft tangerine and lavender clouds. Traffic gathers at stoplights on Hennepin Avenue, and beyond that, office lights twinkle in the windows of downtown skyscrapers. The smell of pizzas baking in nearby restaurant ovens makes me hungry for more than licorice.

"Well, whatever happens," Dad says, lightly punching me on the shoulder, "I'll be there with bail money."

"Dad?" I ask.

"What?"

"Did mom ever tell you why she sent me away?"

"You mean that story you made up about your teacher?"

I shake my head. "I mean before that. Did you know she was thinking of sending me away before all that stuff happened? During the summer?"

"No," he says, tying a knot in a Twizzler, "She wasn't speaking to me then. My lawyer was trying to work out custody, and she kept stonewalling. Why are you thinking about this now?"

"It's just that...she decided to send me away first and found a reason later. She sent me away because she wanted to. But why did she want to?"

Dad pulls on the ends of the licorice knot until one of them breaks. "Grace, if I understood your mother, I'd still be married to her. But there is one thing about her that I can tell you: she was like a porcupine. She'd make you regret getting close to her. But then she'd wonder why no one wanted to be around her."

I imagine my mother as a small, woodland creature with its black-and-white quills erect as it quakes in a tree. I laugh inwardly, but my smile quickly fades. I think about all the invitations I've turned down, all of the people in my life who I've never allowed to get too close.

"Am I a porcupine?" I ask.

"No, Grace, you are not a porcupine."

"I'm serious, Dad."

"So am I! Look, if anything, you're more like a turtle. You retreat sometimes. You hide in a shell that's hard on the outside. But with your mom, it's like...even when she's not sticking you with her quills, she's always reminding you that she has them and isn't afraid to use them."

"Wow," I say. "We have tortured the shit out of this metaphor."

"Yeah," Dad replies, "maybe we should have this conversation at the zoo." Dad puts an arm around my shoulders.

"Dad, did you know that you can make calves' heads taste like turtle meat?"

"Um, no, I did not know that."

"Turtle soup was considered a delicacy in Victorian England, but turtle meat was too expensive for most people to buy, so they made mock turtle soup of of calves' heads. They would scoop the brains out and then stick the entire head in a stock pot and boil it. Then, they would roll the brains into little balls and fry them and plop them in the soup, sort of like Matzo balls."

"That sounds really weird."

"If I put that on the menu at Saveur de Vie, do you think people would eat it?"

"Grace, if *you* made that, people would line up around the block for it."

8

I gave the email I printed from my mom's computer to my dad's lawyer who brought it to the attention of the Roseau County prosecutor. Though the criminal investigation and civil lawsuit we tried to bring against Epiphany Lake Academy eventually fizzled out, I missed so much school going to depositions and hearings that during my senior year, I decided to drop out and get a GED.

Two weeks later, my diploma arrived in the mail. That same day, I caught the number 6 bus and rode it downtown where I transferred to the 17 and went all the way to Northeast. It was cloudy but warm. As the bus crossed the Hennepin Avenue bridge, I looked down at the churning, slate-grey waters of the Mississippi. A year later, I would remember this moment while standing on a bridge overlooking the Seine.

I got off the bus and walked two blocks to Marek's Tavern, which was dark inside except for all the neon. A jukebox faithfully cranked out rock songs from the '70s.

"You look a little young to be in a bar," said a middle-aged waitress.

"I just want to apply for the line cook job," I replied. "It just says I need a high school diploma. It doesn't say how old I have to be."

"Take a seat at the bar," she said. "I'll get you an application to fill out."

After I filled out the application, a husky man with a white hair and a greasy apron appeared behind the bar and picked it up without saying anything to me. I watched his face as he looked it over.

"You're seventeen?" he asked.

"Only for another two weeks," I replied.

"Why do you want to work in a grease pit like this?" His voice sounded gruff.

"I like to cook."

"Tell ya what, kid," he said, setting the paper down and looking me in the eye. "Come back tomorrow. If you can stand the heat, the job's yours."

The next day, I worked my first shift at Marek's Tavern. I spent hours on my feet, cutting potatoes and buttering hamburger buns. By the time I went home, my feet ached so bad I could barely walk to the bus. Grease clung to my hair, and a small burn on my wrist throbbed. My clothes reeked of French fries. Once I got home, I fell asleep right away, and for the first time in months, the only thing I saw in my dreams was Marek's deep fryer.

9

When Jess arrives to pick me up, she's got all kinds of weird shit in the trunk of her car: an axe, chains, dry ice, blankets, gallon jugs of water, a pair of welder's masks, wire cutters, bolt cutters, box cutters, matches, lighter fluid, a sack of charcoal and a grocery bag full of Doritos.

"Do you always drive around with these things in your car?" I ask.

"I didn't know what we would need, and I wanted to be prepared."

"Oh, good. We can go to Burning Man after this."

"Bring the Doritos up front. Those are for the trip."

I toss my backpack into the trunk and grab the grocery bag. Jess rips open a bag of Nacho Cheese Doritos and steps on the gas.

On the drive up north, Jess and I talk about movies, jiu-jitsu, music from the '90s—anything but Epiphany Lake. We argue over whether Eddie Vedder was a better singer than Billy Corgan. We debate the impact that Kurt Cobain's music had on the bands that came after him.

"It's because he shot himself," I say. "They all wanted to be him, so they wrote depressing music."

"Kurt's music was pretty depressing."

"No it wasn't."

"What about that song about him being homeless or the one about how his parents didn't want him?"

"A song can be *about* something depressing without *being* depressing. That's my point. Bands like Stain'd and Seether wrote maudlin dirges that leave you feeling like you just murdered your dog."

"And that's Kurt's fault?"

"Shooting yourself while doped up on heroin is pretty maudlin, don't you think?"

"So why didn't people write depressing music after Jimi Hendrix aspirated his own barf?"

"Well that was an accident. It's not like he left a note."

We pass a dense pine thicket. My stomach tenses. I swallow a mouthful of spit, willing myself not to vomit. I shut my eyes and lean against the window.

"You ok?" Jess asks.

I nod. My heart slams against the walls of my chest. My clavicle aches. "We're getting close," I tell her.

"You sure you want to do this? We don't have to."

I swallow hard, and I turn toward her. The sunlight makes her eyes extra blue, like ocean water, like the clear Dominican sky that I burned under for so many hours.

"We're doing this," I say. Jess nods.

As we get closer, my chest is a mosh pit. The only sound I can hear is my own blood sloshing back and forth in my veins. I point out the turn to Jess and swallow a mouthful of hot, bitter bile as she turns the wheel. Just as we pass the first "Keep Out" sign, I tell Jess to stop the car. I open the door and take a few steps into the woods. I don't stop vomiting until there's nothing left but water.

I get back in the car and shove a stick of Juicy Fruit into my mouth. Jess keeps driving, gravel crunching under her tires. The roar of her loud pipes provides an odd comfort. The canopy of tree branches begins to thin out and the boxy brown bunkhouses come into view. My whole body is vibrating.

"See that?" I say to Jess, pointing to a small white box above the doors on one of the bunkhouses. "That's an alarm. They all have those. Those fuckers blast like an air raid sirens if someone tries to escape."

A row of Level 1 kids trudges toward the main lodge on their way to lunch.

"How are we going to get in?" Jess says as she parks the car near the locked gate.

"Call them," I say. "Tell them you're dropping off your kid."

"Just like that? Don't I need an appointment?"

"Fuck no. They don't give a fuck about anything as long as they get paid. Just call them. And hand me those sunglasses."

I slip the sunglasses on while Jess makes the call. The gate opens and we walk through it. My legs are shaky, but Jess is by my side, her hand tightly gripping my tricep, holding me upright.

As we step inside the bunkhouse, the smell takes me back: dirty socks and rancid mayonnaise. A staffer gives Jess a clipboard full of intake forms and ushers us into a room. As soon as the door closes, scenes from my past flash in my mind. I remember being naked in this room, forced to the floor, a strange woman's fingers inside me.

"What is that sound?" Jess asks. "Some sort of tape recording?"

"A self-help tape," I reply. "Tony Robbins or somebody. They play those at every meal."

"It's so loud! I can't even understand the words."

"It's so you can't think."

"Jesus Christ, Grace," Jess says, "this place is *creepy.*"

I snicker a little. "No shit," I say.

The door opens again and the shadow of a fat man falls across the floor. I stand up and shove the sunglasses up to my forehead.

"Hello, Crandell," I say. "Remember me?"

It takes a moment to register, then he moves in for a hug. "Grace! Grace Haddonfield! It's so great to see you!"

I shove the first two fingers on my right hand into the notch of soft flesh at the base of his throat, forcing him to keep his distance.

"Don't touch me," I say. "This isn't some happy fucking reunion."

"What's going on?" Crandell cocks his head to the side, feigning confusion.

"I want you to take my name off of your website. Immediately."

His face darkens, and I flash back to that morning in his truck after he caught me trying to run away.

"Haven't you ever heard of freedom of speech? Besides, it's not like it isn't true. You were a student here."

"I was a *prisoner* here. And it's *not* true that this place had anything to do with my career."

"You can't prove that."

I take a step closer to him. I notice the small grey hairs poking out of his face and the wrinkles around his eyes. His shoulders have stooped a bit.

"Take it down."

"Now, Grace," he says, his voice treacly with condescension. I watch his hand come toward me, like he's going to grab my collar. I block with my left hand and pass his arm to my right, completing an arm drag. Without even thinking, I step to the side and drop him onto the floor. He grunts. I yank the walkie-talkie out of his belt, pry the battery out and smash the radio against the wall.

"Jess, keep him here," I shout as I run down the hall.

"What are you doing?" She asks.

"There's a circuit breaker panel that controls the whole electric grid for the school. It's somewhere in this building."

"Grace —"

"Just keep him there! Don't let him up."

I run through the dingy hall, past the cafeteria, through the kitchen where a vat of grey chicken legs boils on a dirty stove. I find the closet and rip the door open. The panel has a small padlock on it, but I pull on it hard enough to make the flimsy shank snap off. I flip every breaker. A shiver runs down my spine as the self-help tape goes silent.

A whisper of confusion rises from the cafeteria as I run into it. Fifty dead-eyed kids look up at me like they're slowly waking out of a fog.

"It's over," I say. "You're free. Get out of here. Run and don't stop running. No matter what happens, it will be better than this. I promise."

I run back down the hall, grab Jess, and run back to the car. Before Jess can throw the car into reverse, I tell her to stop.

"Pop the trunk," I command.

"Grace, we've got to get out of here."

"Just do it!"

I grab the axe Jess packed and run back in, past the main lodge. I see some male staffers and upper levels charging toward me, but they freeze in their tracks when they see the blade of my axe. I can hear people shouting, staffers on their radios and kids in the cafeteria, but all I see is the Shed.

The axe starts to feel heavy as I run. My biceps burn from holding it tight to my chest. As the Shed gets closer, so does its smell. Piss. Shit. Vomit. Bleach. That ugly, squat building. I can hear someone crying, but I can't tell if it's coming from a kid in the Shed, or if it's a sound from the past, a ghost on the wind.

Every bone in my body shakes when I'm face to face with the door, but I plant my feet and swing the axe until the wood splits and the door swings open. I hear sirens on the main road.

The Shed is every bit as dark as I remember. There's just enough light to make out the form of a young boy cowering in the corner, his knees pulled up to his chest.

"You're free," I say to him. "Go." I'm out of breath. His limbs unfold slowly. He stands up. He looks like he's not even twelve-years-old. He probably weighs less than seventy pounds. His cheeks are sunken in, and I wonder how long they've been keeping him in here. He's so pale. Three months? Four?

"You don't have to be in here anymore," I say. He walks toward me and throws his spindly arms around my waist. Then he lets out a loud cry and makes a mad dash for the lake.

When I get back to the car, there's a Sherriff's truck parked next to it, and Jess is sitting in the back seat. Word has spread that the electricity is out and kids are pouring out of every building, screaming, running, singing, roughhousing. A trio of girls dances near the main lodge, singing "fuck Crandell" over and over. Through an upstairs window, I can see a boy and girl making out in one of the bunkhouses. The young boy I freed from the Shed is down by the lake, splashing on the shore.

A deputy sheriff approaches me, his handcuffs open. I surrender my axe.

"This is some mayhem you caused," he says as he puts the cuffs on me.

"There was a sheriff just like you when I was a kid," I tell him. "I ran away from here. I hid on a property across the lake. Crandell came to get me and the owners of the property called your office. A young sheriff just like you let Crandell bring me back here. You know what he did? He raped me. He kept me locked up for two weeks, then shipped me off to an island where I almost died. That was fifteen years ago. How many kids do you suppose he's raped since then? How many more have to go through that before your office does it's job and shuts this hellhole down?"

The officer furrows his brow and lowers his head a little. I lean a little closer and speak in a softer voice.

"You know what this place is. You know what goes on here. You know that someday it has to end. If not now, then when?"

He looks into my eyes and slowly lets out a sigh. Without breaking eye contact, he speaks into the radio on his shoulder.

"Send some backup," he says, "so we can execute a search of the property."

An inaudible response comes through his radio.

"Copy that," he replies.

"You can't search this property," Crandell yells, "you need a warrant." Crandell's rictus is the same one he wore the morning he caught me running away, but the officer's shadow dwarfs him, shrinking him down into a defeated Rumplestiltskin.

"Sir," the officer says, "this is a public safety issue concerning the welfare of minors. We don't need a warrant. Step aside, or we'll have to arrest you for obstruction of justice."

A smile spreads across my face, and I feel as if my feet have risen six inches off the ground. The officer smiles back; his cheeks flush a little. He gently helps me into the back of his truck, protecting me from hitting my head as I slide in next to Jess.

Through the windshield of the squad car, I can see that the power has been switched back on and that the staff are trying to regain control of the kids. The officers are going to see it all. Even if they arrest Crandell, they probably won't be able to prosecute him, or if they do, he'll just get a slap on the wrist. He'll be able to change his name, set up another school somewhere in Montana or Wyoming and rake in more millions while raping a new generation of young girls. The thought is like a black cloud pushing its way into my mind, but I force it out as Jess nudges me with her elbow.

I look over at her. Jess's blue eyes glimmer like hot sun on a lake.

"We got the bastard," she whispers.

Jess grins at me. I grin back. We ball up our cuffed hands and bump fists.

Author's Note

I remember hearing about the troubled teen industry for the first time in the mid-to-late nineties, when people like Maury Povich and Montel Williams would interview teary-eyed parents whose teenage children were laying waste to their otherwise-happy homes. Montel or Maury would welcome the teen to the sound stage, at which point the audience would loudly boo while the teen defiantly strutted for the cameras. By the end of the segment, the teen would be crying and passively accept the "gift" of being sent to a boot camp or boarding school designed to rehabilitate "troubled teens."

While tawdry daytime TV shows generate artificial conflicts to hook viewers, the programs they promote are all too real. The troubled teen industry is a billion dollar industry comprising wilderness programs, boot camps and boarding schools that charge more than Harvard and provide even less than the basic standards of living.

While researching this book, I read thousands of online testimonials from survivors of these programs and watched several hours of video testimonials and documentaries. I drew inspiration from books like *Help at Any Cost: How the Troubled Teen Industry Cons Parents and Hurts Kids* by Maia Szalavitz and *Jesus Land* by Julia Scheeres. I communicated directly with survivors on the r/troubledteens sub-reddit as well as on Twitter.

The schools Grace attends are based on real ones. I focused on the now-defunct WWASP network of schools. Epiphany Lake Academy is modeled after Spring Creek Lodge in Montana. Mystic Bay is a composite of Tranquility Bay, which was in Jamaica, and High Impact, which was in Mexico. The character Treblinka was inspired by a video testimonial in which a young woman who attended Provo Canyon School in Utah—which is still operating today and was the precursor for the WWASP schools—says the school staff nicknamed her "Auschwitz" because they had forcibly shaved her head when she arrived, and she suffered from anorexia.

Aaron Bacon's story is true.

As shocking as these stories are, they get precious little attention. As a result, survivors often feel that no one believes them or can understand what they've gone through. With this novel, I hope to not only raise awareness about the troubled teen industry, but also to convince people that a story is worth listening to, even if it seems stranger than fiction. A small thing like being heard can mean everything to someone who feels like they're screaming into a void.

Elizabeth Sowden
Minneapolis
April 25th, 2018

Bio

Elizabeth Sowden grew up in Minneapolis, Minnesota. She earned a Bachelor's Degree from Sarah Lawrence College in 2006. She spent several years working as a marketing copywriter and social media strategist. Her martial arts experience includes Krav Maga and Brazilian Jiu-Jitsu. Her short stories have appeared in a wide range of publications, including VerbSap, Paper Darts, Revolver, Whole Beast Rag and Contrary. She lives in Minneapolis.

Past Titles

Running Wild Stories Anthology, Volume 1
Running Wild Anthology of Novellas, Volume 1
Jersey Diner by Lisa Diane Kastner
Magic Forgotten by Jack Hillman
The Kidnapped by Dwight L. Wilson
Running Wild Stories Anthology, Volume 2
Running Wild Novella Anthology, Volume 2, Part 1
Running Wild Novella Anthology, Volume 2, Part 2
Running Wild Stories Anthology, Volume 3
Running Wild's Best of 2017, AWP Special Edition
Running Wild's Best of 2018
Build Your Music Career From Scratch, Second Edition by Andrae Alexander
Writers Resist: Anthology 2018 with featured editors Sara Marchant and Kit-Bacon Gressitt
Magic Forbidden by Jack Hillman
Frontal Matter: Glue Gone Wild by Suzanne Samples
Mickey: The Giveaway Boy by Robert M. Shafer
Dark Corners by Reuben "Tihi" Hayslett
The Resistors by Dwight L. Wilson
Open My Eyes by Tommy Hahn
Legendary by Amelia Kibbie
Christine, Released by E. Burke

Upcoming Titles

Running Wild Press publishes stories that cross genres with great stories and writing. Our team consists of:

Lisa Diane Kastner, Founder and Executive Editor
Barbara Lockwood, Editor
Cecile Sarruf, Editor
Peter A. Wright, Editor
Rebecca Dimyan, Editor
Benjamin B. White, Editor
Andrew DiPrinzio, Editor
Amrita Raman, Operations Manager
Lisa Montagne, Director of Education

Learn more about us and our stories at www.runningwildpress.com

Loved this story and want more? Follow us at
www.runningwildpress.com, www.facebook/runningwildpress, on
Twitter @lisadkastner @RunWildBooks